Mod...

More pass...

In this volume we ...
novels from one ...

Em...

* * *

"You're mine, Fleur Andersson."

Kit looked directly into her eyes as he continued. "If you even look at another man at the party tonight, I'll probably tear him apart."

The same possessive desire simmered in Fleur's eyes. "I might very well do the same thing to any other woman you look at."

"I want you to myself."

Something else flashed in her eyes—a wild intensity that defied any roping her in. "You don't own me, Kit. I'm yours because I want to be yours. But I won't be kept in a locked vault…"

Emma Darcy nearly became an actress until her fiancé declared he preferred to attend the theatre *with* her. She became a wife and a mother. Later, she took up oil painting—unsuccessfully, she remarks. Then she tried architecture, designing the family home in New South Wales. Next came romance writing – "the hardest and most challenging of all the activities", she confesses.

Look for new novels from Emma Darcy in May and September, only from Mills & Boon Modern Romance.

EMMA DARCY

Mistress to a Tycoon

Jack's Baby

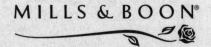

MILLS & BOON®

DID YOU PURCHASE THIS BOOK WITHOUT A COVER?
If you did, you should be aware it is **stolen property** as it was
reported *unsold and destroyed* by a retailer. Neither the author nor
the publisher has received any payment for this book.

*All the characters in this book have no existence outside the imagination
of the author, and have no relation whatsoever to anyone bearing the
same name or names. They are not even distantly inspired by any
individual known or unknown to the author, and all the incidents are
pure invention.*

*All Rights Reserved including the right of reproduction in whole or in part in
any form. This edition is published by arrangement with Harlequin
Enterprises II B.V. The text of this publication or any part thereof may not be
reproduced or transmitted in any form or by any means, electronic or
mechanical, including photocopying, recording, storage in an information
retrieval system, or otherwise, without the written permission of the publisher.*

*This book is sold subject to the condition that it shall not, by way of trade
or otherwise, be lent, resold, hired out or otherwise circulated without the
prior consent of the publisher in any form of binding or cover other than
that in which it is published and without a similar condition
including this condition being imposed on the subsequent purchaser.*

*MILLS & BOON and MILLS & BOON with the Rose Device
are registered trademarks of the publisher.*

*First published as a collection in Great Britain 2005
by Harlequin Mills & Boon Limited, Eton House, 18-24 Paradise Road,
Richmond, Surrey TW9 1SR*

Mistress to a Tycoon © Emma Darcy 2001

Jack's Baby first published in a separate, single volume by
Harlequin Mills & Boon Limited 2004
Jack's Baby © Emma Darcy 1997

ISBN 0 263 84534 6

154-0305

*Printed and bound in Spain
by Litografía Rosés S.A., Barcelona*

MISTRESS TO A TYCOON

BY
EMMA DARCY

Dear Reader,

I think every lover of romance has her own wishful expectations of the stories she reads. I certainly do. For a little while I want to be transported to another life, brimful of excitement and passion and extraordinary things happening, so much so I'm glued to the page from start to finish, completely immersed in the emotional journey I'm experiencing.

I need a lovely admirable heroine who'll make me feel so close to her, I'm virtually living in her skin, my mind and heart attuned to everything she does, everything she feels. I want the man she falls in love with to be oh so special – a hero who makes my blood sing, who has all the qualities I fantasise about in a man and who, I know, will be perfect for the heroine, if only they can cross all the barriers between them and truly reach out to each other; a man who, in the end, will give the heroine everything she needs and desires, becoming true soul partners with her – because love will not allow for anything else.

This is the magic of being a romance author. I can make this happen in a story. My dearest wish is for you to feel this magic, too, especially in this book, *Mistress to a Tycoon*.

With love – always!

Emma Darcy

CHAPTER ONE

BIG changes were highly unsettling. Fleur Andersson was acutely aware of just how big a change she was about to face, and she was just as edgy about it as everyone else gathered in the company boardroom.

Kit Malone was taking over Lancaster Publishing. He'd be here any minute now. Kit Malone, the magazine maestro—what did he know about selling *books?* Would such a fast mover and shaker be patient enough to find out before he made his judgments? Was anybody's job safe?

Having just made one big change in her life, Fleur felt very much afloat on a sea of uncertainties. In fact, she wasn't sure which was unsettling her more—losing her boss of seven years or bringing to an end her two-year relationship with a man who might have made her a very good husband.

At least she could fix the latter, if she really wanted to. Russell would have her back. He couldn't bring himself to believe she'd meant an absolute parting, choosing to interpret her words as simply wanting space for a while. Sooner or later she'd miss their *closeness* and she'd return to him.

He could be right.

Maybe her discontent with Russell was…perverse…unrealistic. He fell in with everything she

decided, everything she wanted to do. It was just that
he never took charge, never made any decisions himself, and to Fleur's mind that wasn't...*manly*. She
wanted...

'They're on their way up!'

Jane Haskell, their fiction publisher, gave the
warning, putting an instant stop to the buzzing spec-
ulation in the boardroom and Fleur's churning over
her private life.

Her work life was on the line right now.

Having been Warwick Lancaster's P.A. for so
many years, she wasn't at all sure she would like
working closely with a completely different style of
person. Or, indeed, that the reputedly dynamic Kit
Malone would want her to stay on as *his* P.A.

She wasn't exactly the type of woman he liked
having at his side, if media photographs were anything to go by. Flamboyantly gorgeous was not a tag
that could be attached to her slender figure, nor her
fair Scandinavian colouring. And what his choice of
companion implied about him didn't sit so well with
her, either. Warwick Lancaster was a solid family
man. Working with him had been comfortable, even
cosy. Kit Malone was...well, she'd wait and see for
herself first.

But it might very well be time to look for another
job, make a clean sweep—newly single, newly em-
ployed. After all, a new year had started—a year in
which she'd turn the dreaded thirty—and January
was the best month for seeking out employment opportunities.

Jane Haskell caught her attention with a host of agitated movements. In a complete tizzy, Fleur thought, as the other woman headed back down the room, obviously having decided to have a word in her ear—purpose in her step, anxious frown on her face.

The fiction publisher was tall, bordering on anorexic, a workaholic with one divorce behind her, and an irritating habit of continually flicking at her long black hair which was cut in one of those wispy styles around the face which led to strands hanging over her eyes. It might be considered sexy but it made Fleur yearn to apply hairclips.

'I'm not sure the champagne is a good idea,' she fretted, fidgeting with everything—her hair, her dress, the silver charm bracelet on her wrist.

Fleur raised her eyebrows. Everyone had agreed it was the right thing to do—the appropriate send-off.

'Kit Malone might think we're frivolous,' Jane ran on, deadly serious about her job.

'It's Friday afternoon. Warwick's last afternoon in the publishing house he built,' Fleur calmly reminded her. 'How many champagne lunches did he give you over the years, Jane?'

She flushed, guilt briefly pricking ambition. Though it didn't stop her from sniping a quick warning. 'Better get it through your head, Fleur. Warwick is yesterday. Kit Malone is tomorrow.'

'And today is today.'

'It's okay for you,' came the resentful sputter.

'Is it?'

'Sweetness and light will get *you* through. *You* won't have to fight for anything.'

Was it a commonly held view, Fleur wondered— that she was safe from being replaced? Maybe she was, if she was prepared to bend with the prevailing wind. But was *safe* all that mattered?

It wasn't with Russell.

And it wasn't here and now.

She'd make sure Warwick Lancaster was given his just due if it was the last thing she did in these offices.

'You're welcome to show disapproval of our frivolity if you think that will win you kudos with the new boss, Jane, but the champagne will be poured as scheduled.'

'It's stupid,' she muttered heatedly.

'So blame me.' With a shrug and a smile to soothe the other woman's brittle edges, she added, 'If Kit Malone begrudges Warwick Lancaster a last glass of champagne with us, he's too mean for me to work with.'

'It's not an issue of meanness. It's attitude,' Jane argued.

'Fine. You show him your go-getting attitude. I'll show him some decent humanity is worth something, too. At least in my book.'

Jane rolled her eyes, shut her mouth and quickly moved away lest she be tainted by an attitude she now saw as risky. Fleur sighed. The champagne was primarily her idea, although everyone had contributed to its cost, maybe in a fit of sentiment that was fast wearing away. Was she the odd one out here?

Sadness rolled through her as she heard the two men coming down the corridor to the boardroom, a cheerful tone in her old boss's voice. Was he really happy about retiring? Or was Kit Malone's offer too good to refuse, given Warwick was now in his sixties? Whatever…the deal was done. No going back.

Her fluttering nerves tightened as Warwick Lancaster ushered his successor into the boardroom. The contrast between the two men was instantly and heart-thumpingly evident. Warwick looked like a benevolent cuddly bear. Kit Malone gave the electric impression of a dark and dangerous panther on the prowl—black jacket, black trousers, black collarless shirt, black hair, all of him emitting an energy that fed on action.

Those who had been sitting around the big table shot to their feet, as though hit by a force that lifted them right out of any comfort zone. No easy smiles were left on their faces. A wary alertness swept the room, heightening the underlying tension of this meeting.

'Well, here we are!' Warwick announced jovially, beaming around at all of them. 'A great staff to work with, Kit. I'll introduce you around, one by one. Ah, Fleur…'

He turned happy, twinkling eyes on her. She'd positioned herself near the doorway, ready to assist with anything he might want of her, not to head the list of introductions. It was slightly embarrassing to be beckoned forward at this juncture when others in far more important positions of responsibility were kept waiting.

It was also somewhat daunting to be the first-up target for Kit Malone's focus. She would have liked the chance to observe him in action with other staff members before being faced with the barely muted aggression he emitted. Nevertheless, his gaze had been directed to her so a response was mandatory, especially since Warwick was burbling on about her in glowing terms.

'Fleur Andersson, Kit. The best right hand you could have in this business. She has a network of valuable contacts at her fingertips, right across the board, and won't let you put a foot wrong.'

'I shall count on that, Warwick,' he said smoothly, holding out his hand to her and nodding an acknowledgment as he repeated her name. 'Miss Andersson.'

Photographs hadn't really captured the man. The rugged handsome face—yes—darkly tanned skin, squarish jaw, a strong, sharply-ridged nose, firmly sculptured lips, straight black eyebrows, hair too thick and wavy to really be tamed, but the eyes had to be seen firsthand—such a piercing silver-grey, Fleur was momentarily stunned by their impact.

'Mr. Malone…' His name tripped out automatically as she took the offered hand. He was bigger than she had expected, too. Her slim hand seemed buried in his, enveloped by an insidious warmth and strength that suddenly made her feel disturbingly fragile. '…welcome to the world of books.'

It was lucky she had prepared that little speech and still had wits enough to trot it out.

'I did cut my reading teeth on books, Miss Andersson.'

Was that a mocking glint in his extraordinarily light eyes? A subtle set down in his reply?

'I need their world expanded,' he added, flashing her a smile of very white teeth—all the easier to gobble you up with, she thought wildly.

'Well, I'm here to assist, Mr. Malone,' she managed rather primly, and thankfully he released her hand, ready to move on.

Fleur quickly stepped back, out of the way. The moment Warwick led him into the next introduction, she surreptitiously took a deep, deep breath and released it very slowly. Someone, she thought, should put Kit Malone in a cage.

He didn't belong in a civilised world. He might have learnt the passwords that unlocked the doors to wherever he wanted to go, but her overwhelming impression of him was of a predatory animal about to seize more territory.

He would take Lancaster Publishing and use it how he willed.

So where did that leave her?

Could a man like him even want anyone else to be his right hand?

CHAPTER TWO

KIT MALONE watched for Fleur Andersson's return. She had slipped out of the boardroom some five minutes ago and he was acutely aware of her absence, especially when none of the other major players in this game was absenting themselves from his presence.

He had the rest of Warwick Lancaster's key staff taped—all types he'd met before; editors, accounts executives, sales reps. A few little personal quirks showing up, probably induced by the uncertainties generated by the changeover, but nothing that surprised him or niggled at the picture he had in his mind.

She was the exception.

For some reason he'd imagined Warwick's P.A. as a comfortably cushioned woman in her forties, well versed in fitting in with his requirements, competent, efficient, probably a mother hen to the staff, complementing her boss's somewhat paternal style.

Fleur Andersson was as slim as a wand, almost childlike young, and stamped with a quiet neat precision that seemed rather unworldly in this day and age. Yet Warwick Lancaster had declared she had an intelligence for this business, second to none, implying Kit would be a prize fool if he squandered what she could give him.

And she had been introduced first—a prime signal in any businessman's language—a sylph-like figure in a light grey suit, lemon blouse, a single strand of pearls around her neck, pearl studs in her ears, a rather small face, delicate features, fine fair skin seemingly untouched by the Australian sun, light blue eyes, ash-blond hair that clearly did not come virtue of a bottle, and cut in a short flyaway style that somehow made her look even more fragile.

An enigma that needed fast resolving, Kit decided. Of course, she couldn't be as young as she looked. She'd held her position here for seven years and wouldn't have walked into it straight from school. Possibly it was the lack of make-up bothering him. Nothing but a touch of soft pink lipstick. He was used to women armouring themselves with clever artifice. Like Jane Haskell, the fiction publisher, a typical career climber, full of nervy hype.

No, the clothes and pearls got to him, too. A woman in her twenties should be more modern. With it. Bright colours and baubles. She'd even worn clear polish on her neatly buffed nails. No concession whatsoever to current fashion. She was like some delicate porcelain doll, existing in some time and place he'd never been.

Music suddenly welled through the room. Kit instantly noted the small Bose speakers tucked into the corners of the wall-length bookshelves. Conversation came to an abrupt halt. The big distinctive voice of Pavarotti broke into the famous aria, 'Nessun Dorma,' which had been used as the theme song for the soccer matches during the World Cup in Italy. Opera wasn't Kit's favourite form of entertainment but this was definitely a great moment in music.

Beside him, Warwick started to chuckle. Kit shot him an inquiring look. The old man shook his head and in a deeply touched tone, murmured, 'That girl…'

Those who'd been standing across the doorway moved aside and *that girl* appeared—Fleur Andersson wheeling in a traymobile loaded with four silver ice buckets containing bottles of champagne and a spectacular platter holding a moulded concoction of seafood in artistic layers—prawns, crab, salmon, caviar set off with slices of boiled egg.

'This is our farewell toast to you, Warwick,' she announced, a big smile lighting up her face. 'We couldn't let you go without some splendid music and a glass of champagne.'

'This is quite marvellous! Thank you!' the old man replied with heartfelt pleasure.

'Okay, guys. Pop the corks,' she instructed, moving aside to allow in another traymobile loaded with glasses and plates and more buckets of champagne.

The corks were duly popped as Pavarotti reached the climax of the aria. Kit wondered if they'd practised it. The timing was perfect, with the artful producer presenting both him and Warwick with brimming glasses of champagne just as the music ended.

'My dear, what can I say?' the old man asked gruffly.

She shook her head. 'We're saying it. Enjoy. We wanted to return a little of what you've given us.' The eyes she turned to Kit held a questioning appeal. 'Please join us. It's just a small honour to a man whose vision has built this publishing house to what it is. I'm sure you wouldn't be here, Mr. Malone, if you didn't see it as a great launching platform for your vision.'

Sweet reason…irrefutable logic.

'A singular pleasure, Miss Andersson,' he replied, nodding an acknowledgment of the achievement while noting she was not assuming anything. Noting also, there was not so much as a flicker of fear in the clear blue eyes directed straight at him.

'And you made your special Norwegian dish for me! I *am* honoured, Fleur,' Warwick exclaimed in delight as one of the assistant editors arrived with plates containing slices of the seafood aspic. They were placed on the table in easy reach for them, along with forks for easy eating.

'You made this personally?' Kit asked, setting down the glass of champagne to pick up his plate.

'I'm afraid you can't buy it, so I had to,' she explained lightly, her neatly curved lips tilting into a wry little smile as she added, 'Warwick has nagged me for a repeat performance ever since I made one for a special launch party. It was a seafaring book.'

'And this is a Norwegian dish?'

She shrugged. 'My mother came from Norway.'

'Your father, as well?'

A slight frown at his inquisition. 'Sweden,' she answered briefly.

Which explained her colouring and perhaps her other world look. It was clear she didn't want to talk about herself. Not to him. He wondered why, given the garrulous outpourings from other members of the staff, eager to have him know where they were coming from and where *he* might take them.

'Please excuse me while I see everyone is served?' she quickly lilted, actively withdrawing from him.

He nodded and she wove her way back to the traymobile.

'I love this stuff,' Warwick remarked, picking up his plate to hoe into his slice.

Kit followed suit, intrigued to find and taste not only the seafood, but peas, capers, olives, bits of beetroot, tomatoes, pickled cucumber, onions, all folded through a delicately flavoured sour cream mixture that enhanced the taste of everything. Definitely gourmet standard.

'It must have taken her hours to put this together,' he couldn't help commenting, unable to think of any woman of his acquaintance who would have gone to so much trouble to please anyone, let alone an employer.

'An angel,' Warwick said indulgently.

'Well, it's heavenly food. I'll give her that.'

'Of all the people here, I'll miss her most,' came the quiet regret. 'She's very special.'

'Yes, I can see she is.'

Wise old eyes cast him an assessing look. 'If I may offer one word of advice…'

'Please do.'

'Don't lose her. It's all too easy for a young lion to stamp on a flower without realising its value. And she'll walk, Kit. She won't try to hang on. And you'll lose by it. Believe me, you'll lose.'

He could be right. He could be wrong. No one was irreplaceable in Kit's world and he'd never depended on anyone to give him a leg up to where he wanted to go. To his mind, Fleur Andersson might be a valuable asset on the journey he had plotted, but she might also be prone to hanging on to the past. Her choice of clothes smacked of a resistance to moving with the times. And in a fast food takeaway world, spending hours in a kitchen was not the current norm.

The Lancaster people relaxed more with the food and drink. The mood in the room rose to convivial. A series of toasts were made to the old man, caution easing as Kit appeared to be accepting all this good-naturedly. Guards were dropped, which was always interesting to a keen observer.

Despite his reservations about Warwick's advice, Kit found his gaze drawn again and again to Fleur Andersson who quietly carried on a subtle hostess act, using pauses to refill glasses and surreptitiously slide away emptied plates, tidying up without being obvious or officious about it.

In fact, she was almost unnoticeable unless one

was actually following her movements. Was that her special skill—a mover behind the scenes? Did she deliberately tone herself down to be more effective in accomplishing what she wanted to accomplish? The grey shadow…

Kit pondered this concept. In a way, it satisfied him. He could even admire a clever deception when it had purpose. Easy enough to work with, but…why not nail it down first?

He moved down the room to where she was now stacking used glasses onto the traymobile. She didn't see him coming. Her hands were quick, efficient, slender and long-fingered, the hands of a pianist, he thought, and wondered if she played.

'Is this cleaning up part of your job, Miss Andersson?' he asked curiously.

She straightened up, a startled flush colouring her cheeks, causing her eyes to seem a sharper, more vivid blue. 'Can I assist you with anything, Mr. Malone?' she parried.

He smiled at her sidestep and gestured to the stacked plates. 'I presume there is cleaning staff.'

'Yes, of course.'

'Then why do it yourself?'

She glanced down the table which she had cleared of all party debris. A quick breath, then a steady, direct look, straight into his eyes. 'Because this is Warwick Lancaster's last day and this was his board-room. When he leaves, I don't want it looking messy. I want it to look right. A last look back, Mr.

Malone. On Monday, we start looking forward...
with you. Okay?'

'Is the division line quite so clear-cut in your
mind? Today is today, tomorrow is tomorrow?'

An ironic twitch of a smile. 'I think it's rather
stating the obvious that you're a very different person to Warwick Lancaster. Doesn't that make a division line clear?'

Clever...answering a question with a question.
'Some people find change very difficult,' he threw
in for her response.

'Others view it as an exciting challenge,' she parried. 'Don't you, Mr. Malone?'

Turning the question back on him now. She was
very quick, revealing nothing of herself, except an
agile mind. 'I note you have a highly developed
sense of rightness—the music, the champagne, the
last feast, the cleared table. What does it tell you to
do with me on Monday morning?'

He was putting her on the spot, his senses alert to
any sign of evasion on her part. A grey shadow
would wait to reflect him, sliding around direct con-
frontation. He expected a political reply.

'Discounting pure luck,' she answered slowly,
'it's impossible to get anything instantly *right* for
someone until you know the person.'

An honest assessment. It surprised him when she
followed it up with a rather playful grin.

'I'm not a clairvoyant. Were you wanting one?'

He laughed, amused and tantalised by this glimpse

of provocative humour. 'Not the least bit afraid of me, are you?' he rolled out, testing those waters.

She shrugged, sobering at what the question might imply about him. Did he want fear? Was that how he worked? He could see the cogitation flitting through the way she viewed him. Her reply was decisive.

'Fear isn't something I care to live with. There are always other options. It's simply a matter of looking at a wider picture.'

Clearly she wouldn't stand for being bullied in any shape or form. A strong backbone in that slim body. 'Ah…a free spirit,' he murmured, smiling to take away any sense of threat.

'Not really.' She cocked her head musingly. 'I'd say more…finding the right box for me to fit into.'

And you might not be it.

Counter-threat?

Lancaster's warning leapt into his mind—*don't lose her.*

Kit moved instantly into persuasive charm. 'That doesn't leave much room for growth.'

It evoked another quick, appealing grin. 'I can always look for a bigger size.'

Impish, he thought. Was she playing with him, trying him on for size? Despite his claiming her attention—her *new* boss—she shot a quick glance down the room to check where her old boss was, currently chatting with the accounts executive. Cute pixie ears, Kit noted, and whimsically wondered if she'd played head elf to Warwick Lancaster's Santa Claus.

The grey shadow didn't fit.

Not with that provocative twinkle in her eyes.

This farewell party was about to break up. It was already five-thirty. Even some last lingering loyalty to the old man would not weigh too heavily against the desire to get away for the weekend.

His night was free.

The urge to pin down the shadow elf called for action.

'It's time to leave,' he stated suggestively.

It snapped her attention back to him. A slight frown at what could be interpreted as an order. 'You mean it's time for you to move.'

'Let's move together, Miss Andersson. Stroll down to Darling Harbour, have a leisurely dinner at The Wokpool, get to know each other.' He smiled. 'Always good to test the box before climbing in.'

She stood very still. He had the strong impression her mind was working furiously, but none of its computing showed on her face. When she finally spoke, the words came haltingly, accompanied by a blush that once again intensified the blue of her eyes.

'You want to be…with me?'

Did she think he wanted to jump on her bones? Surely not! She wasn't the type he liked in his bed. Too thin. He hadn't meant to be sexually suggestive. Damn! He hadn't meant to make her feel vulnerable…certainly not in that way!

'Any reason why we can't talk about the world of books over dinner?'

That put the issue straight. Well, not quite straight, but it moved it right off any harassment question.

Her chin lifted slightly. 'You didn't ask me if I was free, Mr. Malone,' she reminded him in a coolly polite voice.

'You're not married,' he pointed out. 'The choice is entirely yours to make.'

'I may have made another commitment. It is Friday night.'

Pride? It hadn't occurred to him she might be attached to some guy, but of course it was possible. Maybe she was offended by his assumption that she wasn't. Either way…tough! He put the pressure on.

'Then it's a case of priorities, isn't it?'

Her blush deepened. 'And you expect to come first.'

'I always play to win.'

'Interesting to see how far that takes you, Mr. Malone,' she flashed back at him. Very uncool.

'Are you with me or not?'

The bottom line. To hell with pussy-footing around! He had no time for pride games. She'd got under his skin enough this afternoon—a distraction he didn't need. In fact, *losing* her might work better for him than keeping her. Having someone close who interfered with his concentration was not in his best interests.

She nodded slowly, her eyes weighing him against some measure in her mind. 'Yes, I'll come with you.'

Triumph soared through him.

She'd conceded.

As most people did…when he cut to the chase.

Fleur Andersson was no different.

'So your position here is important to you,' he concluded with satisfaction.

Something flickered in her eyes—mocking his judgment or mocking her own? Difficult to tell.

She simply answered, 'I'll go and get my handbag.'

He watched her walk away, leaving him even more intrigued with her. Had he won? Or had she decided to let him win…long enough to see where it led and ascertain if she liked it or not?

And what then?

A very intriguing woman…Fleur Andersson.

CHAPTER THREE

HER cheeks were still burning.

Fleur headed straight for the ladies' washroom, cursing herself for even imagining for one moment that Kit Malone could be attracted to her.

Madness!

If he wanted to tomcat around, it wouldn't be with her. It was just that he had such a strong predatory presence and he was so aggressively *male,* and targeting her like that…it had put her in a total spin. Apart from which, the wretched man had acted as she'd so often wished Russell would, surprising her with a plan he'd already decided upon—one she would certainly be happy to go along with in any normal circumstances.

Except these circumstances weren't normal.

This wasn't a date with a man who fancied her.

Warwick's successor only wanted to pin down what was inside her head and he was ruthlessly determined on doing it.

Fleur pushed open the door into the washroom and hurried over to the basins. She ran cold water over the pulse points on her inner wrists then splashed her cheeks, willing the heat to recede. The worst of it was—Kit Malone emanated sex appeal in bucket loads. He had the kind of animal magnetism that set every female hormone ticking with excitement. Like here was a man worth having—in bed if nowhere else!

Basic instincts—purely physical and highly primitive—causing an insidious disturbance to any common sense.

Fleur turned off the tap, grabbed a paper towel, wiped away all excess moisture and examined her reflection in the mirror. Still too much colour in her cheeks and her eyes were overbright. Nevertheless, she couldn't stay in here forever. Better to get moving and meet whatever had to be met.

The big question was…did she want to work closely with a man whose sexuality would be in her face all the time, undermining her concentration, playing havoc with her hormones? Not to mention the hunter in him always calling for submission to his will.

From the moment he'd entered the boardroom her nerves had been on edge and they were more so now, with the prospect of spending the next couple of hours alone with him. Still, this evening should be a good test of how it would be, working in close proximity.

She wasn't a coward who wimped out of a challenge, but she wasn't a masochist looking for misery, either. She'd parted from Russell because he didn't fulfil her needs. The man she'd just met might be everything her ex-partner wasn't, but that could well mean he had the power to give her even more frustration than Russell had, since he wasn't likely to view her as anything more than a tool he could use.

A pity she wasn't tall and voluptuous and dramatically stunning—top of the pile in the female stakes. On the other hand, from all she'd read in magazines, women built like that weren't any happier with their lives than she was. They could draw guys from the top of the male pile, but keeping them was something else.

At least they had the satisfaction of the experience, Fleur thought, with an uncharacteristic touch of envy. She turned away from the mirror that told her she didn't have a hope in that particular arena, and walked very briskly to her office where she was more than competent in holding her own against all takers. Telling herself she could and would seek a new position, if need be, she picked up her handbag and headed back to the boardroom.

He was waiting just inside the doorway, chatting to a group of editors. His gaze flicked to Fleur the moment she appeared and he instantly excused himself from the conversation, not the least bit concerned about showing a marked preference for her company. The silver-grey eyes did a swift scan of her face. If he had expected her to apply more make-up, tart herself up for him, he was out of luck.

'Ready?' he asked.

'I want to say goodbye to Warwick first. Wish him well.'

'Of course.'

He accompanied her down the room to where the

old man was happily holding his last court. Noting their approach, Warwick broke off from his other well-wishers to give them his attention.

'I'm about to kidnap Miss Andersson and take her out to dinner,' Kit Malone announced, offering his hand. 'It's been a great pleasure dealing with you, Warwick. I hope you have a happy retirement.'

'I wish you well, too, Kit,' came the warm reply. Having shaken hands, he turned to Fleur with a quizzical look. 'Is Russell away?'

'Yes.' She hadn't told him of the changed status in her private life. With a teasing little smile she explained, 'I understand Mr. Malone would like to pick my brain. Did you suggest it to him?'

He chuckled and grasped her upper arms, drawing her close enough to plant a kiss on her forehead. 'Thank you for being you, Fleur.'

She returned a quick kiss to his cheek. '*Bon voyage,* Warwick. I hope it will be the best journey yet.'

'Take care, my dear.'

'You, too.'

Thankfully her *kidnapper* said nothing as they walked out to the elevators. Fleur was fiercely blinking back tears. She'd spent seven very happy years working for Warwick Lancaster—a true gentleman with a heart of gold; generous to a fault, considerate of others' feelings, valuing and nurturing talent, rewarding any special achievement, happy to share his knowledge and experience. Rich years. A treasure house of good memories. She had to be grateful for that, not feel there was going to be a huge gaping hole in her life.

Warwick was moving on.

She had to move on, too. There was more to come. Whether that *more* was attached to the man beside her or not, she would find it, or keep looking until she did. The world was full of paths to take. She just had to seek out the right one for her.

The elevator doors opened.

Goodbye yesterday, hello tomorrow, she thought as she stepped into the compartment, accompanied by the man who might or might not be her next boss. The doors closed, somehow magnifying his presence. The sense of raw power, barely harnessed, was so strong, Fleur concentrated on watching the numbers of the floors tick down to ward off its swamping effect. It was a relief when the doors opened to the street level lobby and they were on their way to open air.

The city skyscraper in which Lancaster Publishing occupied two floors, led out to Market Street which was jammed with people hurrying to catch transport home. The double blast of noisy peak-hour traffic and late afternoon summer heat hit them as they left the air-conditioned building and headed down towards Darling Harbour. It wasn't until they reached the pedestrian bridge at Cockle Bay that they could walk side by side in reasonable comfort.

Kit Malone took off his jacket, slung it over one broad shoulder, unbuttoned his shirt sleeves and rolled them up his forearms—darkly tanned, muscular forearms. Fleur dragged her gaze off them, wishing he wasn't quite so *physical,* and decided she could wait until she reached the restaurant before removing her own jacket.

Not that he'd be impressed by any bared femininity on her part, but even the most superficial undressing near him felt dangerous to any peace of mind. The heat could be borne. Too conscious of his attraction to lay herself open to some derogatory comparison to the women he found desirable, she preferred not to draw even the briefest assessment of her body.

'Who's Russell?'

She was startled by the question, only belatedly recalling Warwick had asked about him in this man's hearing. 'No one connected to publishing,' she answered dismissively, hoping he would let something irrelevant to him slide.

The hint that Russell was none of his business was totally ignored. 'Does he have some claim on you?'

He had no right to this kind of curiosity. He'd already proved he didn't give a fig for any plans she might have made with anyone else. To start probing now into a highly personal area was a bit much. Probably he was surprised she had a man in her life at all, given his own quick denial in having any interest in her as a woman. Which, perversely, scraped her pride into pursuing an information gathering probe on his love life.

'I have more reason to ask if some woman has a claim on you, Mr. Malone, since I'll be taking your phone calls,' she reasoned in what she hoped was a matter-of-fact tone. 'Perhaps you should brief me on any current relationship that requires special consideration?'

He grinned at her. 'I am as free as a bird, Miss Andersson.'

It was a sexy grin. The hell of it was, Fleur realised it wasn't deliberately so. It just was, suggestive of all sorts of possibilities that her rational mind insisted were impossible to relate to herself. Which lent a less than sweet tone to her voice as she remarked, 'I take it this isn't the mating season.'

The grin widened. 'More a time of flitting from tree to tree.'

Her tongue ran away from her. 'Do let me know which tree has your favour as it comes up. Ruffled feathers can be a problem.'

'I'll try not to test your diplomatic skills too far.'

Mortified at her loss of control in pursuing his sex life, Fleur clamped her mouth shut and fixed her gaze on the lowering sun in the west. Daylight saving meant it wouldn't set until past seven o'clock but she had the sinking sensation she was setting her own sun with Kit Malone in double-quick time. Though it probably didn't matter. He was so far under her skin already, working with him would be a constant torment anyhow.

'Can we get back to Russell now that we've established the state of my personal life?' he tossed at her, using the none too subtle blackmail of tit-for-tat.

No point in arguing privacy. She'd just crossed that line with him. A kind of resentment at his careless promiscuity urged her to put Russell up as proof that she could successfully attract and hold a man, demonstrating she was not entirely sexless.

'I guess you could say Russell has been the leading light in my love life for the past year or so.'

'And still is?'

Trust him to pounce on the past tense! She sighed. Stupid to lie. Why let Kit Malone influence any shading of the truth? It gave him a power over her thinking and behaviour which was all out of proportion.

'He asked me to marry him.' At least that said someone found her desirable. 'It made me realise…as much as I care for him…'

'Wrong box,' came the sardonic conclusion.

His use of her own words was jolting. However true they were, the way he dismissed Russell as of no account made her want to reconsider the decision she had come to about their relationship. There had been a lot of good in what they'd had together. It wasn't really Russell's fault he didn't quite measure up to what she wanted. It was his nature to be easygoing, happy for others to take the initiative…

'So Russell is away…as in…gone.'

The satisfaction in that statement riled her into answering with much less finality. 'Right now he's in Tasmania, visiting family there.'

He slid her a mocking glance. 'So you *were* free tonight.'

They had arrived at the flight of steps which would take them down to the promenade around Darling Harbour. Fleur paused before descending, deciding this was as good a time as any to make a stand against the arrogant will of Kit Malone.

'As it happens, yes. But had I made some prior arrangement I would have kept to it.' Her eyes defied the scepticism in his. 'Most people object to being stood up, Mr. Malone. It's not exactly a courteous practice.'

He cocked a quizzical eyebrow. 'You'd put good manners ahead of pursuing the main chance?'

Fleur stood firm on her point, not caring if she sounded critical. 'It's a question of values, isn't it?'

'Rather old-fashioned values,' he drawled, his gaze flicking down to her pearl necklace as though it illustrated where she was coming from.

Her spine stiffened. 'I like living with certain standards, Mr. Malone. Main chances have a habit of shifting. Your own career is a shining example of that. Do you see yourself as providing the only road for me to take?'

'No.' A slow smile, even sexier, more sensual than his grin. The silver-grey eyes glimmered at her beneath lowered lids that held ridiculously long, thick eyelashes. 'I simply like to sort out the sheep from the wolves along any road *I* take, Miss Andersson, and the sooner it's done, the better.'

He was, Fleur decided, a *very* dangerous man, fighting the feeling of being cornered by him.

'Now take you, for example,' he went on, his gaze

travelling down to her sensibly shod feet and up again. 'You're dressed in sheep's clothing. And when you smile I see small, dainty teeth. But I suspect you're a wolf with a bite that Warwick Lancaster probably never saw because you'd circle quietly around him, with your old-fashioned value of respect coating the truth of your inner reality.'

Her heart quivered, recoiling from the image he drew. It wasn't true…was it? Shock held her very still, staring back at him while she fiercely gathered the defences to cope with the idea that he saw or sensed things she didn't recognise about herself.

A wolf?

Part of her did chafe over Russell's inclination to be a sheep, preferring to follow instead of lead, but surely most women wanted their men to show some decision-making capacity. That didn't make her a wolf.

As for her relationship with Warwick, much of her manner to him had been tempered with deference—rightly so—to his decades of knowledge and experience. Of course she had saved him time and trouble on many little issues. That was her job. But the way Kit Malone had said *circling quietly* made her sound deceitful. And she wasn't. Not about her clothes, either. Bright colours would drown her. Pastels were her only option.

'So what happens when two wolves meet?' came the quiet, almost silky question—the tone raising prickles at the nape of her neck.

His piercing light eyes were directly challenging

her now. Closing in for the kill, she thought wildly. Instinct screamed to keep absolutely calm.

'Why don't you tell me, Mr. Malone?' she invited, totally confused about where this was leading.

He laughed, confident he was in control, enjoying the challenge she projected. His eyes glittered with amusement as he answered.

'Two male wolves won't share the same territory. There'd be a fight to the death. But a male and a female…' He let the image linger before pushing home his point. '…a mating could be beneficial to both.'

Her stomach contracted. Her thigh muscles tensed. The physical reaction to his words was alarmingly strong, as though he'd reached into the most primitive core of her and was tugging on it with deep, relentless purpose.

But he didn't mean sex, Fleur savagely told herself.

This wasn't about sex!

Or was it?

This man was used to a pack of women following him. He could very well be using his animal magnetism as a power tool, holding out a promise he had no intention of fulfilling, getting her to fall into line because somewhere down the track, he might choose her if she hung in there.

She needed a diversion and she needed it fast, before he got too sure of his effect on her. 'You know, I suddenly feel quite hungry,' she lightly remarked, forcing her tremulous legs to start descend-

ing the flight of steps to the promenade below. 'Is
The Wokpool a favourite restaurant of yours?'

'The chef has a fine touch with Asian cuisine,' he
answered, not missing a beat as he fell into step
beside her. 'I simply liked the idea of us...eating
together.'

She slanted him a look designed to taunt his confidence. 'Testing my bite?'

His eyes danced with amusement. 'There's always
an exciting edge to living dangerously.'

'Oh, I think you're quite safe with me, Mr.
Malone. I'm not about to pounce on you.'

And if you think I'll join your harem of panting
she-wolves, you can think again.

CHAPTER FOUR

'WOULD you prefer a table inside or outside?' the maître d' inquired, gesturing to the choice he was giving them.

'Outside,' came the swift, firm bite from the she-wolf beside him before Kit could state his preference.

'It would be cooler inside,' he pointed out mildly, more to assess her response than make a protest.

'I've been *inside* all day,' she countered, a challenging glint in her eyes, even as she smiled a charming appeal. 'Can you stand the heat?'

'No problem,' he answered, waving her forward to choose her ground for the skirmish in progress between them.

Interesting that she was intent on evading the kind of intimacy that could be generated at a table inside the more private enclosure of the restaurant's formal dining room. Obviously she saw that as an advantage to him, giving him a more intense focus on her. The alfresco setting in the courtyard was open to the public view, overlooking the promenade and the harbour—more neutral space.

Keeping her distance, Kit deduced, plus ensuring the ready distractions of people and boat traffic to minimise eye contact. She was certainly one very cool operator. But not so cool that she didn't feel the heat at all. Once they were shown to their table, and the waiter appointed to them relieved Kit of his jacket, she was quick to remove hers and hand it off, as well.

The lemon blouse was sleeveless and artfully shaped to fit her figure—no excess fabric puffing out over the waistline of her equally body-hugging skirt. She was not as thin as he had thought. In fact, her slender frame was surprisingly curvy—perky high breasts, a hand-span waist, well-rounded hips, and a cheeky little bottom that was very, very female. All in all, quite a neat feminine package—on the small side—but definitely not without appeal. Even her arms were softly fleshed. No bones sticking out anywhere.

In fact, figure fitting clothes were the fashion this summer and she certainly wore them well. Kit did a quick revision of his previous assessment of the intriguing Fleur Andersson. The grey shadow was emerging as quite an appealing flower whose scent held so many tantalising layers, he kept wanting to sniff out more of it.

A jug of iced water was brought, menus presented, and they were left alone to consider their choices. Kit didn't have to look to know what he would order. The Green Chicken Curry here was always superb. A Margaret River Chardonnay to wash it down, and hopefully the wine might lower barriers. He watched his companion sip iced water while she studied the menu and wondered if she was trying to tip it into her veins.

Twice he'd caused her temperature to rise, the telltale heat in her cheeks signalling that he got under her skin, too. She didn't like it, either. She was probably used to controlling every aspect of her life. Just as he did with his. The trick was to persuade her out of a clash of wills and into a meshing of interests.

'I'll have the steamed fish with soy and oyster sauce.'

'Would you like a starter?' he asked.

She shook her head. 'But please don't let me stop you from having one.'

He smiled. 'I doubt your Norwegian dish can be topped.'

She returned his smile. 'I'm glad you enjoyed it.'

He signalled the waiter, gave the order, then set about drawing her out. 'So you have Scandinavian parents. Are you yourself Australian?'

'Yes. I was born here. My parents migrated to Australia after the Second World War. I was a late child. An only child,' she added ruefully, then sat back as though anticipating he would make some comment.

'Are they still alive?'

'No.'

She lifted a hand to her throat, her fine delicate fingers stroking the pearl necklace as though it gave her some secret, sensual pleasure. For some reason he found the slow fondling intensely provocative.

His imagination zoomed in an image of her, lying languidly in bed, wearing nothing but those pearls, and he suddenly saw them as sexier than any fancy costume jewellery could ever be.

His gaze travelled up to her soft pink mouth. It looked innocent but he was sure it could erupt with passion if restraint was ripped away. The nose above it had delicately flared nostrils. He could see them emitting steam when she was on fire. Her eyes were the blue of the sea on a clear day. They weren't twinkling at the present moment. Deceptively serene, he thought.

Taking in her short fair hair, the overall picture of her face started to remind him of the actress, Meg Ryan, usually cast in movies as the quintessential girl next door. It didn't appear to stop her from having hot affairs off screen and Russell Crowe had certainly found her very sexy.

Russell…

'Are the pearls a special gift from someone?' She was still touching them and Kit didn't like the idea of her thinking of some other guy while she was with him.

The question surprised her into dropping her hand. 'They're special to me,' she answered slowly. 'They were my mother's.'

Back to old-fashioned. 'Do you always wear them?'

'Mostly. Pearls should be worn. Contact with skin gives them more lustre.'

Not sentiment. Definitely sensuality. 'Are they Picard pearls?'

She frowned quizzically. 'Why do you ask?'

He shrugged. 'I've met Jared King. He runs the Picard Pearl Company in Broome and he told me the same thing about skin contact adding lustre. The connection just clicked in my mind.'

'I see. Well, you're right. My father bought them for my mother in Broome and they are Picard pearls.'

Quality, he thought. She valued quality and took pleasure in it—like the Norwegian seafood dish—quality presentation, quality content.

'Best pearls in the world, Jared said. They suit you.'

She blushed, whether from the compliment or his knowing appreciation of *her* quality it was impossible to tell. He liked watching the colour suffuse her cheeks with warmth and the subsequent brightening of her eyes. A naked face, he thought, more fascinating than a painted one.

She leaned forward, picked up her glass of iced water. 'How did you come to meet Jared King? I've read about the Kings of The Kimberley. Quite a legendary Outback family.'

The words were quickly rattled out, diverting his attention away from the personal ground he'd been exploring, away from her. He didn't mind answering since the question led into what he wanted to do with Lancaster Publishing.

'A piece of investigative journalism came up for

one of my magazines. I decided to chase the story myself. It led to Jared and he persuaded me to drop it.'

She cocked her head quizzically. 'He paid you off?'

'No. He made me realise if I printed the story, it could harm an innocent child.' A child who stood to inherit the Kruger fortune—hundreds of millions of dollars—except she wasn't Alicia Kruger anymore, but Alicia King, Jared's adopted daughter, and she knew nothing of the inheritance that could blight her life with unwanted publicity and the threat of kidnappers.

'You dropped a story that fired your interest for the sake of a child?'

Her head was still tilted. In a seemingly idle action, she held the cold glass of water to her flushed cheek—ice and fire. The juxtaposition instantly stirred more erotic images. Was she knowingly teasing him? Could the delicate flower be a subtle Venus's flytrap? He struggled to refocus his mind on her query. Her eyes were waiting, silently assessing.

He flashed her an ironic smile. 'Even wolves protect their young.'

Her mouth moved into an appreciative moue. It was so damned sexy, Kit was stirred into a rampant desire to fling Fleur Andersson over his shoulder and march her off to bed with him. They'd get to first base there in no time at all. A pity there was this work complication. On the other hand, might not the hot spice of sex be the right ingredient to tie her up with him?

Quality…perfect presentation…clever wits and superb timing…such assets would certainly assist in selling his projects. And she had the ground-floor knowledge on book publishing that would paper over any cracks in his expertise.

Mating…

He'd instinctively hit on the answer up there on the pedestrian bridge when she'd flouted any assumption she was sold on working for him.

The waiter arrived at their table with the bottle of Chardonnay and at Kit's nod of approval, proceeded to uncork it and pour it into their wineglasses. Kit sat back, relaxing, content to nurse the plan now evolving in his mind, gathering the pleasurable anticipation of much satisfaction, both physical and mental—the delectable challenge of bedding Fleur Andersson. Tonight!

As soon as the waiter had left them, he picked up his glass of wine and lifted it in a toast. 'To a new beginning!'

She set down the glass of water she'd still been holding and wrapped her fingers around the stem of her wineglass—slow deliberate movements that were innately graceful. Her eyes connected directly with his as she complied with the toast.

'May it lead somewhere good,' she said whimsically.

'Good for both of us.'

She smiled, more to herself than to him—a Mona

Lisa smile—her lashes lowering as she sipped the Chardonnay.

'Fleur…' He rolled her name off his tongue—soft, furry, feminine, seductive—then smiled his pleasure in it. 'I feel we'll do very well together.'

She gave him a veiled look. 'Do you, Mr. Malone?'

'Call me Kit,' he invited, gesturing an appeal for less formality between them.

He sensed her simmering over the familiarity, choosing whether to come his way or not. It lessened the distance between them. It encouraged a more friendly rapport. Was it wise at this juncture?

'Pretend you like me,' he mocked, intent on getting rid of her caution.

It amused her, despite her reservations. A teasing little smile played over her lips and a twinkle appeared in her eyes. 'A journalist who cares more about a child than a story…I think that wins some liking, Kit Malone.'

'Nice to know I have one positive score.'

'Please…feel free to mark up many more.'

He laughed, elated by the challenge, privately promising himself that before this night was over, he'd win all he wanted to win from Fleur Andersson.

CHAPTER FIVE

FLEUR was in big trouble. Her whole body felt bombarded by the signals Kit Malone was putting out. He was flirting with her—eyes, mouth, hands, voice—*flirting,* as though some powerful chemistry switch had been thrown and he was turned onto her full blast.

It seemed incredible. *Why?* she kept asking herself. What had triggered the change? She was sure he hadn't felt attracted to her earlier. Could he just do this at will?

The problem was she couldn't stop herself from responding to it. Her pulse fluttered every time he smiled at her. She drank far too much wine trying to cool herself down or moisten a throat gone hopelessly dry. The steamed fish in soy and oyster sauce, deliciously complemented with julienne strips of chilli and ginger, did nothing to settle the tremulous spasms of excitement around her stomach.

Kit Malone was definitely coming onto her—all guns blazing—and any control she had over this situation was shot to pieces. He even made eating his chicken curry look sexy. Probably because his eyes kept saying he'd rather be tasting her, eating her, gobbling her up like the wolf he was.

And the really, really terrible part was she wanted

him to. Not once in her life had she ever considered a casual sex encounter, yet here she was, semi-squirming in her seat with the excitement this man aroused, wondering what he would look like completely naked, how it would feel being taken, being filled by him. He couldn't be anything else but intensely virile, aggressive in initiating whatever served his pleasure.

Would he care for hers?

Oddly enough, that didn't seem to matter. It was the experience of *him* she wanted—the kind of man he was—exciting, compelling, masterful in mind and attitude. The chance to know was here and now...tonight!

It was wicked, wanton, but oh, so tempting! She couldn't claim she hadn't enjoyed Russell's love-making, and she felt a stab of disloyalty for thinking of it now as *tame*. It had been good, just not highly charged with wild excitement. No all-consuming passion.

Maybe her imagination was running riot, thinking Kit Malone might provide all she felt she had missed out on, all she secretly craved with a man, but if she didn't go with this opportunity, wouldn't she always wonder? And whom would she be hurting? Only herself if the night ended badly.

Besides which, disappointment might cure her of nurturing fantasies that were totally unrealistic. It might even give her a different perspective on her relationship with Russell, get her feet right on the ground and her head out of the clouds. Maybe there was no absolutely *right,* and she should settle for…on the balance, right enough. But with Kit Malone assaulting all her senses…

Surely anyone could be forgiven one experiment.

A learning experience.

An education in…living dangerously…once in a lifetime?

Her mind zigzagged chaotically between what he was doing to her on one level and what he was saying on another. She managed to get through the meal, mainly listening, but once that was over, she had to concentrate more on the plans being propounded.

'I've proved it through the magazines,' Kit pressed, exuding conviction in his beliefs and a passion for pushing them, his eyes inviting her to meet and match the flow of his charismatic energy. 'Good, topical Australian content, reflecting our culture and building it into something even more special and unique. We can sell it in books, Fleur. Both fiction and non-fiction. More than just selling. We can make a very positive contribution to our society.'

He propped an elbow on the table, lowering his forearm towards her, palm out. Then slowly he closed his open hand, fingers curling into a fierce seize position. 'Ours,' he repeated. 'Our society. Our country. Past, current, future. It's time one key publishing house in Australia stopped playing second fiddle to the books shipped here from overseas. Our books need to be pushed to the rest of the world. We have something good to give, too.'

His vision.

It sounded very idealistic to Fleur—strange coming from a man who seemed more suited to pushing pragmatic realities—yet he'd probably reached a point in his life where making money wasn't his top priority. He'd made enough. Time to pour it into something that would make a different kind of mark.

She stared at the clenched hand. He was going to take this project on and make a success of it. Burning to do it. And he wasn't about to let anyone step in his way or hold him back. The sheep would be scattered by this hungry wolf. He meant to win.

'Are you with me?'

In every sense? Or just the job? Impossible to work with him in the state she was in. 'I think it's a fine idea, Kit.'

'But?' His piercing silver eyes lasered into her mind.

Her wits were scattered. She struggled to talk sense. 'I'd have to say the book market is very tight. And overseas countries will resist your initiative. They're very home territory oriented. You're going to have to prove a lot before they reconsider their restrictive policies.'

It didn't faze him one bit. The glint of battle beamed at her. 'We start here. Come home with me now and I'll show you how.'

'Come…home with you?'

Fleur felt quite faint at the invitation. Was the decision upon her? He was talking work but…

'It's not far. I live at Bondi Beach. A short taxi

ride. My study there is stacked with great material I've collected that I want to see taken up and pursued.'

He was pursuing *her*. Every instinct screamed that he was. 'How long have you been planning this move?' she asked, putting off the critical moment.

'A long time. I've been waiting for Warwick Lancaster to see retirement as desirable. I needed a ready-built structure, and you're a vital part of that structure, Fleur.'

He's a takeover man, she thought wildly, intent on taking her over, too. Or was she hopelessly mistaken about a sexual agenda? He was pressing work. Maybe he found it perfectly agreeable to mix the two. Which might be fine for him with his flitting from bird to bird attitude, but if she perched in his tree tonight and was tossed out of it tomorrow…how could she face working with him on Monday?

Was it even possible to work with him, feeling as she did?

He signalled their waiter, handed over his credit card to pay the bill, and asked for their jackets to be collected and returned to them. Time was fast running out and Fleur didn't know what to do. Her inner agitation was increasing by the second, the strong tug of temptation pulling like an undertow, even as she tried to swim towards flags that had seemed eminently sensible in the past.

He smiled, flooding her with mesmerising magnetism. 'Come with me.'

Three little words.

They were like a clarion call to all her unanswered needs.

'All right,' she heard herself reply.

His smile widened to a grin. 'I want you in tune with what I want.'

Did he know what he was doing to her, the chords he was striking? Feeling more vulnerable than she had ever felt in her life, Fleur reached for some defence. 'I'm not the only one you'll need to get onside, Kit.'

'My instincts tell me you and I will be an unbeatable team.'

Which reduced her defence gathering attempt to mash.

The waiter returned with their jackets and set down Kit's credit card and the docket to sign. The paperwork was completed in a matter of seconds. She was on her feet ready to leave, before Kit rose to his. Somehow it seemed important not to invite any physical contact with him.

It wasn't too late to say no.

He didn't attempt to take her arm or hand as they walked out of the restaurant. The pretence of a work-related evening together was still in place. In fact, he chatted on about a recent trip he'd made to the Outback and how struck he'd been by the primaeval feel of so much of the land. There was no doubting his vision for selling what he himself felt about Australia was genuine. Fleur simply didn't know if she could be on his team.

She had the weird sense of not knowing where

she was going at all. Her body was automatically following the direction he steered—into an elevator that took them from the promenade, up to street level—strolling towards the Entertainment Centre and Chinatown—being ushered into the back seat of a taxicab—hearing an address at Bondi Beach being given to the driver. These were exterior signposts, but totally meaningless to the jumble of uncertainties in her mind.

Should she think of Kit Malone as a gift?

Manna from heaven?

Or a piece of sheer wickedness from hell?

'What are you thinking behind that Mona Lisa smile?' he softly teased.

The switch from professional talk to personal comment zapped a charge of electricity through her nerve endings. She quickly mustered a sidestep from the truth.

'You were talking about Aboriginal communities which led me to think about their claim of secret women's business.' She gave *him* a teasing look. 'Not to be revealed.'

He laughed, setting her pulse rate skittering again.

'Why is it that women cultivate mystery?'

The answer sprang to her tongue and she spoke before thinking how it might be interpreted. 'It gives them some power in a world where men think power is their natural right.'

'Do *you* feel powerless?'

She could still say no.

The taxi was travelling through Bondi Junction

now, not far from where her apartment was situated. All she had to do was speak, break the power of this compelling force-field he'd woven around her, take herself out of it. She had the choice. But it felt like an empty choice—a negative not a positive.

'There is only so much that one can control,' she said, her gaze shifting from the passing street, dropping, sliding to the legs of the man sitting beside her—the mover, the shaker, the candlestick maker. *The gift...*

'There's no fun in controlling everything, Fleur,' he murmured seductively. 'It's the risk factor that stops life from becoming static and boring.'

She seized that thought, using it to justify being with him. 'Is that why you're about to pit yourself against the status quo in the publishing scene?'

'What else can a warrior do, except conquer new territory?'

'Take new women?'

The tilt at his purpose shot out of her mouth, and pride forced her to look at him, to see if it hit the mark tonight. He caught her gaze and held it with a simmering intensity that commanded her acceptance and understanding.

'Until one is found who is above all the rest,' he said, turning the challenge back to her. 'Isn't that the quest of both sexes?'

Yes.

But it wasn't as simple as he made it sound.

'Is your past littered with trials and errors, Kit?'

'I'd say you gave Russell a longer trial than I've

given any woman. I've never seen the point of pro-
longing a relationship once you know it doesn't
work for you.'

'It can have…compensations.'

He shook his head. 'I'd rather be alone than pay
the price of compensations.'

It was a provocative argument. Where did pleasure stop and payment start? When did compromise
become a chafing burden? How many disappoint-
ments became too many? Yet was there such a thing
as a perfect match?

Not many people were content to be alone. Undoubtedly Kit Malone would have a network of
friends or acquaintances to call upon if he wanted
company. She suspected he didn't *need* anyone.
Want was simply a matter of reaching out and taking. In fact, she was the object of it tonight, although
she didn't have to answer it. Not completely.

'You know, I've never read anything about your
family,' she remarked, curious now about his personal background. 'Do you have one?'

'The Malones populate the world,' he said dryly.
'I'm the seventh in a brood of eleven. My mother
died of kidney failure before she could produce the
round dozen my father wanted. Since I didn't pursue
the career he had plotted for me I'm considered the
black sheep of the family.' His eyes glittered a savage mockery. 'They don't mention me and I don't
mention them.'

The rebel…the outcast…

'I'm sorry,' she murmured, feeling it was sad to have lost so big a family circle.

'Don't be. I'm the escapee from a prison I'd never want to go back to.'

No caging Kit Malone. *Free as a bird.*

Strange, though, how that background made him more human...defying the rule of a tyrannical father and striking out on his own, burningly intent on making a life that was his. Entirely his.

'Thank you for telling me,' she said quietly, realising it was confidential information, not for public airing. A gift to her.

'You're on your own, too,' he murmured, as though it was an intimate link between them, and the look he gave her sizzled with the desire to forge other intimate links.

Fleur's heart turned over. It was the weirdest sensation. All evening she'd been helplessly aware of her body responding willy-nilly to his strong sexuality. But this was something different, something more than basic instincts. It was as though he had reached out and stroked her heart with an understanding of her that no one else had.

'Here we are!' the taxi driver announced.

Kit paid the fare, opened his door, stepped out, then leaned down to say, 'Better you alight this side, Fleur,' and held out his hand to help her do so.

She took it.

The thought of still being able to say no didn't even enter her mind.

It no longer mattered where tonight might lead.

She was going with him.

CHAPTER SIX

THE house was situated above the southern curve of
Bondi Beach, facing north to catch the sun—a prime
position in every sense and obviously a multi-million
dollar property. From the street the architecture
looked very modern, the building white and stretching up two storeys, balconies dressing the frontage
of the upper floors.

Kit took her up a flight of steps to the ground floor
level, sensor lights coming on to eliminate the dark-
ness. He opened a gate that led to a very spacious
patio. An inground swimming pool was shaded by
an arrangement of white sails overhead and protected from sea winds by a hedge of Hawaiian hi-
biscus and massed groups of palms and other trop-
ical plants. Groups of sun-loungers with blue
cushions promised open-air relaxation with privacy
guaranteed.

Fleur found herself too tongue-tied to comment
on anything. She was overwhelmingly conscious of
the hand holding hers, drawing her forward, locking
her into step with Kit Malone. This was his home.
He was taking her into it and Fleur knew she was
crossing a threshold she had never crossed before.
Her heart was hammering as he opened the front
door, switching on lights, silently urging her on.

She entered a big open living area; terracotta tiles and brilliantly coloured mats on the floor, cane furniture, cushions in green, blue, purple, fabulous paintings of Outback scenes by Pro Hart, Drysdale, Namitjira, hanging on white walls. The whole place had a vivid earthiness that seemed absolutely right for the man beside her.

Somehow it summed up a daring to embrace life in all its colour, to gather it to himself, uncaring of anyone else's opinion or standards. *His* world. And suddenly she felt as though she'd been existing in a much paler world, the shallows instead of the depths, playing safe instead of risking, suppressing her frustrations with it because nothing else had really seemed possible for her.

But with Kit...

The threshold had been crossed.

The door was shut behind her.

She stopped looking at where he was taking her, stopped moving forward, and turned to face the man himself, wanting more than anything else to know *his* depths. She was acutely aware of a heightened tension from him as he halted, alert to any change to his plan and swiftly gearing himself to adjust to it. His gaze snapped to hers.

For a split second she felt an almost violent challenge surge from him—no way was his purpose going to be turned aside or driven into retreat. Then the ruthless glitter in his eyes receded, leaving only a silvery shine that reflected her own urgent searching.

He swivelled to face her, making her acutely conscious of how big he was—the breadth of his shoulders double hers and the top of her head barely reaching his chin. A little shiver ran down her spine. Was she brave enough to take this journey?

He lifted a hand and gently stroked her cheek—a reassuring caress that promised there was nothing to fear. Her skin tingled underneath his touch which drew an instant rush of warmth, her heart kicking with excitement at this first step. His eyes commanded trust and she gave it, wanting him to lead, to show her where they were going.

She heard the jacket he was carrying drop to the floor. He raised his other hand to her face—feather-light fingers stroking both sides now, feeling, softly tracing her features as a blind man would to capture how she looked, but it was more absorbing than that, as though he was subtly drawing on her heart and mind…*come with me, come with me, come with me*…weaving a spell that bound her to him.

He didn't speak.

The silent communication of touch was stronger than speech, more entrancing. And it seemed he was entranced, too, with the shape of her ears, the silky texture of her hair, the line of her brow, the delicate bone structure of her face. It was as though he needed to search out everything about her and was fascinated by his discoveries.

The jacket she was carrying slithered from her arm. It wasn't a conscious decision to let it drop to the floor, any more than it was a conscious decision to let go of her handbag. The need to be free of any encumbrances activated their shedding. She was going with him, wherever he wanted to take her, and nothing else was relevant.

His hand cradled the back of her head. A finger touch under her chin tilted it up. She saw his intent to kiss her, to join their mouths in an intimate locking together, the desire for it simmering in his eyes as his strong male face came closer, closer. She could feel her lips softening, parting, quivering with anticipation, craving the contact.

It came like the brushing of wings, inviting her to soar with him. The soft tantalising caresses of his lips were a taste of excitement, a seductive inducement to try more. Her hands flew up around his neck, eager to press on, ready, willing to explore. No hesitation. No pulling back.

He deepened the kiss, a swift sure ignition of sensation that drove her into invading his mouth, plunging headlong into the passionate entanglement he encouraged and accelerated. It was so easy to let him take charge and simply revel in the power of feeling. It was like a wild release from the responsibility she had carried too long.

He gathered her closer, his hands sliding down the curve of her back, pressing her breasts to the hard wall of his chest, then moving lower, curving over her buttocks, hauling her up so she stood on tiptoes, her thighs meeting the taut muscularity of his, her stomach tremulously aware of his arousal.

Man…woman…

Desire…fiercely exploding through her, seizing the sense of rightness in the feelings he stirred, exulting in them, wanting them pursued.

He swayed to one side and scooped her off her feet. His arms cradled her securely and he seemed to carry her effortlessly, a big man cocooning her in his strength. She clung to the exhilarating power of that strength, loving it, her own arms wound tightly around his neck, her face pressed to the vital warmth of his skin, breathing in the heady scent of him.

He was taking her up a flight of stairs. Up to the sky, Fleur thought dizzily, wanting to fly with him to places she had never been. Curtains swishing back, doors sliding open, the sound and smell of the sea rushing in on them, a light breeze shifting the balmy air of the hot January night…it felt as though they were up in some high eyrie, the rest of the world booming below them.

Kit set her on her feet and began removing her clothes…not fast, more with the slow deliberation of an undressing ceremony, his every touch sure and purposeful, making a ritual of stripping her naked. The fever of wanting ebbed but still she stood in thrall to the sense of what was happening…this gradual stripping away of what she had worn here, as though it had to take place for a new beginning to really start.

He left her with the necklace of pearls, her only adornment, and his eyes told her it was right. She was a woman and it suited her, adding a lustre to her nudity that pleased him. Pearls from the sea…a primitive ornament adding to the pagan feel of shifting to the real elements of life, where water, earth, air and fire all played an intrinsic part of what was to be.

He stood back from her and shed his own clothes in the same slow deliberate manner, not inviting or expecting her to take any active part, watching her watching him emerge naked. A full moon and a clear night brilliant with stars provided a soft gleaming that delineated the muscular power of his magnificent body, shadows adding a mystique that pressed the sense of a noble savage rising out of the mists of time.

Fleur was totally captivated by this image, and the feeling of being the chosen one to share a night that was more special than any other night could ever be. She didn't care if it was fanciful, only that it was happening and she was an integral part of having it happen—a silent pact to let what was possible *be* possible.

He stood before her—a pause to savour the freedom of simply being together like this—the ultimate meeting and mating still to come, anticipation rolling through them like the incoming waves of the sea, reacting to tidal forces that couldn't be ignored or denied.

Then in a wild whoosh he swept her up and laid her on a feather-soft quilt, kneeling over her in all his awesome male splendour, and her heart was thundering at the thought of him coming to her lightning fast. But he chose not to. He chose to touch, to kiss, to revel in the shape of her, the scent of her, to weave a sensual enchantment that drew her into sliding her hands and mouth over him, a gloriously free exploration that filled her with a joy which went beyond the physical.

He made every part of her feel exquisitely female and she exulted in the raw power encased in his flesh, the thick mat of hair on his chest, the taut bulge of muscles in his arms and legs, the hard flatness of his stomach, the strong curve of his buttocks, and most dominant of all, the sexuality that was so aggressively different to hers and more than matching the rest of his intensely virile manliness.

Her whole body was zinging with sensitivity when he finally positioned them both for the inevitable climax of what had seemed like a long and wondrous mating dance. He loomed over her, blotting out the light. The tips of her breasts were teased by the hair on his chest as he bent to kiss her, invading her mouth, erotically stroking as he parted other lips, using the hard hot length of him to stroke her there, too, tantalisingly close…closer…poised on the edge…waiting for the plunge…the sweet quiver of everything inside her attuned to its coming…needing…wanting…

And oh, the ecstatic pleasure of feeling him enter, her body instinctively arching to receive all of him, the rush of excitement at this ultimate commitment to the journey they had taken this night, the last step, the wild joy of it as he filled her, a deep glorious thrust that answered every pulsing promise from the beginning.

But this wasn't the end. It was the start of more and more incredible sensation, a ride that encompassed fantastic peaks and beautiful valleys and raging rivers, holding her to him, taking her with him, together as one, and she clung to their oneness, loving every demand and gift of their union, urging more, inciting more, embracing it with a fervour that poured from her mind and heart and soul, an intense sense of life seizing her, driving her to places she had never been, exulting in the proof that they were possible and not some impossible dream.

There came a time of rest, of slumbrous contentment, their bodies curled snugly together, luxuriating in the feel of each other, skin against skin, softness complementing hardness, a quiet celebration of merging that moved gradually into the slow burning desire for more and more of the intimacy they had forged, compelling action, satisfaction sought and found again, the heat of fusion leaving them drained of energy yet exhilarated that it was still there for them…no diminishment of feeling.

For a while they lay in mutual wonder of what they were experiencing—or so it seemed to Fleur. Then Kit took her hand and drew her off the bed, leading her down from the heights they had occupied, taking her to the terrace below and the pool that lay glittering in the moonlight.

Never before had she swum naked but she did with him, revelling in the silky flow of the water around her, the marvellous sense of weightlessness when her arms were linked around his neck and he swum on his back, pulling her along with him, his powerful legs propelling them forward, the languid slide of their bodies another sensual delight.

He smiled at her.

She smiled at him.

Their smiles said all there was to say.

Words could only dispel the magic of this night.

Tomorrow was another world away.

Decisions…consequences…the future…they were lurking, waiting in the wings to be faced when that time came.

But tonight…*now* was all consuming.

CHAPTER SEVEN

MORNING came.

They moved from lovemaking to brunch on the patio by the pool, to chat about the publishing business, both magazines and books. They spent a few hours in his home office, poring over files of articles that Kit had designated as possible future projects, discussing their viability in the book market.

It was hot. He'd given her a blue sarong to wear, donning only shorts himself. Easy to throw off both garments when they wanted to swim or sunbathe naked or enjoy the sensual pleasure of their bodies. She didn't ask if he kept a supply of sarongs for female visitors who didn't want to be bothered with proper clothes. She didn't want to know. Maybe it was a case of hiding her head in the sand, but the need to keep feeling that what they were sharing was uniquely special for both of them forbade any spoiling questions.

There simply wasn't any break in their wanting to stay together, not the slightest hint from Kit that her company was wearing thin, nor any desire in Fleur to leave his side.

Their sexual awareness of each other was constant. Just a look or a touch and they'd merge, seeking satisfaction, taking it, giving it. Regardless of where they were or what else they were doing, that urge was never denied, simply accepted as natural and mutual.

Yet neither of them spoke of it. Kit seemed to take it for granted, which made Fleur wonder if he conducted all his affairs with women like this, so assured in his own sexuality that he would have been surprised if she'd baulked at falling in with any desire he had. But she wouldn't let these thoughts disturb what was happening. She wanted to revel in this total lack of inhibitions for as long as it lasted.

Saturday slid into Sunday. More of the same. All of it intensely pleasurable. They didn't leave the house. The kitchen was well provisioned, no need to go anywhere else for food or drink. It was fun, preparing meals and eating together. Not for a minute was there any sense of boredom or disappointment. Kit Malone was the perfect man for her, Fleur thought, and he certainly made her feel she was the perfect woman for him.

She didn't want this idyllic time to end, but practical common sense insisted it had to with tomorrow being Monday—a new working week starting. Kit seemed content to ignore that fact as they lazed through the heat of Sunday afternoon in or by the pool, and Fleur let the issue slide, reluctant to face it until it became absolutely imperative.

As a result, when the interruption came, she wasn't prepared for it. The rattle of the gate jolted her out of a blissful doze. She and Kit were lying on a double sun-lounger at the other end of the patio, both of them carelessly naked. Since the gate faced onto a walled alcove, they couldn't be seen from it, but the demanding voice that followed the rattle shattered the serene sense of privacy.

'Kit! I know you're holed up in there! Let me in!'

A male voice, loud and tinged with exasperation.

The fingers that had been idly grazing the curve of Fleur's spine halted. She lifted her head, turning it sharply to see Kit's face, to watch his reaction. He lay on his side, propped up on one elbow, his eyes narrowed under a frown, calculation obviously clicking through his mind.

'Enough is enough!' the voice complained. 'I'm fed up with leaving messages on your answering machine. Since you've seen fit to turn the power off on your mobile, I've dragged myself out here to talk to you and don't pretend this intercom isn't working. Just do the decent thing and let me in, Kit.'

'Who is it?' Fleur whispered.

'My partner in the magazine business. Ben Steiner,' came the low reply, muttered through a resigned grimace. 'I should talk to him.'

'It's time for me to go anyway,' she quickly offered, not wanting to cause a problem with her presence.

'No!' His eyes bored into hers. 'Don't make it a choice between Ben and you.'

'I wasn't.' It startled her that he could assume she'd even try to flex that form of power. 'I just thought...' Her own eyes appealed for understanding. '…I do have to leave soon, Kit. I have washing to do, clothes to get ready…'

'Okay,' he abruptly conceded and swung his legs off the lounger. As he picked up and pulled on his shorts, he stabbed a further warning at her. 'So long as you realise Ben co-exists with me and I don't allow anyone to play games with my business interests. We haven't talked about where we're going from here, Fleur, but that's one place we don't go.'

They should have talked more. Somehow the outside world hadn't mattered, but of course it did! Both their places in it!

'Kit, the least you can do is answer me. Through this damned intercom, if nothing else,' Ben Steiner exploded impatiently.

'I'm coming,' he called out, then swooped to pick up the blue sarong and hand it to Fleur. 'Don't run away. Stay and meet him,' he commanded in a low murmur.

Without waiting for a reply, he strode off around the pool, leaving her struggling to come to terms with this new situation. Gone was the seductive lover. He'd just thrown her another testing challenge and if she didn't meet it, it was clear she'd lose his respect. What he'd virtually told her was not to use the personal pleasure they'd shared as a weapon to threaten or interfere with the set order of his life.

She was stunned that he thought she might. On the other hand, it was common enough for women to use sex to get their own way. Kit Malone had just nipped any such tactic in the bud—perhaps a warning of what she could expect from him at work to-morrow, too. Don't make any presumptions on the grounds of mutually desired sex. He was the boss, both in his business and private life.

Fleur's mind was in such a whirl, she barely gathered herself enough to wrap the sarong around her and knot the ends securely at the back of her neck. Fortunately the fine cotton was not transparent so a reasonably modest appearance was effected before Kit opened the gate to his business partner.

Except it wasn't only Ben Steiner who entered.

'Surprise! Surprise!' A woman's voice trilled, and a lush sun-tanned body in short white shorts and a scarlet midriff top was flung at Kit, arms winding around his neck, a kiss smacking his cheek, long black ringlets being tossed as mock-chiding words babbled forth. 'You bad boy you! Shutting everyone out instead of sharing all your spicy news with us.'

'Ben…' The growl from Kit was not overflowing with pleasure in this *surprise*.

Which was some small relief to Fleur's cramped heart.

'I brought Dolores with me in case you weren't home,' his partner airily excused.

'Then please take custody of her,' Kit grated at him, firmly unclasping the clinging vine arms.

'Back off, baby,' Ben drawled, reaching out to haul her to his side. 'The caveman is not responsive today.'

Fleur breathed again.

Dolores was the kind of flamboyant female Kit

had been photographed with many times. His type of woman, she'd thought. It was unnerving being confronted with one in the flesh, voluptuous curves and cleavage on easy-grab display, but Kit hadn't grabbed. Fleur hoped it was because he hadn't been tempted rather than exercising restraint out of respect for her feelings.

'A drink would be good, Kit,' Ben Steiner suggested. 'We can park Dolores out here by the pool while…' He caught sight of Fleur. 'Uh-oh!'

'As you see, I have company,' Kit stated coolly, his gaze travelling to Fleur, checking that she was standing ready to meet his friends, half smiling as he took in her apparently calm composure.

'Bad timing? Want us to go?' his partner asked, his somewhat leering take on the blue sarong causing Fleur's nerves to tighten. Dislike speared through her. Did she have to co-exist with this man if she wanted a continuing relationship with Kit?

'Why can't we meet her?' Dolores whined, pouting at both men.

Probably posed for some playboy magazine, Fleur decided, feeling her jaw start to clench. She hated pouty women. Such supposed sexiness always seemed so false, contrived. She'd never understood how men could be sucked into responding to it. But then, she wasn't a man.

Which drew her into a sharp appraisal of Kit's business partner who now had Dolores latched to him. He was very good-looking in the slick way that projected *money*—streaky blond hair artfully styled, skin a perfect golden tan, a gym-toned body wearing tailored white shorts, an unbuttoned red and white floral shirt, white loafers on his feet. He probably drove a Porsche, which no doubt Dolores appreciated.

'Actually I'd like to introduce you to Fleur, Ben,' Kit said rather too pointedly, his irritation with his other uninvited guest showing.

'Fine! Fine!' came the enthusiastic response. 'Thought you had to be working, Kit. The usual incommunicado routine. Didn't mean to break in on personal stuff.'

His tone was more curious than apologetic, and as the three of them walked around the pool to where Fleur remained waiting, she was acutely conscious of being the target of hostile curiosity from both visitors...like *they* had been blocked out in favour of *this woman?*

Anger burned through her.

So she wasn't painted up with a truckload of make-up like dolly-bird Dolores, and her hair was probably a limp mess from swimming, and her fair skin wasn't fashionably kissed by the sun, and she wasn't an obvious sexpot...did that make her an alien who shouldn't be here?

As the distance between them closed, making the introduction imminent, Fleur turned her gaze to Kit, a fierce pride driving her eyes into delivering their own testing challenge. *You took me as a partner, too. Make me feel it!*

He smiled, lifting the squeeze on her heart with

the sense that he expected no less a stance from her. 'Fleur Andersson...Ben Steiner,' he announced more than introduced, as though they were contestants in a ring of his making and he was keenly interested in how they would shape up to each other.

'And Dolores Diaz,' Ben Steiner supplied, quickly filling the omission of his girlfriend.

Fleur nodded to the woman who was staring at her with rude incredulity and offered her hand to the man who co-existed with Kit. 'How do you do, Mr. Steiner?'

The formal response startled him. One eyebrow rose. His mouth quirked into an amused little smile. After a brief hesitation he reached out and took the hand Fleur had kept extended to him.

'I do very well,' he returned, green eyes glinting mockingly at the distance she was keeping. 'And please feel free to call me Ben. I don't think Kit regards me as an authority figure here on his home ground. As you must have heard, I come more as a beggar for his time.'

And your time's up, sweetheart, he projected at her.

'I'm sorry you were inconvenienced,' she said in her best professional manner, sliding her hand out of the male-dominant grasp and piling on an appeasing smile as she flicked the ball to the main player here. 'Though I'm sure Kit must have had his reasons for being incommunicado.'

Tell him, she willed behind her smile. *Make me important to you in his eyes.*

But his business partner kept the initiative. 'Which he'll undoubtedly lay out to me as we go get you girls a drink,' he burbled on. 'I'm sure Dolores is dying to get acquainted with you.' A very white smile was flashed at his girlfriend. 'A gin and tonic for you, baby?'

'Lovely!' she trilled obligingly, her dark brown eyes sharpening up to chop Fleur to pieces.

'Fleur, are you happy to stay and have a drink?' Kit asked, not moving to Ben Steiner's hustle, giving her the courtesy of a choice.

She could go now.

Walk away from Ben Steiner and Dolores Diaz— which she was sorely tempted to do—but would that also mean walking away from Kit?

She gave him a very direct look. 'Do you intend to join us?' Being relegated to bimbo territory was definitely not a place she cared to accept, and she was bristling at Ben Steiner's arrogant arrangement. Nevertheless, this was Kit's ball game and she needed to see how he would play it. Needed to see where *she* stood in it from his viewpoint.

'Yes,' he answered unequivocally.

'Then I will have a drink before I go. Just fruit juice please.'

'Right! Fruit juice,' Ben Steiner drawled, as though it was precisely what he expected from her.

He wanted her to bite.

She smiled and nodded, denying him that mean little satisfaction, acutely aware of Kit assessing how she and his partner were dealing with each other.

Intuitively she knew he would favour control above sniping. Nevertheless, it was difficult to fight the sense of having her position here undermined.

'You may not have recognised Dolores,' Kit casually informed her. 'She stars in the television series, "Beach Patrol." I'm sure she'll tell you about it while Ben and I get the drinks.'

Having handed out an easy line of conversation to fill the gap, Kit turned aside, drawing his partner with him. Fleur forced a smile at Dolores and found the other woman's gaze avidly following Kit as he strolled into the house.

So that was how the land lay, Fleur thought, wondering if Ben Steiner realised his girlfriend coveted his business partner. Which explained why Dolores had thrown herself at Kit and why she'd like to take an axe to Fleur.

'So who the hell are you?' Savage brown eyes raked contemptuously over Fleur, the attack coming the moment the two men disappeared from view.

It was a tricky question. In the current scheme of things, Fleur wasn't sure how to answer. Would Kit want their professional connection revealed?

'I beg your pardon?' she temporised, inwardly rebelling against telling this woman anything.

'Oh, don't give me the butter wouldn't melt in your mouth tripe!' No sexy pout now. More an ugly jeer. 'You've been creaming it with Kit Malone all weekend and I want to know where and how he picked on you.' Another contemptuous sweep. 'He's never gone for the *twiggy* type before.'

To Fleur's intense vexation, a flood of heat caused her whole body to blush. 'Perhaps I have more to offer than big boobs,' she retaliated, then wished she'd bit down on her wayward tongue.

Dolores instantly clamped her hands on her hips and thrust out her overflowing breasts. 'Like what?' she challenged, aggressively sure of her winning assets in the female physical attributes.

Determined on cutting off this distasteful conversation, Fleur coolly stated, 'It's really none of your business.'

'Oh, yes it is, little pink girl! Spare me the blushes. You haven't got a stitch on under that sarong and I know damned well you've had what I'd give my eyeteeth for.'

'Then why are you with Ben Steiner?'

'Proximity is always promising.'

'Does he know that?'

'Don't think you can make trouble there. You'll come off second-best, believe me.'

Fleur had no trouble believing her, but that wasn't the point. 'Why would you think Kit Malone would filch his friend's woman?'

She rolled her eyes derisively. 'What world do you live in? All it takes is the right time and a bit of encouragement.'

Had this weekend simply been *the right time* for Kit to have her? Her heart screamed a painful protest. Her mind instantly argued for more information.

'So how long have you been gunning for him,

Dolores? How long have you had to keep Ben Steiner sweet, and still not get what you really want.'

'I'll get him, you whey-faced bitch! He must be on a schoolgirl kick with you. When he's used you up, I'll still be around, waiting for the strike.'

Sickened by the other woman's attitude and disturbed by the idea of being *used up* by Kit, Fleur swung away and moved to the outside dining setting, taking a chair that would give a direct view of the men returning to the patio.

Dolores, of course, couldn't leave well alone, following her with more poisonous snipes. 'You can be as smug as you like, it won't change the fact that Kit Malone is a sexy animal who always moves on. What you are, darling, is simply a different experience for him.'

That could be true. He was certainly a different experience for her, yet she had felt they had communed on more than a sexual level, that the intimacy had reached deeper places than the merely physical. Had she been indulging in wishful fantasy? Or was Dolores Diaz wishfully matching Kit to her own agenda.

No fury like a woman scorned.

Especially when bypassed for a woman she regarded as considerably less than her equal in female attractions. But there was no law for the igniting of a special chemistry between a man and a woman. Fleur took comfort in this thought, doing her best to block the doubts Dolores was intent on implanting as she raged on.

'Okay, I'm obviously a shock to you,' she finally broke in. 'You're a shock to me, too. I apologise for hitting back at you. If all you say is true, then I'm no real threat to your goal, Dolores, so let's drop it, shall we?'

The appeal earned a furious glare, but probably realising nothing more could be gained by attack, Dolores flounced to the chair at the end of the table, pulled it out at a slant, and arranged herself on it with a maximum show of leg for the men who were now emerging from the house.

Another challenge for Kit's interest, Fleur thought, hating the sense of contest. She wanted to feel secure with all she'd shared with the man who'd claimed her as no other man ever had. Yet looking at him, seeing how his powerful physique and sexy magnetism completely overshadowed Ben Steiner's more superficial flashy appeal, she knew there would always be women like Dolores Diaz, waiting to offer themselves to him.

The question was…had all Fleur could offer on a sexual level—and on a business level—been used up?

One intense weekend of *mating*.

He couldn't just shut it off…could he?

CHAPTER EIGHT

KIT was angry with himself. Angry with Ben, too. It had been a mistake letting him in. Their connection went back eight years, deserving of considerable personal consideration, but consideration went both ways and Ben was fast overstepping any leeway he had ever earned.

'What? Taking to cradle-snatching now?' he had chortled, the moment they were out of ready earshot of the two women.

Kit was not amused. He'd fixed Ben with a knifing look and coolly stated, 'Fleur is older than Dolores. And more of a woman than your *babe* will ever be.'

To Ben, all women were viewed as babes to be bedded or bypassed—a crass immaturity Kit had tolerated up until now—but he was not about to tolerate Fleur being measured on that scale.

'You're kidding!'

'I'm deadly serious.'

'Come on! You can't be! What's she got for you?'

Impossible to explain. Kit hadn't even tried to define it for himself. He didn't want to. Besides, something as deeply instinctive as the feelings Fleur had tugged on would be incomprehensible to Ben who worked on the principle that men understood each other and women were a separate species.

'She's got plenty for me. Better believe that, Ben, and keep your judgments to yourself.'

'Well, give me a hint because it sure ain't visible.'

'Probably because you're fixated on big breasts.'

'Yeah? Well, I've never seen you lust after anything less, my friend.'

It was probably fair comment, yet it had irritated Kit out of all proportion. 'Fleur is different,' he'd tersely muttered.

'How different?' Avid curiosity. 'You mean she knows some great tricks?'

'Is this what you came here for, Ben? To pry into my sex life?'

Finally the message that his remarks were not welcome had registered. It sparked a resentful accusation. 'You were supposed to come to my party last night.'

Another mindless party, boozing on with boring people. Hardly a tragedy that he'd missed it. But… 'Sorry. I forgot.'

'You forgot.'

'Completely slipped my mind. What do you want to drink?'

'A long cold beer. And since when do you forget anything?'

Losing patience with what came over as rather childish resentment, Kit had tried to give some reasonable perspective that would be understood.

'Ben, I start a new enterprise tomorrow. Fleur happens to be in publishing. Being with her was more important to me than making small chat at a party with people who are too stoned out of their minds to offer one stimulating thought.'

'Ha! So she's useful to you.'

Kit had fixed the drinks, letting Ben think whatever he liked. There was no point in correcting him. There was none so deaf as those who didn't want to hear and it was perfectly clear Ben didn't want to hear that any woman could be more in tune with Kit than he was.

At the present moment, if it came to a choice of having Ben or Fleur in his life, he'd choose Fleur, which was probably irrational, given the longevity and profitability of his partnership with Ben. He didn't want the two to clash. It would be much, much easier if they would accept co-existence without judgment.

'You're having fruit juice, too?'

The critical comment had been one too many, earning a laser-like glare. 'Why not? It's refreshing.'

Ben didn't like it. 'Have a beer with me.'

The boys' club!

Kit had given him one straight warning. 'You tried to put Fleur down out there, Ben. I didn't like it. Now you either toss your prejudice away, or stay out of the way, because Fleur Andersson is going to be in my life for some time and I won't have anyone putting her down.'

'Fine! Fine! I won't cruel your pitch now I know what it is.'

He didn't *know*.

As they carried the drinks out to the two women, Kit regretted answering Ben's call. Yet how could he keep both Ben and Fleur entirely separate? It was inevitable that they meet. Spaces for them had to be worked out. Some pragmatic cross-referencing had to be put in place.

Ben was yabbering on as they crossed the patio. Kit looked at Fleur. She had a beauty all her own. In a way, he was glad Ben couldn't see it. She was…a woman apart. One glance at Dolores Diaz certainly underlined the difference. A hot-house red carnation held no allure whatsoever. A blast of primary colour. No subtle scent. A commonplace flower, available to be bought anywhere.

Whereas Fleur…was sitting absolutely still, her air of alertness very sharp, her expression guarded. Kit knew instantly she felt under attack. She was holding her ground, not backing off yet, but bullets had undoubtedly been fired by Dolores, and Fleur was not the kind of woman who'd submit to being target practice for anyone.

Bad scene.

She won't hang on, Warwick Lancaster had warned. *She'll walk.*

Her choice, Kit thought, sensing she was only waiting to see what support she'd get from him. Which was fair enough. But he silently cursed Ben again, not only for his untimely intrusion and his mean response to Fleur, but for bringing Dolores Diaz with him.

*   *   *

Every nerve in Fleur's body had tightened as Kit's gaze had turned from her to Dolores and slowly back again. Comparing the two of them? Reconsidering the weekend he'd spent with her instead of with his usual taste in women? Ben Steiner would undoubtedly have been critical of his choice. No mistaking *his* resentment at finding her in residence here.

He was probably still pouring poisonous comments into Kit's ear. He was certainly doing all the talking as the two men walked across the patio. Whether Kit was listening or letting the barrage of words float past him was impossible to tell. There was an air of self-containment about him that reminded Fleur he was very much his own man, which surely meant he would do whatever was right to him.

Best remember that, especially in this particular minefield of uncertainties. It was one signpost she could trust. Her stomach ceased its nauseous churning as she suddenly recognised another.

Ben Steiner held a large tankard of beer in one hand, the gin and tonic for Dolores in the other. Kit carried *two* long glasses of fruit juice. A gesture of solidarity? Fleur wondered. Or a reproof to his friend for the supercilious attitude he'd struck towards her? Either way, she felt much less out on a lonely limb than she had a few moments ago.

He set her drink on the table in front of her and took the chair at the opposite end to Dolores, bringing a powerful domination to the scene even though he didn't say a word, apparently content to let Ben Steiner take centre stage with the conversation. After a bit of non-consequential banter with Dolores, Ben sprawled himself in the chair opposite Fleur's, and directed his attention at her, glittery green eyes seeking to get under her skin.

'So…you've been giving Kit the inside track on book publishing, Fleur.'

Out of the corner of her vision she saw Dolores' mouth curve in a smirk of satisfaction. No doubt her presence was now explained and the conclusion being reached was that her usefulness to Kit would soon run out.

She shrugged. 'More listening to what Kit wants to achieve with the innovative concepts he has in mind.' She smiled at him. 'Would you call me an inside track or a sounding board?'

'Ben has a habit of putting people in pigeonholes,' he said dryly. 'Even if I put tags on you, none of them would fit the box labelled Fleur Andersson.'

Her heart lifted. This was no easy dismissal of her. He was saying she was someone special…telling Ben Steiner and Dolores Diaz so, too.

'Oh, come on! Everyone can be typecast sooner or later,' Ben argued. 'Psychologists have written books on the various personality types. I've read them.'

'They're generalisations,' Kit pointed out.

'But they can be uncannily accurate,' Dolores chimed in. 'Like with astrology.' She gave Kit a full blast of flirtatious admiration. 'You're a perfect fit for the description of a Leo.'

'Star signs…' Kit rolled his eyes.

'Don't scoff. Dolores knows a lot about that stuff, don't you, baby?'

Ben's defence of her forced Dolores to simper pleasure at him. 'I sure do.' Catty eyes turned to Fleur. 'What's your star sign?'

'Libra.'

'Ah, The Balancer! Always balancing the scales. I bet you're very good at that, too,' she said with enough sly emphasis to imply Fleur was a fool if she didn't see she was on the short end where Kit Malone was concerned. 'Now Ben and I are both Sagittarians. We go after what we want, don't we, darling?'

Fleur decided she'd had enough. *On balance,* she had better things to do at home than sit through this superficial dissection of character when it was only too obvious these people wanted her gone. Besides, it was up to Kit to let them know what her place in his life was. She didn't really know herself. Tomorrow might determine it for her, and right now tomorrow couldn't come fast enough.

She finished her drink, excused herself from their company, asked Kit to call her a taxi while she got ready to go—'Ten minutes'—and headed straight inside and up the stairs to the bedroom where she had left her things. Action was better than thinking or feeling. It kept her from feeling hopelessly vulnerable from laying herself open to Kit Malone.

Not bothering with a shower or make-up, she dropped the sarong on the bed, dressed in the clothes she'd worn on Friday, brushed her hair into a semblance of order, collected her handbag, and was back on the patio just as the taxi tooted its horn.

Kit instantly rose from the table to see her off. She waved a farewell to the others who were once again staring at her as though she were some alien apparition. This time she refused to be shaken by it. What they thought didn't matter, particularly since Kit chose to be at her side. And he hadn't let her down. Not yet, anyway.

'I don't think I'm quite Ben Steiner's style,' she murmured ironically as they walked towards the gate.

'Life moves on,' Kit answered. 'Ben just hasn't made the step yet.'

'He might not want to.'

'Then he'll get left behind with his own limitations. I won't be held back from where I want to go.'

It was a cool ruthless statement. Fleur wasn't sure if it was an assurance that his partner would have no influence over their relationship, or a warning that she held no reins on him. For the few seconds it took him to operate the gate, she tried to tune in on his feelings, but his energy force seemed withdrawn from her at this moment of parting.

Then he turned to face her and the silvery eyes simmered with sensual memories. 'It's been good, Fleur.'

'Yes,' she agreed, not knowing how much the past tense encompassed, not wanting to ask.

'I'll look forward to working with you tomorrow.'

She nodded.

Tomorrow she would know.

It was only a matter of waiting.

There was no embrace, no goodbye kiss, no touch at all. She felt him watch her down the steps but she didn't look back. Somehow it was important not to do that, to be as self-contained as he was in effecting their parting. She heard the gate clang shut as she stepped into the waiting taxi.

Was that the end of it?

Would it be all work tomorrow?

What would be would be, she told herself. Trying to cling on to something when it was gone was futile. Logic told her that. But she hoped—she desperately hoped—that what had started this weekend, hadn't ended.

She'd been right to go, and he'd been right to let her go, Kit argued to himself, listening for the taxi to pull away, sealing Fleur's departure. Ben's arrival with Dolores Diaz had broken the bubble of enchantment and the reality check had been too abrupt. Damage had been done. Not too much, he hoped. Still, it was an inescapable truth that damage was always done in the real world.

Very little was perfect.

Very little remained perfect.

The taxi took off, marking the end of two incredibly marvellous days in his life. Fantasy or fact, he briefly wondered. Tomorrow was another day and if Fleur couldn't absorb the damage and keep moving on with him, she wasn't the woman he thought she was. It was as simple as that.

He activated the lock on the gate and walked back to finish off Ben's visit—the payback for failure to attend the party last night. Though even if he'd remembered it, Kit knew he wouldn't have gone, wouldn't have wanted to share Fleur with anyone else. Still, Ben could hardly be expected to appreciate that viewpoint. He'd never been enthralled with a woman. Neither had he before this.

Would it last?

Too early to tell.

'Honestly, Kit! What planet does Fleur come from? Those clothes…' Dolores drawled.

The grey suit, lemon blouse, sensible shoes…the comment echoed his own thoughts when he'd first seen Fleur, yet looking at Dolores now in her skimpy shorts and top—everything about her so *obvious*— he found a new appreciation of the pleasure in mystery and discovery.

'You may not understand this, Dolores,' he said with a taunting edge, sure in his own mind she'd been bitchy to Fleur, 'but there is a subtle power in understatement.'

'Power…' Ben curled his mouth around the word as though he wanted to spit it out. 'Did *she* persuade you not to come to my party last night?'

Kit frowned at him, vexed by his lingering resentment. 'How could Fleur know about it when I'd forgotten it myself?'

'Making you forget is one hell of a power,' Ben flashed back at him. 'Better watch that, Kit.'

'Get over it, Ben. I apologise for not letting you know I wouldn't be there, but what's another party in the scheme of things?'

'I had Press people there to pick up on your celebrating your new move.'

'On the society pages?' Kit mocked.

'Any publicity is good publicity.'

'I thank you for the thought and I'm sorry that I unwittingly frustrated it. I'm sure you handled any disappointment with your usual deft touch with the media.'

'That's not the point.'

'You're right,' Kit snapped, annoyed by the persistent tunnel vision. 'The point is that attending your party would not have helped my move on the company people tomorrow.'

'And Fleur Andersson could do that?'

'Yes.'

'Is she attached to the company you've taken over?'

Aware of Dolores' big ears and big mouth, Kit gave Ben a hard look. 'I don't wish to discuss this any further. I have work to do and I want to do it. Understand, Ben?'

'Didn't look like you were doing much work when we arrived,' Dolores put in sulkily.

'Shut up, Dolores,' Ben shot at her, rising from his chair. 'Just stay put while I have a private word to Kit.'

She pouted. 'Don't talk to me like that.'

'Pretty mouth. Stupid words. Better watch that, babe,' Ben tossed at her as he took Kit's arm and steered him towards the house.

'You're pushing it, Ben,' Kit grated, detaching himself, though accepting talk between them was necessary.

'For your own good, my friend.'

'So spit it out and let's have done with it.'

'What position does Fleur Andersson hold within the publishing company you've taken over?'

'As of tomorrow, she'll be my personal assistant.'

'Oh, great!'

Kit could feel his jaw clenching. He waited until they were inside the house before tersely stating, 'I know what you're going to say. As far as I'm concerned, it's irrelevant.'

'Sleeping with the staff? Are you mad?' Ben swung on him, eyes biting with scathing scepticism. 'You think she's not going to take advantage of having you in her clutches?'

'It's not in her character.'

'She's a woman. They think sex is power.'

'I told you she's different.'

'Oh, yeah! Different until she's sure she'd got you by the balls. Which she has already achieved since you've gone off the deep end and made the most elementary mistake in business.'

'It's my judgment call, Ben.'

'And bloody stupid it is, too. You've given her a power no staff member should have over a boss.'

'She won't use it.'

'What if she does? You can't sack her. She'll have you up on sexual harassment.'

'You don't know her.'

'I know women. Let them get their hooks in and they'll hang on for all they can get.'

'Not this one.'

'You've lost it, Kit.'

'Maybe…just maybe…I've found it, Ben.'

'Found what?'

'What I've been missing out on all these years of being on my own.'

Anger flared. 'What you've found is trouble. With a capital T. Big, big trouble!'

It ignited the anger Kit had contained up until now. 'Then it's trouble I'll handle myself. *My* way.'

'You've obviously been knocked so cockeyed you can't see straight.'

'*My* way, Ben. Don't meddle with this.'

He shook his head. 'I can see there's no talking sense to you.'

'You could try trusting my instincts.'

'Right now they're all below the belt.'

'Enough!' A surge of rage blew away any further attempt at reasoning. 'You've given your advice. I've told you it doesn't apply. No more argument, Ben. And I do not care to listen to any further derogatory comments on Fleur. Have you got that?'

It gave Ben pause before blathering on with more offensive strikes at the situation. He took a deep breath and raised his hands in a peace gesture. 'Sorry! Fine! Don't say I didn't warn you.'

The fire in Kit's belly was not appeased. 'Warn or insult?'

'I'm backing off. Okay?'

'Fine! And I'd appreciate it if you didn't blab my business to your *babe* out there.'

'I *never* mix business with pleasure. A golden rule, Kit.' He left one hand up in a mocking farewell salute. 'Not another word! I'm off! Good luck tomorrow!'

Kit was never so glad to see the back of his business partner. And his screw-anyone girlfriend. Who was a prime example of precisely what Ben had been warning him about. But Fleur was not in the same category as Dolores Diaz. She was so far distant from it, the warning was almost laughable.

He was well aware he was breaking a golden rule.

But there was always an exception to any rule.

He'd decided this was it.

If he was wrong...

Well, he'd be learning a lesson he'd never forget.

CHAPTER NINE

MONDAY morning…with a vengeance, Fleur thought, given the amazing highs of a very private and personal weekend with Kit Malone, and the all too probable complexities she'd be facing at the office today. There was no anticipatory bounce in her step as she alighted from her train at Town Hall Station and started walking towards Market Street. Every minute since she'd left Kit had made her more nervous and wary about how it was going to be when they faced each other again.

Could she set aside the intimacy they had shared if she had to? Apparently he could. He'd done it the moment the outside world had intruded on them yesterday. But when they were alone together, would he relax back into it? Or had the Ben Steiner/Dolores Diaz combination succeeded in killing off what they undoubtedly viewed as an undesirable situation between her and Kit?

The main problem was not knowing how Kit viewed the time he'd spent with her. The recollection of his words in the boardroom last Friday afternoon—*I play to win*—kept fretting at what she wanted to believe. Was he congratulating himself on a useful connection made? A trouble-free rapport established? A valuable ally secured? Submission to his will guaranteed?

The questions—not even raised when they'd been together—were now causing her considerable heartburn. She couldn't come to any decisions and she shied away from making any assumptions.

The only certainty was that nothing was going to be the same as when Warwick Lancaster had ruled his publishing house, not for her, nor for anyone else.

'Fleur…'

The call halted her. She turned to see Jane Haskell skipping around the slowed traffic in George Street, typically ignoring the pedestrian crossing—fast-lane Jane, charging for what she wanted.

'I tried to call you all weekend,' she shot at Fleur accusingly. 'Where the devil were you?'

'Was there some problem?' They were hardly bosom friends and Fleur was not about to confide in her.

'Oh, for heaven's sake!' A roll of heavily made-up eyes. 'What we all face this morning is *a problem!*'

Having reached Fleur's side, she paused to check her dress was straight, shimmying until it fell right. Fleur suspected the lining was a bit askew. It was one of the sheer dresses that were very *in* this summer, a swirl of bright colours—turquoise, lime green, orange, bright lemon—on a black background. Jane had chosen turquoise accessories; a *Cab* handbag and high-heeled backless sandals. Her legs were bare, which Fleur regarded as unbusiness-like, but everyone had different standards these days.

To her mind, Jane was dressed more for a party than the office. On the other hand, maybe Kit Malone *was* the party in Jane's mind, and she'd dressed to kill. In which case, she might very well be peeved if her target didn't respond as she wanted him to. Or worse, showed a preference for Fleur.

Problems…yes. There was a lot of truth in the saying—never mix business with pleasure. Kit had crossed that line on Friday night and she'd been fool enough to cross it, too. Yet she couldn't honestly regard her choice as foolish, not when it had resulted in what she could only call a once-in-a-lifetime experience. No regrets. It was just that the price to be paid for it was nerve-rackingly uncertain, as yet.

Jane flicked the irritatingly long bangs of her long black hair from her face and continued her accusing train of thought. 'You got the inside track, having dinner with the new boss on Friday night.' Her eyes flashed dark envy. 'Warwick told me, so don't bother denying it.'

Fleur shrugged as she began walking again. 'It's true we had dinner together. You might remember I was busy with Warwick's farewell on Friday afternoon and he wanted to have a chat with me about the business.'

Jane sighed her exasperation. 'Why you?'

'Why not me? I was Warwick's P.A. Perhaps he wanted to know if I'd suit him or not.'

In every way, as it had turned out. And she'd thought she had. She'd thought...

'I take it you passed with flying colours,' came the waspish comment.

Fleur pushed the memories away. 'He didn't suggest I resign, if that's what you mean,' she answered.

But she might have to if she couldn't cope with the situation Kit presented today.

Or if he flitted to another tree.

Instant recoil at that thought. Somehow he'd touched her too deeply for her to stomach another woman superseding her as *above all the rest.*

'So what did he talk about? What did he want to know from you?' Jane quizzed.

Fleur did her best to push her private torment aside. They were turning into Market Street. She had to get her mind focused on the business of today.

'Nothing for you to worry about, Jane. He didn't discuss people in the company. More his purpose for taking the company over.'

'Which is?'

'I'm sure he'll be telling you personally.'

'You can give me a hint, can't you?' Acid impatience.

Fleur gave her a level look designed to force a backdown. 'Would you breach confidentiality if you were in my position, Jane? With a new boss?'

Her grimace conceded the point. She changed tack, her dark eyes twinkling wickedly, inviting a woman-to-woman chat. 'Did you find him sinfully sexy?'

Again Fleur shrugged, hiding her personal vulnerability to Kit's strong physical attraction. 'I imagine most women would see him that way.' Certainly Dolores Diaz did.

'And how!' Jane affirmed with lustful fervour. 'My toes are curling just at the prospect of being in the same room.' A sly look. 'I don't suppose you even batted an eyelash, sitting over a dinner table with him.'

'It was business, not a date,' Fleur reminded her somewhat tersely.

'Well, I sure would have turned it into something else, given the chance,' came the feeling reply.

Along with every other woman in the world. Which hammered home the kind of competition she could expect for Kit. Not that she was going to compete, she fiercely resolved. Either she was above all the rest for him or she wasn't. That was his decision. Fighting every other woman for his interest was simply not on. She'd rather walk away with pride and dignity intact, remembering what had been uniquely special for however short a time it had lasted.

'But I guess having Russell makes a difference,' Jane argued, happily excusing the apparent lack of response to their new boss's magnetic sex appeal.

Russell!

Fleur's feet almost faltered in shock. She hadn't given Russell a thought—not one thought!—since she had left the taxi outside Kit's home on Friday evening.

'After all, he's a very hunky guy, too,' Jane prattled on. 'And he obviously thinks the world of you, always ready to do anything you want.'

A stab of guilt pierced Fleur's heart. She hadn't loved Russell. A whole year of their lives had been wasted, pursuing a relationship that was never going to build into what Russell had hoped for. Yet it hadn't really been a deception on her part. She simply hadn't known better. It had seemed…promising. Yet virtually in the wink of an eye, Kit Malone had wiped out any prospect of her ever getting back together with Russell.

Jane maundered on about her own failed relationships, putting the fault on the men she had mistakenly chosen. Fleur barely heard her, so consumed was she with the memory of all she had experienced with Kit. But was it more a dream shaped from her own secret yearnings than anything she could really base life decisions on?

How did *he* view what had happened between them?

They reached their building and turned into the huge marble lobby, heading for the elevators at the far end of it. The heels of their shoes clacked on the floor, sounding like a drum-roll leading them towards a moment of truth. Fleur let Jane press the button to summon an elevator. She suddenly felt tremulous, unsure of being able to control anything, not even her hands.

It was the same elevator that had transported her and Kit down on Friday evening. Seeking immediate distraction from any lingering sense of his strong presence, Fleur snatched at the first question she could think of to get Jane off her subject of men she had bedded.

'What did others on the staff think of Kit Malone last Friday?'

'A new broom,' she replied in an ominous tone. 'And one that's not likely to leave any old dust in corners.'

'A man with a mission,' Fleur murmured, not realising she'd spoken out loud until Jane pounced on it.

'A mission to do what?'

'Sell more books,' tripped straight off her tongue.

Jane huffed her frustration. 'You can be an infuriating person, Fleur Andersson.'

'Sorry. I don't mean to be.'

'I know. It's just the way you are. Makes me wonder, though, how Kit Malone will like working with you...' A sceptical eyebrow raised. '...all that high octane energy of his running into your mountain of calm.'

The calm was totally deceptive this morning. It was Fleur's only shield against the effect of Kit's power to turn her inside out—mentally, physically and emotionally.

The elevator halted, its doors opening onto their floor.

They stepped out.

'I wish you luck,' Jane muttered before sheering off to head down the corridor to the editorial offices.

Luck was not what this situation was about, Fleur

thought, her heart fluttering nervously with the feeling of being completely at sea, with no idea which way the tide would be flowing today. She forced herself to walk steadily towards the executive offices, knowing Kit would be at his desk already. A man with a mission did not arrive late.

One way or another he would set the tone of what she could expect from him.

Then she would be able to decide what to do.

If she could keep her wits about her.

Kit heard her enter the adjoining office, noting it was still ten minutes short of nine o'clock—early enough to be in good time, not so early as to appear anxious.

Good, he thought, not wanting her to feel anxious about working with him. He pushed his chair back from his desk, intent on greeting her and putting to rest any concerns she might have about intimate dalliances in these rooms, or anywhere on official business. If his reading of her character was right, she wouldn't invite them and any dubiously familiar word or action from him would be anathema to her in their work environment.

The carpet muffled his footsteps. He'd left the door between their offices slightly ajar so he would hear her arrival and it made no noise when he pulled it back. She was behind her desk, removing some personal items from her handbag. He paused in the doorway, feeling an intense sense of satisfaction.

He hadn't been wrong about her. Fleur Andersson was uniquely herself. The pale blue suit she wore was perfectly tailored to her slender figure. She'd chosen a white blouse today with little sprigs of blue on it, probably tiny flowers. The string of pearls hung around her neck and pearl studs clung to her earlobes.

This was her style of dress and Kit could see now how perfectly it suited her. He had been intuitively sure that nothing was going to change or divert the essential Fleur—the quiet inner strength, the sense of what was right to her mind—but it felt good to have his judgment affirmed. He wasn't in the habit of respecting many people. Most of them led messy lives, swayed every which way by others' opinions. Not this woman. This woman walked to her own drum. Just as he did.

Her short flyaway fair hair looked soft and shiny, temptingly touchable, and the light feminine pink on her lips had an incredibly sexy allure, reminding him of wildly erotic sensuality and uninhibited passion that was a long way on from mere pleasure in his desire for her. Yet she emitted a seductively female submission that appealed so strongly to him, the urge to feel it again...

No, this wasn't the time nor the place.

Kit threw the governing switch in his mind and moved onto the path that would serve him best today.

'Good morning!'

Instant stillness. Then the slow turn of her head, guarded blue eyes focusing directly on his, watchful for any signal she might not like.

He smiled his pleasure in seeing her—a simple *glad you're here* smile.

She relaxed enough to return it. 'Good morning, Mr. Malone.'

He was amused by her formality. 'Is there a correct length of time before it's appropriate to call me Kit in the office?'

Her chin tilted slightly. 'If you're asking my opinion, I think formality will serve you better with the staff until you've sorted out the level of friendliness you want to establish with them.'

'Informality can slice through resistance,' he argued. 'Make them open up more.'

A blush whooshed into her cheeks but her gaze remained steadily on his. 'Whatever you think best. It's your decision.'

He didn't want a *you're the boss* cop-out from her. 'But...' he prompted, testing for where she might lead.

A slight shrug. 'People tend to take themselves very seriously in the book world. Familiarity can be misinterpreted if used too quickly.'

His inclination was to instantly smash the barrier she seemed intent on putting in place, yet her view of the bigger picture could be valid. Magazines were aimed at a quick turnover. Books were intended for a long haul in the marketplace. The people involved probably did carry different attitudes towards their work.

To ignore the advice of his personal assistant who had years of this territory under her belt could very well be unwise, yet Fleur could be pursuing a private agenda here, establishing *her* standard for reasons of her own.

'Playing to others' rules goes against my grain,' he stated unequivocally.

Shoulders squared, backbone stiffening, chin lifting higher. 'I always thought a conqueror sent in scouts and listened to their reports before deciding on his line of attack.' Her eyes flashed a testing challenge. 'Of course how much value he places on those reports comes down to his judgment.'

She was measuring his ego level!

And subtly pushing the point that if he was so big-headed or pig-headed not to listen to her advice, the blame for any costly mistake he made from ignoring it lay fairly and squarely on his shoulders.

'You're saying don't move too quickly.'

The irony of that dictate in reference to themselves was impossible to keep out of his voice, and his eyes transmitted the memory of just how quickly he had acted and how quickly she had responded.

Kit knew instantly he'd pressed the wrong button with her. The air between them was suddenly charged with negative electricity. Her cheeks once again bloomed with heat but the eyes above the infusion of warmth were blue ice.

'You know best how successful your own modus operandi is, Mr. Malone,' she stated flatly. 'Please excuse my questioning it.' The ice snapped to let through a blaze of scorching emotion. 'On second thoughts, I'm sure all the women attached to the company will appreciate whatever rules you play to.'

The message was crystal clear. If he'd used sex to get her onside with him, and intended to use sex to generally get other female staff and authors onside with his projects, Fleur Andersson would henceforth be a block of permafrost as far as he was concerned.

It belittled what the two of them had shared to such an extent, Kit found himself bristling with anger that she would even think he'd use such tactics to get his own way. He hadn't made his fortune via a stream of beds. In fact, experience had taught him there were as many negative aspects to being attractive to women as there were positive, especially in business. If expectations were raised—even unwittingly—and left unanswered, a stab in the back was a very common and costly reaction.

His pursuit of Fleur Andersson had been the exception, not *his* rule, and here he was, damned in her eyes for it! He gritted his teeth and commanded a cooler head to deal with the problem. No way was he about to excuse what had happened between them, to which she had been an equal party anyway. He'd meant to draw lines between business and pleasure today and they would now be adhered to with a vengeance.

'I appreciate your advice, Miss Andersson, and will take it under consideration with each person I deal with.'

She needn't think she'd won! The game was his to play, not hers.

No backchat this time. The blast of emotion had shrivelled up. She looked as though she'd been turned into a block of stone.

'If you're ready to step into my office now,' he clipped out, still seething at her attempt to set him down and determined on asserting his authority, 'I'd like to run through today's schedule with you.'

She unstiffened herself enough to incline her head, acknowledging his request and her readiness to accede to it.

Kit didn't wait for her to move towards him. He turned and strode back to his desk, privately vowing not to allow one word or look carry anything she could interpret as ambivalent in any personal sense.

He didn't *need* her.

He'd got this far on his own wits, in spite of his father's prediction of abject failure for not submitting to *his rule*. If Fleur Andersson thought she could dominate any aspect of his thinking, she'd be out of his life before she could blink.

The golden rule…

Was Ben right after all?

Had that little exchange erupted from a sense of possessiveness she thought she had every right to have?

If so, Fleur had better learn one lesson very fast.

No one *owned* him.

And no one ever would.

CHAPTER TEN

FLEUR had to drag herself out of the shock she'd inflicted upon herself.

He was going to run through today's schedule with her. Which meant he still expected her to work with him, to assist in any capacity she could.

It was a wonder he hadn't sacked her on the spot!

She'd been faced with Kit Malone for only a few minutes and a jealous snipe had sliced off her tongue for no good reason at all! So what if he'd seemed to deride her advice against moving too quickly, his eyes telegraphing just how effective it had been for both of them on Friday night! To leap into applying what he'd done with her to how he'd deal with every other woman was utter madness.

What had got into her?

He had, came the swift stark answer, to a depth she'd never experienced before, tapping feelings she hadn't yet learned to control—primitive possessive feelings. Just one look at him and she'd wanted what Dolores Diaz and Jane Haskell were hunting for. Only more. Much more. And it killed her to think of any other woman getting even the smile he'd greeted her with.

Having slipped hopelessly out of control, she wasn't even sure now if her professional advice to him had been honest, or tainted with the wish for him not to get close to anyone else. A need for some control had pushed for a formal distance to be kept between them at work. Or was it a form of self-protection in case he didn't want her anymore?

Whatever…there was certainly no pleasure in achieving her objective. Mr. Malone…Miss Andersson…it was pompous nonsense, underlining what was now a very cold chasm between them. Fleur hated it as she followed him into his office. She wanted the intimacy back. She wanted him to turn around, sweep her into his embrace and kiss her senseless, completely smashing any care about what anyone else thought. Better still, demonstrating to all and sundry that he was taken. By her.

But he walked straight to the chair behind his desk without so much as a glance at her, and Fleur felt miserably chastened as she closed the door behind them, then settled herself gingerly on the chair she'd always used when taking notes from Warwick. It was on the opposite side of the large executive style desk which provided a very solid physical barrier to letting any lustful desires get out of hand. Although Kit was perfectly capable of hauling her across it and…

'I want to review our non-fiction list this morning,' he stated matter-of-factly, a cool denial of any heated thoughts about her.

It jolted Fleur out of her feverish fantasies. She gripped her pen tightly, forcing control on at least one part of her body. It took more effort to meet his gaze levelly, projecting an expression of waiting for his instructions.

'I've been looking at the bestseller lists, month by month for the past two years,' he went on. 'We've done well with diet and exercise books, cooking, gardening, biographies of our sporting heroes, but we haven't even tapped the relationship market.'

He paused, subjecting her to a keenly assessing look. Fleur struggled to climb out of the mess in mind. She'd lost his respect with her dreadful gaffe. If she didn't regain it, there was nowhere for them to go. Resignation loomed as the inevitable end.

'Is our non-fiction publisher, Peter Shaw, a go-getter or the type to wait and see what literary agents present to him?' he asked, seeking her supposedly informed opinion.

Being put on the spot about a fellow employee did not sit well with her, knowing how anxious everyone was about their jobs, yet her own job was to assist Kit in what he wanted to do. It was *his* interests she had to serve now.

'I know he has commissioned work which has sold well, mostly about local celebrities,' she answered, realising even as she spoke, it was not a great record of go-getting.

'Easy and obvious targets,' Kit muttered. He shifted restlessly. 'I need people who can see holes in the marketplace and fill them brilliantly.'

In fairness to Peter, Fleur had to say, 'There aren't many risk-takers in publishing. Perhaps if you give him a directive, he'll rise to the challenge.'

It evoked a grim smile. 'We have to move beyond playing safe. If that puts our Mr. Shaw out of his comfort zone, he doesn't belong on my team. Set up a meeting with him for ten o'clock. We'll use his office so he can put his hands on any material I might ask for.'

The new broom…in ruthless action. She was instantly reminded of the words he had spoken just before they'd parted yesterday—*I won't be held back from where I want to go.* Not by her nor anyone else.

'Do you want me to sit in on this meeting?' she asked, unsure what role he had in mind for her, if indeed she really had a role at all.

'Yes, Miss Andersson, I do. You need to be up to date on everything I'm aiming for and…' His eyes took on a hard mocking gleam. '…I'm interested in hearing your slant on how my ideas are received. I trust your scouting instincts will be very sharp today.'

And loyalty to his mission had better be even sharper, if she was reading him correctly. He intended playing hardball with no quarter given and Fleur fiercely wished she'd kept her mouth shut earlier. She should have realised Kit had set a path from which he would tolerate no deviation and their sexual connection had no relevance to it.

'What about Jane?' The words slipped out of a well of concern for the people who had worked happily under Warwick Lancaster.

'Jane?' His eyebrows rose in a challenging arch.

'Jane Haskell, our fiction publisher. She has equal status to the non-fiction publisher within the company and it will look bad if...' It would definitely unsettle the staff even more, but she bit back those indiscreet words. 'Do you intend to meet with her today?'

'You call her Jane,' he drawled pointedly, 'but you advise *me* to call her Ms. Haskell?'

Fleur wished a hole would open up that she could drop into. Her face flamed with guilt and shame. She couldn't bring herself to keep arguing for formality. It was wrong. Especially in-house. She knew—*knew*—Jane would find it threatening, making her too nervous to perform well. The same could probably be said for Peter Shaw.

'I'm sorry,' she blurted out, driven by her sense of rightness to correct what she'd done. 'I was trying...there are some older authors who...' She floundered. 'You could be regarded as...' No. No excuses. She took a deep breath and forced out the truth. 'It was protection.'

He frowned. 'Protection?'

'For me. For you. Not letting anyone think we're too...too familiar with each other. But you don't need it, Kit.' She shook her head at her own stupid folly. 'I'm sorry. And I'm sorry for what I said about...about your effect on women. It was totally uncalled for. Totally.'

In an anguish of shame, she shot to her feet, too agitated to sit still. 'I'll go and set up the meeting with Peter. I think he'd feel more at ease, be more

open and receptive if you call him Peter,' she babbled, already on the move towards the door, desperate for some recovery time.

So much for *the mountain of calm!*

It was utterly shattered.

'Wait!'

She had her hand on the doorknob, escape within
her grasp. Her heart screamed a protest at the command from Kit, yet even the muddle in her mind
insisted he was still her boss and to ignore him
would compound the professional sins she had already committed.

She waited, her whole body a tremulous mess. It
took a few seconds to muster the strength to turn
around and face him. His chair was swung towards
her, a big leather executive chair, the seat of authority. He filled it, dominated it, and what Jane had
called his high octane energy was trained directly on
her with raking intensity.

He kept her waiting, his silence tearing at her
nerves. Was he weighing up whether to keep her or
not, whether she'd be a hindrance or a help to his
grand plan? Had her *confession* proved how unreli-
able she might be? Was he thinking he wouldn't be
able to trust her advice on anything?

This was the price to be paid!

And still his eyes burned into hers, making her
feel like a butterfly writhing on a death-delivering
needle. When he finally spoke, it was like a strike
to the heart.

'Are you with me, Fleur?'

It hurt. It clawed at so many raw and sensitive places, there was no easy answer to it. She'd said yes on Friday night, yes to the experience he'd offered and given, and while there'd been just the two of them, it had been all she wanted. But there was a difference between leading and dominating, and she couldn't help feeling Kit had crossed that line.

She wanted to be with him, wanted it very badly, and the tug of his sexual magnetism was so strong, she could barely lift her mind above it. Only a weak and wavering sense of self whispered that she needed some acknowledgment from him. Being a slave to his will was not acceptable—*now I want you, now I don't, just wait in the wings until I want you again.*

She wasn't even aware of the question forming. It just spilled from her lips, a ragged hope, a nagging fear. 'Are *you* with me, Kit?'

He tilted his head to one side as though weighing his reply. She stared at him, half expecting to be crushed, yet knowing the words she'd spoken had poured from a need she could no longer suppress.

'I would have thought that was self-evident,' he said musingly.

'No.' She shook her head. Her eyes shot her truth at him, no longer caring that the feelings being expressed were personal, not professional. 'You disconnected from me yesterday. I was trying to disconnect from you this morning. I made a hash of it.'

His eyes narrowed, still concentrated on her but

Fleur sensed the running of memory tapes through his mind.

'If you're referring to when Ben came,' he said slowly. 'You had my support. I didn't know you needed me to hold your hand.'

A half-hysterical laugh broke from her throat. 'Oh, I can stand alone. I'm actually very good at it. That's not the point.'

'What is?'

She dragged in a deep breath and tried to steady her voice, determined to lay it out now even if it led to her resignation.

'You took my hand on Friday night. Then when other people turned up, you dropped it. Cold. No more sharing. No more…mutuality. So how am I supposed to reply to…*am I with you?* I don't know where you are, Kit.'

His mouth slowly curved into a wry grimace. 'Well, I could say I'm sitting in this chair, where I've planned to be for some time.'

The boss!

Fleur's stomach contracted around a sick hollowness.

'On the other hand…'

He pushed out of the chair with a lithe powerful surge, making her heart skip at the instant sense of a dangerous animal staking his territory, primed to fight any threat to it. And she was in his sights, no escape, no letting her go. The aggression emanating from him was mesmerising as he closed the distance between them. She didn't move. Didn't think of moving. Only her heart moved, pounding into a wild gallop.

His arm swept around her waist, hauling her against a hard wall of muscle. He cupped her face, his thumb tilting her chin high. She looked into eyes that speared her soul.

'I didn't want to expose what we shared to Ben. Nor to Dolores Diaz. It wasn't for their eyes. But how could I not want to be with you, Fleur?'

And his mouth carried those words to hers in a storm of kisses that obliterated any defences she might have raised, any questioning she might have thought of, any lingering sense of disconnection. Her arms flew up around his neck, winding, binding, and all sense of self was lost in a raging flow of passion.

This was how it had been. This was how it was…the quick craving for each other, unabated. Kit's hands were in her hair, pressing possessively down her back, clutching her buttocks, lifting her to fit more intimately with him. Torrents of sensation poured through her, exultant desire running rampant, her mouth as erotically driven as his, her breasts straining to feel the beat of his heart, acutely sensitised from the heat of his chest, her stomach glorying in the hard roll of his erection—such intensely satisfying proof that he wanted her as madly, as needfully, as urgently as she wanted him.

He backed her up against the wall, locked the door. 'I hope you're not wearing pantihose,' he growled between kisses—kisses on her eyelids, her nose, her temples.

She caught breath enough to answer, 'Stockings.'

'Yessss…' It was a hiss of triumphant pleasure, his hands gathering up her skirt and reaching the bare tops of her thighs. Then his mouth was invading hers again, driving anticipation for the ultimate act of intimacy, his tongue darting, plunging, rolling around hers, teasing, exciting to fever-pitch, raising excitement even higher as she felt him unzip himself, felt the slip of silk between her legs being moved aside, felt the hot hard naked length of him sliding between her soft folds.

Yesss…her body sang, and it was a song of fierce exhilaration.

He hitched her up. Her legs found purchase somewhere behind his knees. Her shoulders were hard against the wall, her hands raking down his back, fingers digging in, calling on the strength and power she knew was his. It pulsed from him, pulsed through her as he took the path he'd opened, thrusting forward, driving to the innermost depth of union, filling her with such intense satisfaction, she quivered in sheer ecstasy.

His arms tightened around her, preventing any slipping away as he swivelled and carried her with him to the desk, laying her on the broad surface of it, planting his hands on either side of her, doing precisely what she'd imagined he could when she was afraid he might not ever want to.

It was incredibly marvellous, watching the powerful rhythm of his body drive the rhythm of their joining, the inward concentration of pleasure in his eyes, the strain of working muscles against his shirt, the taut need on his face, feeling inside her the constant cresting waves of sensation, building, building, breaking faster, tension climbing.

The desk telephone rang.

She thought he would ignore it.

There was a leap of wild wickedness in his eyes as he plunged deeply, picked up her legs and fastened them around his waist. Then he snatched up the telephone receiver.

'Yes?'

He made teasing little movements as he listened, twinkling eyes laughing at Fleur as he finally answered.

'I'm conducting a vital meeting. Hold all calls until I let you know I'm available.'

Had to be the receptionist, still speaking as he started lowering the receiver. He raised it to his ear again, grinning down at Fleur.

'Miss Andersson is not available, either. She's with me.'

The receiver crashed down. He leaned over her, his face coming closer, closer, his eyes dancing with devilish joy, lips brushing hers. 'You are with me, aren't you, Fleur?' he murmured teasingly.

Laughter gurgled from her throat. It was mad— mad and bad and beautiful, and she loved it. She squeezed him with her inner muscles. He laughed and started again, revelling in the control he took, speaking to her between thrusts.

'I *want* you with me.'

'I want to ride through this day, knowing you're with me.'

'Pushing the program.'

'Lighting fires in their bellies.'

'Reaching for more.'

'Making it happen.'

'Come with me…come with me…come with me…'

Fast now…gloriously fast…a mighty drumming of explosive sensation spinning her into an exquisite climax of coming together. And still he rested inside her, holding the sweet sense of fusion while his eyes commanded her to keep it, too, keep it long beyond this moment.

'Work with me today, Fleur. Whatever I do, whatever I say, stay connected to me. As I'm connected to you. And when the day is done, we'll stroll down to Darling Harbour, relax over a fine dinner at Chinta Ria, eat and drink at our leisure, remembering, celebrating, how we feel now. And we'll think of how much more we might feel when I take you home and time is ours and ours alone.'

He kissed her with long, lingering sensuality as he slowly, slowly withdrew from her. 'All right now?' he murmured.

'Yes,' she whispered, silently vowing not to let anything ruin their connection.

She was with him.

He lifted his head, took a deep breath, gave her a rueful smile. 'There is one thing we must agree upon, Fleur. As good as this was, and as much as we both wanted it, there will be no more of it in the office. Strictly business here. You do understand…'

He was switching off again. It was happening right now. How could he do it? How could she?

A weird flutter of panic raced through her. He was asking her to play a part—take on a double life. Lovers in private but here…no one was to know?

'It doesn't mean I'm disconnected from you,' he assured her. 'It means there will be other levels in operation. Professional levels.'

She could accept that. What he said was common sense—so why did she feel in such conflict about it?

'You'll have my support,' he went on. 'Tell me I can count on yours, Fleur.'

There was no question about that.

'An assistant assists,' she said, forcing a wry little smile. 'I'll support your projects as best I can.'

His smile was rich with satisfaction. 'Then let's get to work.'

He helped her to her feet. She couldn't bring herself to look at him while they re-established respectable appearances. Business now, she kept reciting to herself. Hide the intimacy. Button up. Nothing but business in the office. And Kit rammed it home, moving straight into instructions.

'Inform Peter Shaw of the ten o'clock meeting and let Jane Haskell know I'll be looking at the fiction list with her at two o'clock this afternoon.'

He'd listened to her.

He'd responded positively.

What more could she ask of him in these circumstances?

'Jane will be pleased,' she said, wondering if she could stomach the fiction publisher playing up to Kit without wanting to scream, 'Hands off!'

'I'm only interested in performance,' Kit answered dryly, rounding the desk to his chair again.

She nodded and headed for the door. No being stopped this time. Kit had set the course. Wanting him as she did, Fleur knew she had to accept his rules and play by them, right down the line.

Tonight, she thought, I'll get my reward.

Something deep inside her rebelled at that idea.

It was wrong.

But she'd worry about it later.

Today she would follow the plan.

CHAPTER ELEVEN

THE days in the office were not so difficult to manage as Fleur had expected them to be. Kit's personal magnetism focused everyone's attention on him, his drive and energy galvanising the staff into a flurry of enthusiastic activity. Even as his personal assistant, almost constantly at his side, she went virtually unnoticed. She was viewed, as usual, as the facilitator of directives given, a channel to and from the boss, an advisor behind the front line.

Kit, of course, made no move that would alter this view. Neither did she. Occasionally a look passed between them that didn't belong to strictly business—an understanding that might have been read as intimate if anyone had suspected their private relationship. No one did. And Kit was very particular about keeping the female staff in general at arm's length. They could earn the flash of a smile from him. That, alone, melted most of them at the knees. But if anyone besides Jane was hoping for more, they didn't get it.

As long as Kit stayed true to her...as long as there was no other woman...Fleur told herself she could live with not having their more personal connection acknowledged. The nights they spent together made up for it. When the work of the day was done, he shared all his thoughts with her on what had happened, and what he intended to do next, making her feel an integral part of his book world. And the sex with him was too addictive to give up. It felt as though he was making love to her and she knew she was making love to him, but it didn't seem to follow through into anything more from him.

The demarcation lines stayed in place.

The bad time came when he left her to herself and she was faced with living this life with him in separate boxes. It wasn't just the box for work, and the box for away from work. There was the box with Ben Steiner in it, too. That was Kit's magazine world and he didn't want her overlapping into it. Ben wouldn't like it and Ben was the major player in place, taking care of business while Kit extended himself into the book market.

Fleur wondered if he ever spoke about her to Ben. If she even entered his mind when he was with Ben. It was probably weird feeling jealous of a business relationship between two men but she did. Because she was locked out of it.

All the same, the highs she did share with Kit were so high, Fleur kept the lows to herself, nursing them in silence, quelling the rebellion that occasionally demanded she really look at what she was accepting. Even if she was short-changing herself, when all was said and done, Kit Malone was a man apart—exciting, challenging, passionate, a dynamic leader—and it was all too easy to argue she was lucky to get some of him.

Three weeks slipped by.

Three weeks of playing to Kit's rules.

Then the roses came.

Friday morning…Kit was in the boardroom with Jane and one of her authors, discussing the kind of Australian story Kit wanted to push. Fleur was on the telephone in her office, touching base with booksellers on her personal contact list, canvassing interest in Kit Malone's new initiatives, dropping names to drive up curiosity.

She had just finished one call and was checking the next one to be made on her list when a knock on the door was followed by the cheerful face of Sally Jethroe poking around it.

'Ah! You're free!'

'What for?' Fleur asked, smiling at the receptionist whose perky nature invariably drew smiles. She was slightly plump but very pretty with a mass of brown curls and merry brown eyes. Her generosity of spirit reached out to everyone, making visitors always feel happily welcomed.

'Just hold it right there,' came the teasing command. 'Stay off the wretched phone. Leave the door open. I'll be right back.'

Fleur did as she was told, glad to have a relaxing break for a few minutes. She liked Sally who had been her biggest helper in organising Warwick's farewell. Which had only been three weeks ago, Fleur reflected, heaving a sigh over the incredible change in her life since then.

She hoped Warwick was enjoying his retirement.

He would undoubtedly be shocked at what she was doing with her new boss. It would be appallingly wrong for any number of reasons in his book. As it was, her relationship with Kit had very little to do with reason. More primal instinct. In any event, she had no one to answer to except herself over the decisions she had made.

'Here we are!' Sally backed her way in, pushing the door wide open as she swung around, carefully carrying a stunning arrangement of red roses. 'You were on the phone when the delivery boy arrived so I held them for you in reception.' She grinned. 'Pretended they were for me. Probably used up most of their scent, smelling them.'

Red roses?

They couldn't be from Kit...could they?

'So what's the big occasion?' Sally's eyes twinkled. 'Is Russell going to pop the question tonight?'

Russell!

Fleur's heart had begun to jiggle at the possibility that Kit might be surprising her but...it dropped into a heavy thud at Sally's reminder of the man who had promised her love for the rest of their lives.

Red roses for love.

Lots of them to convince her of it.

Of course, they had to be from Russell.

He'd be back from Tasmania by now. No doubt he figured he'd given her enough time to reconsider her decision, enough time to miss him, and an extravagant gesture like this would tap straight into a well of sentiment that would favour their getting back together.

In fact, it was one of the endearing things he'd always done, giving her flowers—a bunch of spring blooms, a potted tulip, Christmas bells, a posy of violets. Flowers for Fleur.

Now red roses.

Having carefully set them down on the desk, Sally stood back to admire them. 'Well?' she pressed, batting her eyelashes. 'No exciting news to tell me?'

Fleur shook her head. 'It's not what you think, Sally.'

'Oh! Pity!' A sympathetic grimace. 'I'll leave you to it then. Card pinned on the side. If this is about an argument, I'd forgive him if I were you.'

Having delivered this sage advice, she sailed out of the office, closing the door after her to seal Fleur's privacy.

Forgiveness wasn't the issue.

Fleur stared at the attached card in its little envelope, wishing she didn't have to open it, or answer it. No way could she take Russell back in her life now, which left having to dash his hopes and dreams all over again. He'd be waiting to hear from her. It was only common decency to respond. Which meant she had to read the card.

Reluctantly she leaned over and unpinned it, catching a waft of rich scent from the roses. If only it had been Kit who'd sent them… Her heart caught for a moment. Maybe it was. She didn't know for certain.

Her fingers tore open the envelope and extracted the card, flicking it open for her to read the message.

'I miss you. Can we meet? Name the time and the place and I'll be there. All my love, Russell.'

She heaved a long, deflated sigh.

Definitely not from Kit.

And so typical of Russell, leaving arrangements to her.

The office door flew open and Kit strode in, Jane Haskell at his heels. 'Fleur, we need you to…' He stopped, catching sight of the unmissable display of roses on her desk, his gaze snapping quickly from the luxurious blooms to the card she still held in her hand.

'Ah-ha!' Jane crowed. 'Big weekend coming up? Got to hand it to Russell. He sure knows how to do things in style.'

Russell… Fleur found her jaw clenching. They all thought *Russell* because no one knew about her and Kit. And he was standing there, his eyes burning into hers, not liking this scenario one bit and possibly blaming her for it though it wasn't her fault.

'You were saying?' she prompted him, ignoring Jane's interest in the gift and suddenly wanting her *secret* lover to stew a little over what the roses meant and what the card said. How did he feel about her glossing over a part of her life *he* was shut out of?

'If you're caught up in something personal…' he clipped out.

'Business comes first in the office,' she quickly

inserted, barely keeping a mocking edge out of her voice.

'Fine! Can you lay your hands on the file I put together on Far North Queensland? Our author is more drawn to that area than western New South Wales.'

'Cooktown, specifically,' Jane chimed in, instantly taking the hint that personal gossip was a *faux pas*. Warwick Lancaster would have happily played along with a little teasing but Kit Malone was a different kettle of fish.

'No problem.' Fleur rose from her desk and led the way into Kit's office where she had organised filing cabinets to store all the material he'd brought in from his home at Bondi. It only took her a few moments to extract the bulging manila folder from where she'd placed it. She handed it to Kit who passed it over to Jane.

'Give the author photocopies of any material he wants to take with him,' he instructed. 'Let me know when you're leaving for lunch and I'll join you.'

'You're not coming back to the boardroom?'

'You're his editor. Pin him down to a definite project. I'll pick it up and run with it over lunch, get him fully committed.'

'Okay.'

Jane's dark eyes were sparkling with excitement over this joint venture with Kit. She'd completely forgotten the roses. There was not even a glance at Fleur as she turned to go, her jaunty walk to the door expressing confidence in Kit's trust that she would deliver what he wanted.

Everyone on the staff responded to him like that— the intoxicating pleasure of being inspired by great leadership, being on a team committed to breaking new ground, pursuing new fields to plow. It *was* exciting. And Kit's belief that he could bring these projects off in the marketplace, made eager followers of all of them.

Besides which, he'd made it clear he took full responsibility for where he was taking them. If anything failed, they'd learn from it and move on. No blame attached to anyone. He was leading them in every sense. He'd invited them to come with him and not one of them had declined.

Fleur knew she was caught up in Kit's compelling net, too. Far more intimately than any of the others. She didn't want to leave, either, yet Russell's roses had stirred a deep discontent with how things were between them, and as she watched him follow Jane to the door, seeing her out of his office, then deliberately shutting himself and Fleur inside together, an angry rebellion simmered in her mind.

No exit for Fleur.

He turned around and stood right where he was, blocking any escape, eyeing her with ruthless purpose.

'So Russell's back,' he said grimly.

'Yes,' she answered, tearing her gaze from his and busying herself, closing the drawer of the file cabinet.

'Pleading his cause with roses?' came the sardonic comment.

Resentment voiced her reply. '*Red* roses have a very specific message.'

'Are you swayed by it?' An even more sardonic edge.

No, she wasn't, but his tone goaded her to turn around and flout his self-assurance. 'It has appeal,' she stated defiantly. 'In fact, the delivery of those flowers here reminded me that Russell never had any problem in showing anyone how special I was in his life.'

His eyes narrowed on the biting challenge in hers. 'That doesn't make him right for you.' A decisive claim.

She bristled at the lack of any giving from him. 'Is anything ever absolutely right? Those roses reminded me that while the box with Russell might not have fitted perfectly, I wasn't kept hidden in it. My role in his life was on full display.'

Having fired that highly satisfying broadside at him, she walked steadily towards the door, determined on making him move to give her exit room, if nothing else.

He didn't move.

She stopped in front of him, recklessly revelling in the tension emanating from him. One score to me, she thought savagely.

'If you don't require anything else, I have work to do,' she stated, deliberately provocative in ramming his *work* ethic down his throat.

For a few electric seconds, Kit's eyes bored into hers, demanding she place a value on everything they'd shared. Her stomach quivered as she realised he was not about to change anything.

'You know it's wrong to have our relationship on display here,' he tersely argued.

Fleur's chin went up. 'I know it's wrong for you, yes.' But trailing in his wake all day, just like everybody else, diminished what they shared at night, and she didn't like the yoyo feeling, nor the sense of being kept under wraps.

'Do you want to leave?'

The bottom line. If she didn't share his work here, what else would they share besides bed? It was all tangled up together and the truth was she couldn't let it go. Not yet. Perhaps not ever.

'Not at this moment, no,' she answered, pride insisting he shouldn't get a complete surrender from her.

Having wrung that lack of ultimate decision from her, he pushed further. 'I had assumed we'd spend the weekend together. Am I wrong in that assumption?'

The message was loud and clear. *Don't play games with him. No shilly-shallying. In or out.*

'The whole weekend? To ourselves?' she asked, refusing to let the fear of losing him override the need for some demonstration of how much he valued her. Other weekends had been broken by meetings with Ben Steiner and various unexplained calls on his time.

He paused to weigh the depth of her alienation before slowly answering, 'I have an invitation to a party tonight—the launch of a new product by Platinum Boutique who buys big advertisements in our magazines. Ben wants me to be there. I thought I'd give it a miss, but if you'd like to go…we can do that.'

It was a concession. A public outing in his social scene around the magazine trade. And right under Ben Steiner's nose, whether he liked it or not.

'Fine! Since you'll be going to lunch with Jane and her author, I might spend that time buying a new party dress.'

His face relaxed into an ironic little smile. 'I hope you'll take pleasure in it.'

'I won't know until I'm there, will I?'

And see how you deal with me in your social circle.

'Always interesting to share an experience with you, Fleur,' he rolled out, his eyes gleaming some private satisfaction as he stepped aside and opened the door for her to exit.

She was instantly certain the party was inconsequential to him and she'd probably hate it, but wild horses wouldn't stop her from going now. It represented one small victory for her self-esteem.

'The *whole* weekend?' she queried, needing that claim staked before she stepped past him.

'Yes,' he confirmed without hesitation. 'Since you'll want to shed some things…' He paused meaningly, and Fleur had no doubt he meant Russell.

'...and collect whatever items you need, I'll pick you up at your place at seven o'clock this evening. Okay?'

She nodded, and satisfied she hadn't acted like a doormat that he could walk over as he liked, Fleur continued on into her own office.

Where she was faced with the roses again.

She had to call Russell straight away, not leave him thinking there was any chance of their meeting and getting back together.

But first...the roses had to be removed from her desk. Keeping them there implied an acceptance that simply wasn't true. Besides which, it was dishonest, deceptive, to let Sally, Jane, or anyone else keep thinking she was still involved with Russell. They might never know of her relationship with Kit but it felt really sleazy to hide it behind another man.

She carried the extravagant arrangement out to reception and set it on Sally's desk. 'They look better here,' she explained. 'And more people can enjoy them.'

'But they're for you,' came the bewildered protest.

Fleur shook her head. 'I told Russell it was over. I feel wrong about having them. Take them home with you if you like, Sally.'

A pained look. 'If you say so. Sorry it didn't work out, Fleur.'

'No point in hanging on when it's wrong.'

But she was hanging on with Kit, despite the wrongness she felt, hanging on in the hope that time would take the hard edges away and make it possible for the boxes to be thrown open. Early days yet, she told herself, and she had the whole weekend ahead of her to revel in what *was* right between them.

Brilliantly right.

CHAPTER TWELVE

ONCE Fleur had gone, Kit walked slowly over to his desk, remembering how he'd taken her on it their first morning here, then laid down the law on not letting it happen again at work. Strictly business.

Had he demanded an agreement she hadn't wanted to give?

He'd thought she'd understood.

These past three weeks had run so well. Surely she could see how it had to be—one leader holding all the reins of control. It was the only way to inspire confidence. Any suggestion of unfair influence would break that. Everything had to be conducted on a purely professional level.

He sank into his chair, feeling distinctly needled by the situation that had just blown up in his face. And his reaction to it. The sense of competing with another man for Fleur had knifed straight into his gut. All his instincts shouted she was his, and he'd barely restrained himself from sweeping her into his arms and proving it to her. Only the knowledge that breaking his own rules—dangerously so—had held him back.

Had she been subtly daring him to do it—wanting to measure the strength of her power over him? If he'd fallen into that trap, he would have lost the ground he'd established here in the workplace, ground that he knew served his best interests. As it was, she'd forced his hand against the deep urge he felt to keep her to himself.

He cursed the roses from Russell—stirring feelings that had no place here in the office. The she-wolf in Fleur had definitely been snapping—*give me some ground or I might go back to where I have all of it.*

He didn't want to take her to the party. But he would. It was a done deal now. And it wouldn't do any harm. The magazine trade was a world unto itself. There would be no crossing of lines tonight. He would keep Fleur at his side and cut off any questions he didn't want answered.

Which reminded him Ben had to be notified of this decision. Seating arrangements at the table had to be organised. Probably re-organised since he'd left his attendance up in the air and here he was taking an extra person. Which could cause a problem.

The moment Ben came on the line, Kit informed him, 'I'm bringing Fleur to the launch party tonight.'

'You're *what?*'

'You heard me. I want her seated beside me at our table. Can do?'

'If that's what you want, Kit,' he answered slowly.

'Consider it settled. Are you taking Dolores?'

'No, I'm not.'

Kit felt relieved of one potential problem. Dolores Diaz was a bitchy piece. He hadn't wanted her near Fleur again. Ben was well aware of the need for discretion and was unlikely to slip up on anything he considered unwise—always having his eye on what served his best interests—but Dolores had definitely been a wild card.

'She was getting too pushy so I dumped her,' Ben went on in a rather pointed drawl.

How *pushy* was Fleur getting was the implied question.

Kit ignored it.

'So who has your favour now?' he dryly asked.

'The very tasty Tessa Templeton.'

The girl who'd recently won the model competition run by one of their magazines. She was eighteen, just out of school, and Kit hoped she was wise enough to know Ben would be no more to her than a useful connection.

'And you accused me of cradle-snatching.'

'Man, this baby left the cradle a long time ago!'

Kit didn't doubt it. Ben invariably went for women he classified as 'users.' Easy to pick up, and even easier for him to discard because the essential Ben was never really engaged with them. Getting *hooked,* as he put it, messed men up. Getting laid kept things simple.

'Well, I trust Tessa knows the score,' Kit remarked.

'Does Fleur?' came straight back at him.

'Different situation.'

'Yeah, right! I look forward to seeing the two of you together tonight. I'll go fix the table now.'

Ben wasn't ever going to understand how it was with Fleur. It had nothing to do with some superficial appeal. She matched something inside him, filling a place that had always been empty. When he was with her, even during work hours, she added a special zing of sharing that spurred him into going for more, doing better. Winning was sweeter because she was watching, listening, sharing. No other woman had ever affected him like that, lifting the ordinary into the extraordinary.

Had she done it for Warwick Lancaster in a less physical way? Was that what his warning had been about—*It's all too easy for a young lion to stamp on a flower without realising its value. And she'll walk, Kit. She won't try to hang on. And you'll lose by it. Believe me, you'll lose.*

A flower.

Roses from Russell, determined on getting her back with him. Kit had no doubt Fleur had brought that something extra special into Russell's life, too.

But she was *his*. Kit knew it in his bones. They were *right* together. Okay, if she needed some public proof that he wanted her by his side, he'd do it. But Ben was right, too. Fleur had to understand the score here, and not push him too far. He'd planned this move into book publishing too long to have it messed with by anyone. Even Fleur. Especially Fleur.

By the time Jane Haskell called him to keep the lunch appointment with her author, Kit had himself well in hand, and as he passed through Fleur's office and noted that the roses were gone, he felt a surge of triumph.

'Happy shopping!' he said by way of acknowledging peace between them.

'I hope your lunch works well,' she returned,
holding the business line, though her lips curved into
one of her Mona Lisa smiles.

He walked into the reception area and his sense
of triumph took an instant knock. The roses were
there! She hadn't got rid of them. She'd simply
moved them out of his face from her desk. Was this
a sign she hadn't completely put Russell out of the
running? Was he being held in the wings while Fleur
measured the level of satisfaction their relationship
gave her this weekend?

Kit felt his hands clench.

Be damned if he'd be drawn into some contest for
her!

She either made a decision clear-cut tonight or
he'd walk away.

Seven o'clock… Kit was in a fighting mood as he
fronted up to the door of Fleur's apartment. Some
sorting out needed to be done. And not only on the
Russell question. He'd conceded this totally useless
party and if it salved her pride, okay. But if she had
ideas of pushing him into a corner… No! He would
not be pushed!

Having rung the doorbell, he stood back, determined on getting the burning issue of Russell out of
the way before they went anywhere. Yet when the
door opened, every male instinct in him rose in a
fiercely primitive wave, demanding sole possession
of this woman, whatever it took.

She had a breathtaking allure that contracted his stomach and shot sharp signals to his groin. The dress she wore was a sensual concoction of filmy fabric embossed with velvet flowers, all black, clinging to every female curve of her body, erotically sexy, and ending in a flirty little flare above her knees. Her legs were bare, suggesting absolutely minimal underwear, and her dainty narrow feet were strapped into high-heeled sandals that were a long way from being *sensible*.

Her fair hair looked sleeker, very stylishly shaped into a smooth cap around her head, but still soft and shiny and even more temptingly touchable. She'd emphasised the sea blue of her eyes with some subtle make-up, and her mouth was a brighter pink than usual, her soft lips more artfully defined and delectably kissable.

Pearls on her earlobes. Pearls around her neck. That hadn't changed, yet with the frame of the low-scooped neckline of her dress and snug three-quarter length sleeves, they shone with a perfect elegance that lifted her overall sexiness into something very special, very classy.

The rampant desire she stirred was stronger than anything Kit had felt in his whole life. It took iron discipline to hold it in check, and only the sense of losing himself to a power he couldn't control forced him into it. He sucked in a quick fix of oxygen and spoke, dragging out the bone of contention that he'd been gnawing on.

'Well, having knocked my eyes out, tell me you're finished with Russell.'

The words came out in a harsh rasp, surprising her. She gave a slight shake of her head, as though mystified he would even put the question to her.

'I was finished with Russell before I met you, Kit. That hasn't changed and it won't change.'

'You've told him that?'

'Yes. Again today. I don't want him wasting any more time hoping there's a chance of my thinking any differently.'

'No chance?'

'None.'

So it should be. And it was, Kit thought, elation at this outcome bursting through his inner tension and making everything feel right again. He caught sight of the overnight bag standing just inside the doorway. The weekend beckoned. He stepped forward and picked it up. The action brought him very close to Fleur. He could smell her perfume—a musky scent that called on the wolf in him. He took a deep breath and looked directly into her eyes.

'You're mine, Fleur Andersson. If you even look at another man at the party tonight, I'll probably tear him apart.'

The same possessive desire simmered in her eyes. 'I might very well do the same thing to any other woman you look at.'

'I want you to myself.'

Something else flared into her eyes—a wild intensity that defied any roping her in. 'You don't own me, Kit. I'm yours because I want to be yours. But I won't be kept in a locked vault. Either you take me out with you or what we have will die. Understand?'

A *locked vault*…the evocative image sent a chill down Kit's spine. Was this what his father had done to his mother, locking her into pregnancy after pregnancy, tying her into such a closed domestic life, there was never any chance of her straying from his rule? Owning her, owning their children, directing and dominating all their lives…was the same trait in him?

He shook the idea away. He wasn't like that. He wouldn't be like that. This strong sense of mating with Fleur had been a private thing and it was best on their own. No outside distractions. But she was right. They couldn't stay closeted alone forever. His business demanded a certain level of social life and it was wrong to keep her out of it…like a denial of what she was to him.

He lifted his free hand and gently touched her cheek. Her skin was burning, reflecting the deep heat of her need to have the choice of running beside him. 'I'm sorry I made you feel as though I was holding you in a constricted space. Let's move out of it right now. You're ready to go?'

'Yes,' she said huskily. 'I just have to grab my handbag.'

It was a little black beaded affair on a thin strap which she slung over her shoulder. As they left her apartment and headed down the staircase to the street, Kit caught her hand and deliberately interlaced their fingers in a firm grip, wanting the pleasure of tangible togetherness.

Fleur flicked him a look that carried a touch of vulnerable uncertainty. 'Where is the party we're going to?'

'Doulton House. It's right on the harbour at Pyrmont. Used to be the casino before Star City was built. Now a function centre.'

'Do you know how many people will be attending?'

'Probably about a hundred and twenty.'

She took a deep breath. 'Do you intend to drop my hand once we arrive there, Kit?'

He glanced sharply at her, frowning over the carefully level tone of the question. She kept her gaze trained on the stairs they were descending. Suddenly the hand in his felt very fragile—like a flower that could easily be crushed. She'd dressed herself to fit into what she perceived as his social world, but she wasn't sure it was enough to keep him linked to her in public.

He did have other agendas.

Not tonight, he vowed.

She not only had the right to his first consideration, but looking as she did in that dress, he wasn't about to risk anyone at the party not knowing she belonged to him.

'No,' he said decisively. 'You're with me, Fleur, and I'm with you. All night.'

CHAPTER THIRTEEN

THE big day—nine months in the making and here it was at last—the launch of Kit's first group of Australiana books in time to catch the Christmas market! Nine months seemed particularly appropriate, Fleur thought whimsically. This was the birth of Kit's brainchild, and from where she stood, it was getting a great welcome into the world.

She cast her professional eye around the highly satisfying crowd of people who'd been drawn to The Outback Centre at Darling Harbour. She'd suggested this venue to Kit and it was working brilliantly. Not only did it give background colour to the books he wanted to push, but it heightened interest, as well.

Of course, the event had been highly publicised—radio, television, newspapers, magazines—interviews with Kit, interviews with the authors involved—and the media had turned up in impressive numbers to cover the launch. The important booksellers were here, as well, noting the rush of sales and the line-ups at each author's table for autographed copies.

The books were walking out the door—*Murder at Ayers Rock, The Red Heart Grab, The Cooktown Castaways, Battle of The Sexes—Aussie Style, Tripping into Tibooburra*. Teasing titles, eye-catching covers, no expense spared in presenting these babies to the public. This was a full-on drive for big sales. Kit Malone did not intend to fail in his mission.

She caught sight of Ben Steiner sidling around the crowd, obviously aiming to reach her. Fleur couldn't help tensing. He always made her feel like an interloper in Kit's life, someone who shouldn't take up as much of his time as she did, though he seemed to have accepted her as a fixture at Kit's side at the various social functions they attended. Since their very first meeting back in January, Ben had never once been rude to her, yet the feeling persisted he'd prefer her to go away and stay away.

He carried two glasses of red wine. Kit had ordered cases of Australian wine to be on tap today, pushing the home product as a general theme. A buffet of Australian finger food was also available to anyone who wanted a nibble of barramundi from Cooktown, Outback beef, aphrodisiac oysters, passionfruit tarts...

'I've brought you a drink. You deserve it,' Ben declared, thrusting one of the glasses into her hand.

'Thank you.' Surprisingly his green eyes held a twinkle of approval so it was easy for Fleur to smile at this unexpected accolade from Ben. 'It's going well, don't you think?'

He grinned. 'They're all playing Kit's game. He brings it off every time, gets them in his hand and drives them into his net.'

They watched him for a few moments, exuding

his charismatic energy to the mesmerised audience around him. Fleur couldn't help dwelling on Ben's expression—*Kit's game*. It summed up where she was—a member of the team—uniquely placed as his bed companion, but he still stood alone as team leader. Always would. It was the nature of the man.

'I've got to hand it to you, Fleur,' Ben remarked somewhat ironically. 'Most women in your position would be up there, trying to get a share of the lime-light.'

'It's not my place,' she said quietly.

He looked quizzically at her. 'You're quite rare. You know that? Sharing so much with him, yet not messing him around, demanding he perform for you.'

Her smile was wry, reflecting the bitter-sweetness of a relationship she had no way of controlling. Months ago she'd come to terms with the reality of accepting what Kit gave her of himself or having none of him at all. She could always sense the lines he drew—the lines that weren't to be crossed. She'd learnt not to mind because it wouldn't win her any-thing. And the bottom line was…she loved him, loved being part of his life, loved the intimacy of being his woman.

'Anyhow, I owe you an apology,' Ben rambled on. 'I thought Kit was making a big mistake, taking up with you. Truth is, I kept waiting for you to get your hooks in and turn the screws, while he kept saying it was a different situation.' He paused, cu-riosity sparking. 'Want to tell me the difference?'

His rather backhanded apology was probably the best Ben could do, Fleur decided, and his bid for understanding could possibly be more sincere than it sounded.

'I guess it's in sharing things you can't share with anyone else, Ben,' she answered, careful not to be judgmental about the way he ran his life.

'Yeah…well, can't say it hasn't worked. Might look for a bit more of that myself. Which reminds me, who is the tall, whippy brunette flitting between the authors?'

'Jane Haskell, our fiction publisher.'

'Attached to anyone?'

'Not that I know of.'

'Right!' He grinned. 'Great day for her, too. I might just help her celebrate it.'

Fleur found herself grinning as Ben drifted off. Jane had given up on Kit. It was now generally known that Fleur accompanied him on social outings, though their private intimacy remained strictly private. Jane would probably lap up any attention Ben Steiner gave her and if they ended up having breakfast together, she'd make the most of that, too.

Go-getter Jane. After all the hard work she'd put into Kit's projects, she deserved a reward, and after the comments Ben had just made, maybe he was a little less prejudiced against women as people.

Fleur did a slow circle of the huge room, picking up favourable comments from booksellers to relay to Kit later, ensuring that the catering was being kept up—no empty plates—stopping to chat to media people, checking the best quotable lines with them, listening to the buzz of interest from the book-buyers.

'Fleur…'

She spun around in surprise as she recognised the voice of her old boss, Warwick Lancaster. There he was, beaming his benevolent smile at her, and somehow his fatherly figure and the cosy familiarity of their old relationship brought a prickling of tears to her eyes.

'…had to come and see my girl in action again,' he teased.

My girl…he'd often called her that, rolling pride and pleasure through it, almost as though she were his daughter. It made her realise how much she'd missed his generous approval—how easy it had made her working life.

'Warwick! It's lovely to see you!' She quickly kissed his cheek while she blinked the moisture from her eyes. 'How goes the retirement?'

'I must say I've had a marvellous time, tripping around the world at leisure, not being limited to book fairs.'

'You don't miss them?'

He shook his head. 'I'm past them, my dear. But thank you so much for the complimentary books Kit has just published.'

'He was happy to send them.'

He wagged his eyebrows at her. 'Think I don't recognise a Fleur touch?'

She blushed. 'How do you feel about Kit's push into Australiana? Do you mind?'

'Good heavens, no! Part of why I sold to him. About time it was done. Just didn't have the drive and energy to do it myself.' He waved around at the surrounding crowd. 'From what I see and hear, he's made a great start.'

'Yes. It's looking good,' she fervently agreed.

His eyes twinkled at her. 'Ably assisted by you. And don't deny it, Fleur. I know your worth. Glad Kit was astute enough to see it, too.' He leaned forward and whispered. 'I hear you two are an item.'

Her blush deepened.

He chuckled, took her hand and patted it. 'No need to comment. Better man for you than Russell. Gives you a challenge, doesn't he?'

'Yes,' she admitted.

He pulled back and rustled in a plastic bag that hung on his wrist. 'Got something for you.' He lifted out a gift-wrapped box and presented it to her with a big happy smile. 'Happy birthday, Fleur!'

'Oh, Warwick!' No stopping a blur of tears now. 'It's so kind of you to remember.'

'Unwrap it! I saw it in Hong Kong and thought instantly of you.'

It was an exquisite Lladro mermaid in pale pink and beige and blue-grey. She wore a lei of tiny pink flowers around her neck and was looking down at a sea-shell in her hand—a shell containing a single pearl.

'It's just beautiful, Warwick!' she murmured huskily, then looked worriedly at him. 'It must have been terribly expensive.'

He waved away any protest. 'My wife says the best part of travelling is the duty-free shopping. It's my pleasure to think of you having it, Fleur.' He handed her the plastic bag for easy carrying.

'I'll love it forever,' she accepted gracefully. 'Thank you.'

'Happy times, my dear,' he said by way of a farewell, and moved off to chat to other people he knew here.

The gift had choked Fleur with too many emotions to resume her role of general overseer of the launch. She slipped out of The Outback Centre and walked briskly along the mall to the ladies' washroom, needing some private time to pull herself together again.

Kit had forgotten her birthday.

She'd told herself it wasn't important. Today was the culmination of all the wheeling and dealing he'd done in the industry to get his publishing program off the ground and running. His mind was totally focused on making it a new landmark in the book trade. She understood this. Forgetting her birthday was forgivable. Yet the disappointment she'd tried to bury, rose up again in a sickening wave.

Warwick had remembered.

If she was still with Russell, he would have remembered.

But Kit...in all the time she'd been with him, he'd never presented her with a gift, not even a simple bunch of flowers. Wasn't she *more* to him than she'd been to Warwick? Did he think of her at all when he wasn't with her? Warwick had been half a world away in Hong Kong, yet he'd seen the mermaid and thought of her.

Still, it was probably unfair to make that comparison. Kit had cut free from his family so many years ago, he'd lost the sense of caring about such things as remembering birthdays. His own would probably have been ignored if she hadn't asked him about it, recollecting Dolores Diaz saying he was a Leo. August the first, he'd replied, and had been somewhat bemused when she'd cooked a special birthday dinner for him on that night.

His family background had a lot to answer for, she'd decided. It seemed the ruction—particularly with his father—had driven him to care more about what he could achieve in the world than how he related to people. Sometimes, she wondered if his sharing with her would stop when the challenge of this project had been won.

How much did their togetherness mean to him?

Would he ever come to love her as she loved him?

More tears welled.

Stupid to be getting into a state when there was work to do. Her birthday simply hadn't been important to Kit, so she might as well accept that and forget it herself. Besides, Warwick was right. Kit did suit her far more than Russell ever had. There were moments between them of utter perfection. Better to remember that than stew over a disappointment.

She washed her face, touched up the light make-up she'd worn, and braced herself to carry on as usual. The face reflected in the mirror above the washbasins didn't look any different to yesterday's face. But today she was thirty years old.

Thirty...

Just a number, yet it felt like an emotional assault, making her feel more uncertain about where her life was going with Kit. She wanted something solid to hang on to. She just didn't know how to get it.

Heaving a sigh to get rid of the weight on her heart, she went back to work, wanting to concentrate on activity, needing it to keep other things at bay.

The day wore on. The launch officially finished at three o'clock. The authors had writers' cramp from signing books. The management of The Outback Centre was delighted with business. The media had long since departed. The caterers were packing up. Kit was still re-inforcing his strategy to a number of booksellers. Ben Steiner proceeded to kidnap Jane Haskell, apparently with Kit's blessing. Fleur skirted the scene, ensuring people were properly thanked and nothing was missed in the general packing up.

When everything had been seen to, she signalled to Kit she was going back to the office. He excused himself from the group he was talking to and she watched him stride towards her, exuberant energy almost crackling from him. In keeping with the venue, he'd worn Outback gear; R.M. Williams boots, snug blue jeans, a royal blue sports shirt and an Akubra hat. He looked incredibly macho, his powerful physique shouting dominant male, his sex appeal sending tingles down Fleur's spine, even now after all these months with him.

He grinned at her, his eyes dancing with the adrenaline of success. 'It's gone well.'

She smiled at the absurd understatement. 'Definitely your day, Kit.'

'*Our* day,' he corrected her. 'Don't think I'm not aware of all your contributions to making it happen. And keeping everything running right today. You're a marvel, Fleur.'

His appreciation added a special glow to her own satisfaction in today's success. 'Thank you.'

'I saw you with Warwick Lancaster earlier. Nice of him to come.'

'Yes. It was good to see him, looking well and enjoying himself.'

Kit glanced down at the plastic bag she was still carrying. 'What did he give you?'

It amazed her that he always seemed to be aware of what was happening between her and anyone else. Did nothing escape his eye?

'A figurine of a mermaid. He saw it in Hong Kong and thought of me.'

He frowned slightly and asked, 'May I see it?'

She shrugged, wondering why he was so curious. 'If you want to.'

Having handed him the box, Fleur felt slightly uncomfortable when he took out the mermaid and studied it with what felt like too much intensity. It occurred to her he might think it too extravagant a gift from a former boss.

'Yes,' he murmured. 'It does capture the essence of you, Fleur.'

Embarrassed, she blurted out, 'Warwick bought it for my birthday. He always bought birthday gifts. That's just the way he is.'

He looked sharply at her beneath lowered brows. 'Your birthday?'

The disappointment stabbed again. *He ought to know. He should know.* 'It's today.'

'Why didn't you tell me?'

'I did. Twice,' she told him flatly. 'When I was talking about star signs before your birthday and when you set the date for this launch.'

He grimaced at his forgetfulness. 'I'm sorry, Fleur. It went right out of my mind.'

She nodded, quickly excusing, 'Too much else on it.'

Though resentment whispered she'd worked hard on everything that was important to him. Which, of course, was all he cared about. In fact, if she wasn't so *useful* to him... Fleur pulled herself back from going down that track. It was wrong. There was more than *usefulness* to their relationship.

He carefully replaced the mermaid in its box and handed it back to her. 'Have dinner at home with me tonight. I'll order in something special.'

'I'd like that,' she murmured, stowing the box in the bag again. A special dinner was something, she told herself, though it would only take him one phone call to arrange.

He reached out, cupping her face and tilting it up, forcing her to meet his gaze. The silver eyes seemed to bore straight into her heart. 'Roses from Russell. A mermaid from Warwick. And I give you nothing. How do I make it up to you?'

The answer came out of nowhere, leaping into her mind, a wild need that made no rational sense, yet more compelling than any thought she'd ever had.

You can give me a child.

Maybe it was turning thirty. Maybe it was the feeling she would never really have Kit—not all of him. A child would be a part of him that she could have…for the rest of her life.

'Just give me you,' she replied, and meant it far more comprehensively than the physical connection Kit took it to be.

'Tonight will be your night,' he promised, the anticipation of their sexual pleasure in each other instantly simmering into his eyes.

Yes, it will, Fleur thought fiercely.

Kit had had his nine months.

The next nine months were hers.

CHAPTER FOURTEEN

HE'D ordered lobster, grilled to perfection with a light butter sauce—sinfully expensive but it was Fleur's favourite meal for extra special occasions and Kit had remembered. The sweets she had also raved over at a previous dinner together—a mousse concoction of white and dark chocolate with raspberry coulis.

It was a happy start to the night.

Kit had opened a bottle of Dom Pérignon, and when they'd finished eating, they took what was left of the champagne up to the balcony that led off his bedroom, and sat in deckchairs, drinking it under the stars, listening to the roll of the sea. It was only mid-Spring—the tenth of October—and it was cool outside, but the night was clear, and Fleur enjoyed the crisp air and the salty smell of it.

She thought of the mermaid and wondered if it did capture the essence of her—a creature of fantasy, a pearl in her hand. It was said pearls were for tears. Her hand lifted instinctively and touched the pearls at her throat. She'd lost her mother, her father. She felt no real security with Kit. A child would at least give her a sense of family…something *solid*.

'Libra—The Balancer,' Kit mused, smiling at her.

'Is that your secret, Fleur, keeping everything in balance?'

The thought instantly came—*If I have my way, I'm about to throw everything out of balance.*

'I didn't think you held much stock in star signs,' she dryly remarked.

'I don't as a rule. I think people are responsible for their own lives.'

'There are some things one can't do by oneself, Kit.'

It evoked a soft laugh. He reached across and took her hand in his. 'Finished your champagne?'

'Yes.'

'Then come and have a shower with me.'

His eyes said—*And we'll proceed to what can't be done on one's own.*

Fleur's heart thumped with nervous excitement as she stood up with him. He led her into the bedroom and slowly undressed her, his hands grazing sensually over her bared flesh. Her breasts tingled with a sharp awareness of what they were really for…not this touching…the suckling of young…a baby. And when his fingers stroked down her stomach, removing her underwear, she thought only of the emptiness in a womb which was made for carrying a child.

As his magnificent male body emerged from his clothes, Fleur felt her inner muscles contracting with a desire that went far deeper than the wanting to revel in the power of the sexual pleasure he promised. It went straight to the primitive core of mat-

ing—his seed inside her, pursuing an act of crea-
tion—a child for her…from him.

Showering together…

In her mind it was like a cleansing ceremony, and
she took intense satisfaction in touching him, feeling
him all over, the perfect proportions of him, the
strength encased in taut flesh and muscle. She enjoyed the fun he made of soaping her, loving the
wicked mischief in his eyes, imagining the little boy
he had once been.

If they had a son…what a wonderful adventure
life would be with him! Like having Kit from the
beginning and being able to shower love on him,
love that let him grow as he wanted to grow, no
constrictions caging him into a space that didn't fit
his need to spread wings and fly on his own. A new
Kit, a different Kit, a Kit who would love her back
for being the mother she would be to him.

The man who could be the father of this child was
turning off the taps, reaching for a bath towel, wrapping it around them like an intimate cocoon. His
eyes teased her as he rubbed them dry. His body
teased—man and woman.

'Tell me how old you are, Fleur,' he commanded,
his smile suggesting some provocative purpose behind the question.

'I'm thirty,' she answered, and the plain truth was
she could have borne a child at half that age. Fifteen
years gone. If she was going to have a baby, it was
best done now. She certainly wasn't about to get any
younger.

The smile widened to a grin. 'Then I shall give you thirty kisses.'

Seductive kisses, exciting kisses, erotic kisses, loving kisses... Fleur gave herself over to them, letting herself feel all Kit had made her feel on countless nights together. From bathroom to bedroom he kissed her and once they were on the bed, there was no part of her he didn't kiss, an intensely sensual and passionate possession of her entire body.

Yet even as she revelled in the sense of Kit loving the woman she was—*his woman*—she was waiting, her whole inner being poised for the moment he would join with her. She didn't try to hasten him. The waiting made her all the more exquisitely aware of what was coming—all that made him a man driving towards all that made her a woman because it was right for them, a force of nature as old as time, compelled by a deeply implanted instinct to reproduce life, to survive.

She closed her eyes when it started...the strong full rush of him plunging to that innermost place where it could happen if they let it. Her whole being was focused on it, riding the rhythm, silently urging it on, the sweet tension building, pulsing through her, clenching muscles that strained to draw in the essence of the man, to capture, to hold.

And oh, the sublime ecstasy of it when it came! The infusion of warm liquid life that soothed the need and promised so much more! She clasped Kit tightly to her, wanting the sense of all of him joined to her, and she kissed him with joy and wonder in the glorious rightness of this union, and it felt as though she was sharing with him the breath of life itself.

Lying together afterwards, Fleur wondered what Kit felt, whether he ever thought about what mating really meant. She was half sprawled across him, her cheek pressed against the strong beat of his heart, one leg resting between his, her thigh rubbing the hair that grew there, savouring the soft-hard power of his sexuality. She grazed feather-light fingers down his rib cage, his taut stomach, the highly sensitive area of his groin, stroking…

'Kit, do you ever think…' What were the right words?

His chest rose and fell in what sounded like a contented sigh. 'I'm not into thinking right now. You're distracting me and I'm finding the distraction just fine.' His voice was a low throaty purr, making her smile.

'It's about this…seriously.'

'Mmh…?'

She raised herself up to watch his expression. His eyes opened to a narrow glimmer. His mouth had a soft indulgent curve.

'When you're inside me, do you ever think of what could happen…if we let it?' she asked softly, hoping that being so close like this, still warm with each other's heat, it would be easy for him to accept what she yearned for, to want it, too, because surely it was the natural outcome of where they were.

A long pause before he slowly answered, 'You mean...producing a new life?'

She nodded eagerly. 'A child. Yours...mine... ours.' She almost sang the words, a siren song, calling to the same instinct in him.

'No. I haven't thought about it.'

It was a disappointing reply, though it still left the way open to talk and Fleur pressed on. 'But the power *is* there, Kit. We could be creating life when we're joined together and we reach that incredible pinnacle of...of not just physical sensation...it's more like everything coming together right...totally, totally right...and that's when a baby should be conceived, don't you think?'

'A baby...' he repeated, frowning as though it were a concept that had never occurred to him. 'You are on the pill, aren't you, Fleur? You told me...'

'Yes, but if I stopped taking it... I might have life growing in me right now, Kit...'

'You can't want that,' he cut in, a hard edge to his voice. 'We have our own lives to live, things to do.'

The negative charge from him stopped her heart. For several moments it was frozen in suspension, then tripped into painful life, beating in panicky bursts against the constriction Kit had just placed on it. She looked down at him—this man who had just denied her dearest wish—and the unfairness of his judgment burned into her soul.

'You didn't even ask me if I wanted it.'

Having spoken that quiet, deadly indictment, she

could not bear to be in contact with him. The heat of their physical intimacy mocked the coldness he'd struck by removing any sense of mutuality. He'd decided. And she wasn't one with him anymore.

She rolled away from him.

He flung an arm around her waist, halting her from leaving the bed.

She didn't try to fight him. Pointless against his strength. Besides, she suddenly felt too drained to bother resisting as he pressed her back onto a pillow and hitched himself up to argue his case.

'You haven't thought this through, Fleur,' he started. 'A child consumes a woman's time. You'd have to give up your work to tend to its needs. You wouldn't be free to pursue your own interests for years.'

She lay there, her eyes silently mocking his supposed concern for her future. 'You asked what you could give me,' she reminded him. 'I want your child, Kit. I'll handle the rest.'

That swept the mat out from under his argument.

He frowned, finally muttering, 'I don't want children.'

'Why not?' she snapped back at him, goaded into fighting this elemental ground. 'It's a fairly natural desire for both men and women.'

'What?' A dark savagery leapt into his eyes. 'To run off extensions of themselves? To hang on to their children as lifelines to a sense of immortality? Little gene-pools to carry on...'

'I'm not your father,' she cut in just as fiercely.

'I'm not him, either, Fleur. I don't need some kind of affirmation of myself in a child. What I do with my own life is enough.'

'Would you prefer never to have been born?'

'No, of course not.'

'Yet you would deny life to any child of ours.'

His mouth thinned, robbed of ready words to throw back at her.

'I am a woman, Kit,' she pressed more calmly. 'I want my body to produce something beautiful, something that comes from us—you and me together—yet a person who is uniquely herself or himself.'

He had no answer to that. There was no answer to it. She wanted a baby—his baby—and he couldn't make that *want* go away, not by force of will or any other power he had. It was *right* to her.

He dropped back onto his pillow, defeated by that rightness. She would not surrender it. They lay side by side, but apart, waiting, letting the silence press for some change of mind, any little shift of position.

No words were spoken.

No move was made.

The realisation gradually seeped into Fleur that she couldn't go on with Kit. Even with someone you love, as much as she loved him, there was a limit to giving when the giving wasn't returned.

The possibility did exist that she could take what she wanted from him—throw away tonight's pill in the hope—probably a million to one chance—that a child would eventuate from their earlier lovemaking. A child thieved from him...

But that could never be called *right,* not for anyone, least of all the child, who deserved to have both parents. It was a hopeless situation, and tears of hopelessness welled into her eyes and started trickling down her cheeks. She could feel herself choking up. Any moment now the grief building up inside her would burst through all control mechanisms.

She swung her legs off the bed and was on her feet, moving to scoop up her clothes and head for the bathroom before the damn of tears broke in earnest. She would not cry in front of Kit. Her grief was her own.

Movement behind her. 'What are you doing?' The quick curt question seemed stupidly offensive. He had to know there was nothing left to say.

'I think I'll go home now,' she replied, unable to keep a furred edge of emotion out of her voice.

No glancing back.

Almost blind with tears, she collected the last of her clothes, blundered into the ensuite bathroom and closed the door.

Kit was off the bed and striding after Fleur before it struck him that any forceful action would not save this situation. It wasn't simply a door closing between them. What he had to face here was a life choice.

He pulled himself up short of hitting the door, his hands clenching with the need to fight with something physical. But feelings weren't physical and they could be far, far stronger than bone and muscle.

Primal need...that was what Fleur had been telling him. A woman...made for having a child. All the argument in the world was not going to change that. He'd lain there beside her, chewing over all his reasons for not wanting a child in his life, angry with Fleur for raising the question and driving a wedge between them, but for all his gut-recoil to the idea, he couldn't deny she had every right to what she wanted.

Except...*not with him.*

He had a choice in this, too.

He didn't want a child. He didn't. Yet he could lose Fleur over this. Already she had withdrawn from him—mentally and physically. Perhaps emotionally, as well.

He stared at the closed door.

What would his life be like without her? He could barely remember how it had been before. Full of activity. Women who'd entertained him for a while. Sex he'd found satisfying enough...but not like it was with Fleur. Not that sense of soaring together, the intensity of feeling, and knowing...*knowing* it was shared. So much shared.

He shook his head.

Be damned if he would lose her! She had to understand there were other things in life that more than compensated for not having a child. He'd take her out more, do some travelling, get her excited about planning trips together. Maybe...sometime in the future…he'd consider…*one* child. It was probably her birthday stirring her up tonight. He should have remembered, bought her something. He'd do that tomorrow—think of something better than the mermaid.

Determined on getting her back in his bed right now, Kit moved straight to the bathroom door and dispensed with that barrier—only to be stopped dead in his tracks by an image that instantly destroyed all his self-serving reasoning.

Fleur was sitting on the tiled rim of the spa-bath, still naked, but hunched over the bundle of clothes she had clutched in her arms, hugging them over her stomach as though they were taking the place of the pregnancy he had denied her, rocking herself over them. The motion stopped as soon as his entrance impinged on her consciousness, but the slowness of the reaction told him her consciousness had travelled a long way from connecting with him again.

Her anguish was so stark, the shock of total devastation held Kit paralysed. It seemed an agonisingly long time before she lifted her face to look at him and even then he wasn't sure she was seeing him. Her cheeks were streaked with tears and her eyes held a bleak emptiness that knifed straight into his heart.

He'd done this to her.

She'd given him more than he'd ever believed a woman could give him and he'd just ripped away at her need to fulfil herself as a woman by having the child of the man she had chosen to mate with.

You didn't even ask me if I wanted it.

Shame and guilt drove him forward. He scooped her off her cold, comfortless perch on the rim of the bath, cradling her gently in his arms, sweeping his mouth over her hair in a rain of healing kisses, choked by an overwhelming wave of tenderness. She felt so slight, fragile and he couldn't bear the sense of her being broken inside.

Her head dropped onto his shoulder—weariness, despair—he didn't know. Words tumbled out of him and he no longer cared what their consequences were.

'We'll give it a chance, Fleur. Throw away your pills. If it happens, it happens. Our child. Okay?'

He laid her on the bed, grabbed the clothes she still held and tossed them away. He spread his hand over her stomach and willed his own eyes to laser through the glaze on hers, to mend the wound he'd inflicted without any real thought for how deeply it went.

'We'll put life in there, Fleur. If it's meant to be, then you'll have your baby. Our baby. I don't know if I'll be a good father. I haven't had much of an example on that front. But I'm sure you'll make up for any failures on my part. Nothing can go too wrong for any child of ours, with having you as its mother.'

And that was true. Fleur managed everything so perfectly, Kit had no doubt she would bring every skill she had to motherhood.

'Is that all right with you?' he pressed.

Her throat moved in a convulsive swallow. Her eyes gathered more focus though it seemed there was still some distance to travel before she could accept what he was saying.

'I promise you I won't backtrack on this,' he stated fervently. 'No more contraception between us. Just come back to me and we'll try all night if you want to.'

Her focus sharpened. Her eyes searched his. Finally a hesitant whisper fell from her lips, a whisper that ached with longing.

'Do you want to, Kit?'

'Yes,' he answered. 'Yes.'

Anything to keep her.

Anything.

And he carried that affirmative into a kiss he hoped would obliterate any doubt in her mind.

CHAPTER FIFTEEN

KIT was feeling particularly pleased with himself. Definitely a stroke of genius, getting in touch with Jared King to order a special gift for Fleur. The moment she came into the office he'd surprise her with it, prove he did care enough to think of her.

It was three weeks since her birthday, but to Kit's mind, the time-lag was irrelevant. It was the thought that counted. As it was, Jared had given his request top priority. The purchase had arrived by special courier after Fleur had left to attend a meeting yesterday, and he'd been tied up with magazine business last night, but this morning...work could wait. He wanted to see the pleasure on Fleur's face when she opened the box.

He'd only just settled in his chair behind the desk when he heard her arrive, earlier than usual. He didn't even have time to get completely to his feet before she burst into his office, her face beaming joy, her eyes all sparkles of excitement.

'Kit! I'm pregnant!'

He was so stunned, only automatic action carried him upright.

'Can you believe it?' she bubbled on. 'It's only been three weeks but the test was definitely positive!'

Positively pregnant!

He wasn't ready for this. Fleur had barely gone off the pill. Some couples took years to strike conception. Some never brought it off.

'You're sure there's no mistake? It's early days,' he said weakly, struggling to get past the shock of having fatherhood thrust upon him within a few weeks of agreeing to it. *In theory.*

'That's what I thought.' She laughed, clearly delighted there had been no mistake. 'My period was late but I reasoned it was probably messed up by going off the pill mid-month. It was only when my breasts started feeling sort of tight and tingly...'

'Your breasts...'

'Mmh...one of the first signs of pregnancy.' She grinned, flicking her hands up over their peaks with uninhibited pleasure, then carrying through the movement into an open happy gesture. 'So I did the test this morning and there I was...in the pink!'

'The pink?' He shook his head, still too dazed to take this in. 'You mean...it's a girl?'

'No! The test showed up pink! Means I'm pregnant!' She waltzed over and flung her arms around his neck, her eyes mischievously teasing. '*This girl* will get down to work in a moment. She just has to kiss you first. Okay, Dad-to-be?'

Dad-to-be?

His mind was totally blown! Kit swiftly decided a kiss might knock some sense into him and the longer it took, the better. In fact, she gave him a kiss that strongly reminded him why he'd agreed to all this. Besides which, it was impossible to recant now he was faced with the reality of having a child. He just hadn't expected it so soon.

'Now you mustn't worry about this affecting our book program. I'll stay working as your P.A. as long as I can, Kit,' Fleur assured him.

That rattled him some more. She was vital to keeping the project on track. How long would she stay assisting him in her own unique and highly effective style?

'In fact, if you don't mind...' Another brilliant smile burst from her as she rubbed her stomach—still flat—against his. '...my pregnancy *showing,* I could probably go on working until the baby's due.'

The baby. *His* baby. Showing. The whole publishing company knowing if she stayed on. The whole publishing *world* knowing! And he *needed* her to stay on. There was only one solution to this. The only solution that would keep harmony everywhere.

'Best we get married right away,' he said firmly.

It was her turn to look stunned. Hot colour raced into her cheeks and the wild joy in her eyes faded into vulnerable uncertainty. 'You don't have to do that, Kit.'

His certainty surged. He didn't stop to think whether it was protection or possession or something else entirely. The equation seemed very straightforward to him. 'You're having my child. We get married.'

She frowned. 'I didn't set out to trap you into…into marrying me.'

'No trap.'

'It's not necessary these days. I mean…'

'Are you saying you don't want to marry me?'

'No…I…'

'Then it's settled. We get married. You come and live with me and we bring up our child together.'

Kit knew he was acting on automatic pilot here, but the plan sounded right, felt right, so it had to be right. He'd work out details later.

Her arms slid down from his shoulders, her gaze dropped, and her hands plucked nervously at his shirt. 'You haven't given this much thought, Kit. I don't want you to feel obliged…'

'Fleur…' This concern of hers was completely out of kilter. Hadn't he already demonstrated his commitment to her well-being? Did she think he'd just let her sink or swim on her own, now that the life she'd wanted was growing inside her? He tilted her face up to show her his conviction that marriage was the only reasonable course to take here. 'Aren't you already my wife in everything but name? Do you have some objection to making it official?'

'Your…wife?' Wonder in her eyes.

'Wife…partner…mate…call it what you will. That's how it is for me.'

'You've never said…'

He remembered the box. A winning stroke. 'Then let this say it for me.' It was sitting on the desk. He stepped back, scooped it up and presented it to her. 'Open it!'

For several moments she simply stared down at the small box sitting on her palm. Then she took a deep breath and opened the lid with her other hand. The ring was nestled in black velvet—five exquisitely crafted petals in gold, and in the centre, rising from a nest of five diamonds, one perfect glowing pearl.

A flower for Fleur. One that wouldn't wilt and die. One to keep all her life if she wanted to, and it would be as beautiful at the end of her days as it was now.

She shook her head as though in awe of it. 'You bought this for me?' Her voice was barely a husky whisper.

Kit grinned, triumph zinging through him. He'd done it. Taken her breath away. Completely knocked her out with *his* gift. An absolute winner!

'I had it made for you. It's a Picard pearl and Jared King's wife, Christabel, designed the ring. I told her I wanted a flower to give to a woman who was very special to me.'

Again she shook her head. 'I don't know what to say, Kit.' Her voice was still husky. 'I'm just so overwhelmed. It's the most fabulous ring I've ever seen.'

Time to press the advantage. 'You can say you'll marry me. And...' He took the box, removed the ring, picked up her left hand. '...you can wear this on your third finger.'

It was a touch loose but wearable. He'd had to guess her size. She could have it altered if she thought it necessary. She didn't seem to notice, holding her hand out with her fingers still spread, her gaze locked on the pearl as though enthralled by it. He hadn't meant it to be an engagement ring. Marriage hadn't entered his mind. No reason for it. But there was now and he wanted to hear her agreement.

'Well?' he prompted.

She looked up at him, her eyes all shiny, like the sea on a sunny day. 'Yes. I'll marry you. Oh, Kit!'

Her arms were around his neck again and what could he do but kiss her—his wife-to-be and mother of his child? There were times when breaking rules was totally justifiable. After all, this wasn't an office affair. They were getting married. And no doubt everyone would know it before the day was out.

Which was fine.

Best to get it out in the open straight away, then everyone could get back to work.

Including him.

Fleur was floating on Cloud Nine for the rest of the day.

She'd no sooner tried to get down to work than Sally Jethroe popped into her office to say, 'Good morning,' and relay the happy news that the guy she'd had her eye on had finally asked her out. Her eagle eye had spotted the ring on Fleur's engagement finger and she'd almost jumped up and down with excitement at the news of Kit's proposal.

From then on a stream of bright-eyed staff had dropped by, congratulating her and admiring the ring. Jane absolutely drooled over it, wondering hopefully if Ben Steiner had as good a taste in jewellery as Kit. They were all happy for her, but none so happy as Fleur herself.

Kit…wanting to marry her, thinking of her as *his wife,* ordering this fabulous ring for her before either of them knew about the baby…it was like every dream she'd ever had coming true.

He must have planned it after he'd told her to throw her pills away, made up his mind that very night—if they were going to have a child, they should get married. Except he'd given her no hint of it. She'd been totally stunned this morning, not even sure she had any solid place in his life, then…those incredibly wonderful, telling words… *his wife, partner, mate…*and the ring!

Her heart seemed to swell every time she thought of it, every time she looked down at the magnificent pearl in its exquisite setting. Maybe Kit didn't think in terms of love, but he must love her. After all, he hadn't wanted a child but he'd given in to her need. More than given in. This morning he'd made it abundantly clear he was committed to having their child—joint parents, right down the line!

It had to mean he really loved her, and Fleur had even more reason to believe it that night when they sat over a celebratory dinner together and Kit in-

sisted they start planning the wedding—a big wedding—which he wanted to take place as soon as it
could be arranged.

'I've been onto Ben about this already,' he informed her.

'Ben?' She shook her head dazedly, wondering
what a swinging bachelor like Ben Steiner would
know about weddings.

'I called him this afternoon. We publish a bride
magazine and he'll be getting advice from the editor
on who's the best wedding co-ordinator.' He shot
her a look of concern. 'You won't have time to do
all the planning, Fleur. And I don't want you tired
out by it. As it is, pregnancy can sap your energy.'

She smiled teasingly. 'You've managed to get
expert advice on that, too?'

He grimaced and it seemed a shadow marred the
usual keenness of his eyes. 'I saw my mother worn
out by pregnancies, Fleur. I won't have that happen
to you.'

Eleven children... He'd been the seventh—three
years old when his mother had had the next baby,
then five, seven, and nine when she'd died, soon
after giving birth for the eleventh time. He would
have been aware of at least the last three pregnancies. Perhaps, watching his mother struggle with
them—at such impressionable ages—had contributed to his attitude of not wanting children himself.

'I'll be fine, Kit,' she promised him. 'I've always
been a really healthy person.'

'And we're going to keep you that way,' he said

determinedly. 'Which is why we'll have a wedding co-ordinator doing all the legwork. Besides which, I need you with me at the office. Can't let the book program slide.'

'Okay,' she happily agreed. 'What about a list of guests?'

'You can make up the book publishing list, Ben can make up the magazine people list, we add in old friends, and that should do it.'

'What does Ben think about all this?' she asked curiously.

Kit laughed. 'He said if I wanted to strangle myself by tying the knot, at least you were the kind of woman who didn't want to take all my air. And he expected to be best man at the wedding.'

'I don't think he likes women much,' Fleur ruefully commented.

'Doesn't trust them enough to let them close. His mother deserted him when he was five and his father proceeded to bring home what Ben called one manipulative bitch after another. Two-faced Eves. All sugar to his father while he gave them what they wanted, and all vinegar to Ben for being a nuisance kid they didn't want to bother with.'

It explained a lot.

Fleur couldn't help reflecting that both Ben's and Kit's family backgrounds were very different to hers. Being the only child, born when both her parents were in their forties, she had always known herself dearly loved. The apartment she lived in had been theirs and all the family photographs and mementos were still in place there.

She'd been a contented child, probably more self-sufficient than most, having no siblings. Her parents had always encouraged her interests, sharing in them. She had no quarrel with her upbringing and only wished her mother and father had lived longer—to see her married to a man she loved, to see their first grandchild.

The sense of loss she felt made her think of Kit's, and she began wondering whether or not the existing estrangement from his brothers and sisters could be crossed—if just any one of them would reach out. It seemed so wrong to actually have a family, yet have no connection with it.

'Kit, I have no relatives to invite, but what of yours?' she asked impulsively.

His mouth twisted. 'They wiped me off their list a long time ago. I've made my own life and I don't need them in it.'

The fierce flash of dark pride denied any void left by his family's rejection. For a few moments the blast of negative energy from Kit on this sensitive subject held Fleur silent. Maybe it was best to let sleeping dogs lie, yet how could he not feel a hole where his family had been?

His childhood and adolescence had been shared with ten brothers and sisters, and they were still out there somewhere—people who belonged to him in ways only a family knew. To let pride be a barrier to any reconciliation seemed wrong to her.

She might be treading dangerous ground here, getting completely offside with Kit, yet with the right push, might there not be a chance to achieve something worthwhile?

'I can't help wondering if wiping you off their list was your father's doing, Kit,' she pressed quietly. 'You told me they wouldn't go against him.'

His chin jutted aggressively.

He had, Fleur instantly read. Nevertheless, few people were as strong as he was. Maybe he couldn't forgive the others for being weaker. But was that fair? To be completely cut out of one's family—to be alone in the world—wouldn't most people think twice about taking that step?

She pushed on, risking Kit's anger. 'You did tell me your father died last year. He's gone. So your brothers and sisters don't need to fear his reaction anymore. Might that not make a difference?'

He waved a curt dismissal. 'I don't know them anymore. If they wanted to know me...'

'They might think you'd just turn away from them after all this time. You've been a high-flyer, Kit. Extremely successful. Lots of publicity. It could be very daunting for any of them to approach you.'

He frowned, seemingly considering the point. After several minutes of brooding silence he remarked ironically, 'My oldest sister did say something like that—she didn't want to intrude on my life.'

'When was that?' Fleur pressed.

'When she contacted me about Dad's death. And

the funeral. Maggie would have felt it her duty to tell me.' Again his mouth twisted. 'The dutiful eldest daughter who was appointed to take over the household when Mum died. I have no doubt my father used up her life.'

To Fleur, the comment revealed some wanting to know what had happened to all of them over the years he'd been gone.

Though he immediately shrugged it off. 'I said I wouldn't be attending the funeral and the conversation ended.'

'Would it hurt to invite them, Kit? I mean…if they refuse, they refuse, and nothing's gained nor lost. I just thought…well, it would be nice to have some family at our wedding, maybe get to know them a bit.'

'Apart from Maggie, I don't even know where they live,' he said pointedly, still resisting.

'I bet she'd know.'

'Oh, yes.' Very dry.

'Then…could we ask her for their addresses?'

He looked at her, puzzled by her persistence. 'What does it mean to you, Fleur?'

She paused to think it through. 'Apart from my parents, I had no relatives,' she answered slowly. 'I envied other kids who did—brothers, sisters, cousins, aunts, uncles, grandparents. I guess I'd like our child…not to feel that gap.'

'The mermaid,' he murmured on a whimsical smile.

'Pardon?' It was her turn to look puzzled.

'Swimming out of the normal stream of humanity. That's you, Fleur. Part of what makes you very unique.'

She supposed it was one way of describing her life. 'It can feel very lonely.'

'But at least we own our lives, Fleur. We don't have to account to anyone or serve someone else's interests,' he said in a burst of vehemence.

She held her tongue. Enough was enough. He had made his own life and clearly there was still a very raw place in Kit where his family was concerned. It wasn't her place to be prodding at it. She hadn't experienced what he'd been through. However much she might wish to make it better, there was no way she could make a fair judgment.

Besides, broken families could bring tensions to weddings, tarnishing what should be a happy, harmonious atmosphere. It was probably stupid to even bring up the issue, let alone invite possible problems. It was their wedding, and what mattered most was how they felt about each other.

'I'm sorry for bringing up your family,' she said in a rush of concern over spoiling tonight's harmony between them. 'It's none of my business, Kit.'

He shook his head, a wry little smile negating any need for apology. 'Maybe…for the sake of our child…I should give it a chance,' he said slowly. 'As you say, it wouldn't hurt to invite them. I'll call Maggie and see what response I get.'

For the sake of our child…

Fleur's heart swelled again.

Already he was caring about their child. For a man who hadn't wanted children, Kit was being amazingly wonderful about her pregnancy and now...wanting what she wanted for the life they would bring into the world, wanting it enough to risk another rejection from his blood relatives.

He reached across the dining table and took her left hand in his, half smiling down at the ring he'd given her. 'The perfect ring for Fleur,' he murmured. Then his gaze sought hers and his eyes were rueful. 'I can't make everything perfect for you. It's not a perfect world. If the rift can't be crossed, don't be too disappointed.'

She nodded, deeply moved that he was prepared to try.

'We'll be making our own family,' he went on, and his eyes gleamed with fierce resolution. 'I won't be like my father. I can promise you that. It will be different. We'll make our family as it should be— connected because the connection is good.'

'Yes,' she whispered, loving him so much her throat was almost choked by the welling of emotion. 'Thank you for giving me the happiest day of my life, Kit.'

His face relaxed into lines of pleasure, his eyes warmly caressing hers. 'For you...anything.'

She believed him.

He was his own man.

He had many agendas because that was the kind of man he was, seeking more, needing challenges, wanting to conquer new territories.

But he wanted her with him—wife, partner, mate—and he'd always clear the way for her to stay at his side. He would do what he could to keep her happy there…as long as she let him be who he was.

Fleur understood that now.

It had taken her a long time, but she finally understood.

This was Kit Malone.

She loved him…and in his own way, he loved her.

She hoped his family would respond, not so much for their child-to-be, but for him. He shouldn't carry the brand of an outcast with him all his life. A re-connection should be made—a good one—and Fleur silently vowed she would do anything to help it happen.

CHAPTER SIXTEEN

LUNCH with Maggie Malone!

'She wants to meet you,' Kit had said offhandedly, reporting on the call he'd made to his eldest sister. 'She's coming down from Newcastle for a couple of days in Sydney. Asked if you'd join her for lunch on Saturday.'

'Just me?'

A nod and a shrug. 'Maybe more comfortable with woman-talk. Who knows? Anyhow, she suggested twelve o'clock at a restaurant called *City Extra* on Circular Quay. It's up to you, Fleur.'

It was hardly a meeting she could refuse, having set the contact ball in motion, but why was Kit being bypassed in favour of his fiancée? It was like choosing neutral ground in a war, and there was no war. It was also a snub to Kit—*no, I won't meet you but I'll take a look at the woman you're going to marry.*

Fleur didn't like it. On the other hand, she might gain some insight on Kit's family, giving her a better understanding of the rift and why no one had tried to mend it. With this hope, she presented herself at the nominated restaurant precisely at noon on Saturday.

Butterflies occupied her stomach as the waiter led her up the stairs to the top floor dining room. She'd been to the restaurant before. It was handily placed on the quay, providing a great view of the ferry traffic on the harbour, as well as the bridge and the opera house, but surprisingly, the menu was moderately priced, not over-the-top expensive. For a meeting of strangers, it was a safe choice—nothing intimidating about it and easy to escape from to other activities if the meeting didn't work out well.

Fleur was very conscious of a heavy responsibility sitting on her shoulders as she moved up the stairs. The feeling was very strong that she was about to be judged by Maggie Malone, and on that judgment would rest any future connection with Kit's family.

Having arrived on the upper floor, the waiter directed Fleur to a table where a woman was already seated. It was just on twelve o'clock, but a glass of white wine in her hand indicated that Maggie Malone had been here for some time, possibly calming *her* nerves with a drink. She gave Fleur a cursory glance, then apparently dismissed the possibility of her being Kit's fiancée, turning her gaze back to the view outside.

Further unnerved by the visual dismissal, Fleur braced herself to make the approach, wondering what Maggie Malone *was* expecting? The answer— probably one of the more flamboyantly glamorous women Kit had been photographed with over the years—did nothing to boost her confidence. Nevertheless, she knew she was Kit's choice, and if his sister was unimpressed, well, maybe getting acquainted might help.

'Miss Malone...Maggie?' she said invitingly, stopping right at the table to draw an acknowledgment of her presence.

The woman's head jerked up to her. Grey eyes, not as light as Kit's, but the similar bone structure of her face marked her as his sister, and the grey streaks in her short dark hair placed her as older. She wore no make-up apart from a red lipstick. No jewellery, either. Her black suit was the type of outfit that covered most formal and semi-formal occasions.

She looked stunned as Fleur held out her hand and introduced herself. It took her a few moments to collect herself enough to push up from her chair, in rather awkward haste, still struggling with disbelief as she finally grasped the offered hand.

'You're Fleur Andersson? Kit's Fleur?'

'Yes.'

A sigh of relief, then an apologetic grimace. 'I didn't think it could be you. Sorry to be so thick. Please...let's sit down and I'll try to make up for my rudeness.'

'It's okay,' Fleur quickly excused with a smile. 'I could see you were Kit's sister. You would have no idea of me.'

They settled at the table. After an awkward little silence while Maggie simply gazed at Fleur, a rueful little smile broke out on her face.

'You're right. I know nothing about you. Would you mind telling me about yourself, how you and Kit met?'

Her interest was so keen, Fleur's inner tension

eased as she talked, telling Kit's sister the background she wanted to know. They both ordered lasagne and salad for lunch, sipped glasses of Chardonnay, and while Fleur still felt judgments were being made, she sensed they were not unfavourable. Eventually the atmosphere between them seemed friendly enough to ask some questions of her own.

'What about you, Maggie? Kit said you took over the household when your mother died. But the younger children must be grown up now. Are you involved in something you like doing?'

She sat back, a musing smile on her lips as she considered her reply. 'I know Kit thinks Dad sucked up my life, but I had my own escape from him. Mum taught me to love books, too. And all those years of telling the younger ones stories...well, I started writing stories of my own. Children's books. They've sold quite well, given me financial independence.'

'That's marvellous! What publishing house are you with? I should have seen your name...'

'No, I don't write under Maggie Malone. It was...my secret life.' She shrugged off all that implied about her father's tyrannical domination. 'My author name is Kay Tierney. It was my mother's maiden name.'

'Kay Tierney,' Fleur repeated, wanting to remember it. 'I haven't read any of your books, but I will.'

Maggie gave a self-conscious little laugh. 'You don't have to do that.'

'I want to.'

She shook her head, her eyes regarding Fleur in a slightly bemused fashion. 'You know, I didn't think it could work. I thought Kit would have moved too far from us. I didn't expect someone like you.'

'Like me?' Fleur prompted, needing to understand where Maggie was coming from in her assessment.

She opened her handbag and passed over a typed list of names and addresses. 'Send the invitations. I'll let everyone know it's all right. They'll want to come to the wedding.'

Somehow, that was too blanket a statement. It felt wrong to Fleur. For one thing, how could Maggie speak for everyone else? For another, the decision shouldn't be resting on what Maggie thought of her. What about Kit and what he might feel? Didn't she care at all about her brother?

'Why?' she asked, needing her confusion sorted. 'I mean...I'm glad they'll want to come, but...what difference have I made?'

'The person you are reflects the person Kit is inside,' came the too simple reply.

Fleur looked her bewilderment.

Maggie smiled. 'You have a giving nature, but you're strong within yourself. It shines through. I don't think you'd ever let yourself be dominated in any negative way. Which means Kit respects that in you, and it's part of why he's chosen you to be his wife. It says a lot about him.'

'You thought he might be...'

'Too much like Dad.' She leaned forward to explain more fully. 'You see, Fleur, he's the spitting image of our father. And Kit had the will and the fire to fight him. They were like two powerful bulls locking horns. Dad wouldn't bend and neither would Kit. We all remember that.'

'So his brothers and sisters think Kit's another version of his father?'

'He is, in a way. I don't know if Kit has told you…Dad was a union leader at the mines. He was always fighting injustices, wanting to change the world, plotting how to take on the establishment. He had his plan for all of us…like fighting pieces on his chessboard, telling us what we had to achieve, what we had to win. And of all his children, Kit was the star. He excelled at everything—sport, school— a natural winner. Except Kit didn't want to play in Dad's world. He wanted to make his own.'

'And he has,' Fleur murmured, wondering what this was leading to.

'Yes. But we didn't know what kind of world he'd made. Whether it was good to be in it.'

'It's good. The whole staff at the publishing company love working with him and for him,' Fleur assured her. 'He's pushing something positive—laying it out for people. But it's up to them whether they want to buy his vision or not. That's not dominant force, Maggie.'

A wry little smile. 'You don't have to defend him. I've seen what I needed to see for myself.'

Judgment.

But it wasn't really fair judgment. It was all from the family's point of view. Particularly *Maggie's* point of view. Had any of them paused to consider Kit's side of things, being the outcast they'd made him after the break with his father?

'You know,' she started tentatively, looking for some *giving* in the grey eyes that made judgments. 'Kit has felt...cut off by you all...because he didn't knuckle down to his father. He calls himself the black sheep. You might think about that, Maggie. All these years he's spent alone. At least the rest of you had each other. Kit forgets his own birthday because he has no family to remember it. You just...let him go, like he was nothing to any of you.'

She frowned. 'Kit left...and we paid for it.'

The resentment underlying those words made the picture much clearer to Fleur and it was a picture she didn't like. It was false and it wasn't fair to Kit, so she shot it down, as it deserved to be shot down.

'You paid because you stayed, Maggie. That wasn't Kit's fault. But you made him pay for going. Let's get this straight because nothing good can be built on false foundations. There are two sides to this family ruction and I don't think Kit's side should be ignored. None of you held out a hand to him.'

Angry sparks in her eyes. 'You have no idea of the pressures put on us. Especially after Kit left.'

'No, I don't. But you are *free* of them now. There's no reason left to keep treating Kit as a black sheep.'

'I told you we thought he'd be just like Dad.'

'Yes, you told me.' Fleur shook her head. 'There's nothing to fear from Kit. There never was. And I don't understand why you couldn't risk one meeting with him. You could have walked away if he made you feel uncomfortable.'

'I saw no reason to put myself in that position when I could make a judgment from you.'

Judgment.

It was precisely what Kit had cut free of… judgments made for him, about him, not being seen as the person he was—a person who wanted something different to the judgments.

Fleur looked at his sister and realised exactly what was going on here and it was not good. It was wrong for Kit. Yet it was possible that Maggie Malone didn't see she was repeating an abuse that she herself had been a victim of. Maybe her perception—her judgment—needed a jolt of truth. Fleur decided to give it a chance.

'I'm just wondering if it's you who's most like your father, Maggie, ruling the roost now he's gone, telling the others what to do.'

It jolted her all right. Something flickered in her eyes—a recognition of the power she held? It pushed Fleur to go on.

'If that's the case, let me tell you Kit wouldn't want any of you to come to our wedding, because he's about people making their own choices, and he wouldn't respect anything else.'

Silence. A very stiff silence.

The lunch was over. The bill had been paid. They'd been sitting over last cups of coffee, now empty. Fleur put the printed list of names and addresses in her handbag and stood up.

Maybe she'd taken too strong a stance, yet all her instincts had been twigging something very wrong here—an abuse that was probably too deep-rooted to shift. Which was a shame. The man who had perpetrated it was dead. The family could be free of it if they worked at putting it in the past.

'You know, Maggie, this meeting shouldn't have been with me. It should have been with Kit. It's time you stopped using a back door. Your name is Maggie Malone not Kay Tierney. Start feeling good about yourself, good enough to stand up and be counted for who *you* are. Not your father. Not your mother. You. I know Kit would be very proud of having a sister a published author.'

She stared back as though a foreign language was being spoken.

A sense of failure pressed heavily on Fleur's heart. Kit had given her the child she'd wanted. If she could have given him back his family…

But he was right. There was no perfect world. Some dark and twisted places were better left unvisited. Even shining light on them could be painful. Nevertheless, Fleur couldn't stop herself from reaching out one last time.

'Thank you for the list. I'll send out the invitations. You said Kit's relationship with me says a lot about him. To my mind, how your family responds will tell a lot about them. And you. Why not make it good, Maggie? Why not?'

She left her with that challenge.

She didn't tell Kit what had transpired between her and his sister, simply showing him the list and adding it to the paperwork for the wedding.

'Why did Maggie want to meet you?' he asked.

Fleur wrinkled her nose at him. 'I think to see if I was a socialite snob.' She wasn't about to add hurt to hurt by telling him how he'd been viewed by his family.

He laughed and that was the end of it until the responses to the invitations came in. Not one formal R.S.V.P. from his family. Every brother and sister wrote a letter, some pouring out feelings that brought tears to Fleur's eyes, all of them expressing pleasure in the invitation and the desire to come to the wedding and wish Kit and his bride well.

Kit, also, was moved by the response. 'You were right. It only took reaching out...and they were there.'

She smiled, happy that he was happy, sad that so much damage had been inflicted over the years, hoping that their wedding day would form a bridge from a negative past to a positive future for all the Malones.

To Kit's eye, it was her Mona Lisa smile.

He knew instantly it was her subtle but very effective hand behind all this. It didn't really matter what she'd said or what she'd done because the end result felt great!

Amazingly, his family was coming to their wedding. And some dark sense of oppression he'd forced himself to ignore all these years, lifted from his soul.

He wasn't like his father. Fleur would not have stayed with him if he'd been in his father's mould. He was Kit. And she…she was the light of his life…a pure steady light that would always steer him right.

He'd been wrong.

He did *need* her.

And always would.

CHAPTER SEVENTEEN

KIT couldn't stop smiling. The Malones might not quite populate the world, but they were certainly populating a number of pews at the front of this chapel. It was good to see them, all spruced up for his wedding, and from their greetings—handshakes and kisses—they really were glad to be here for him.

Beside him, Ben muttered, 'I thought your family was on the outer rim of your life, Kit. How come they've all come in today?'

He shot his best man an amused look and simply answered, 'Fleur.'

'Hmm…' A wagging of eyebrows. 'That's a dangerous woman you're marrying. Sure you want to go through with it? We could still nick out…'

'No, my fate is sealed,' Kit happily declared. 'In fact, I think my fate was sealed the first night I met Fleur. You're right—a very dangerous woman. Goes straight for the heart. She was tugging on mine before I knew it.'

'You think it will last? You've only been with her a year, you know.'

A year—January to January—one complete revolution of time—and so many changes. There was no doubt whatsoever in Kit's mind where he stood now. No doubt where Fleur stood, either. Side by side. Forever.

'We fit together, Ben. Nothing is going to break us apart.'

'Yeah…right!' He nodded a few times then off-handedly commented, 'I'm getting the feeling that Jane and I might fit. She understands what work means to me, you know?'

Jane—whom Fleur had asked to be her brides-maid, partnering Ben. A little assistance there, too?

The marriage celebrant took his place in front of the bank of flowers Kit had told the wedding co-ordinator to put at the head of the chapel. Huge displays of white flowers. It had felt right for Fleur… for his bride.

Strange how the knowledge of what she was to him had become so clear these past few weeks. He'd acted on sheer instinct when he'd proposed marriage, yet he'd spoken the truth when those words had tumbled out—wife, partner, mate. It *was* what he felt.

The organist started playing. He and Ben turned to watch Jane walk down the aisle, her pearl grey dress gleaming elegantly as she moved to the pace of the music—*Song of Joy* by Beethoven—chosen by Fleur. Absolutely appropriate, too.

Kit caught Maggie's eye on him from the aisle end of the front pew. He smiled at her, delighted she'd made a career for herself writing children's books. He made a mental note to approach her about a special project for his publishing company—stories with an Outback setting.

The Australian-theme books he'd launched had made a killing in the Christmas market. No doubt about their success and no reason why Maggie shouldn't jump on the bandwagon. If she wanted to.

'Jane sure looks great with her hair up like that,' Ben murmured.

'Sure does,' Kit agreed.

Her long black hair was coiled around a rope of pearls—no bangs hanging over her face today. She was smiling at Ben who must have winked at her because she winked back. They *were* two of a kind, Kit decided.

Song of Joy finished. Jane stood beside them. Kit's heart zinged with anticipation as the sound system took over from the organ, producing a marvellous fanfare of trumpets. From Verdi's opera, *Aida,* Fleur had told him. Which just went to prove there was something to be said for big classical music. Perfect!

The double doors at the back of the chapel were opened.

And there she was...*his bride!*

His breath was completely blown away. She was a vision of almost ethereal loveliness—otherworldly—yet somehow essentially Fleur, exquisitely feminine, tugging strongly on every male instinct he had.

Organ music swelled again—Mendelssohn's Wedding March. She started down the aisle, seem-

ingly gliding towards him, the big skirt of her gown
hiding the steps she took. No father to escort her, to
give her into Kit's keeping. She came alone, not
needing anyone to hang on to, serenely confident in
her sense of self and where she was going...to the
man of her choice. And Kit felt very privileged to
be that man. This woman who stood far above all
the rest—the one to make him feel complete.

She was three months' pregnant with their child
now but it didn't show. The bodice of her gown
fitted her curves very snugly—a low sweetheart
neckline and filmy flowers forming shoulder straps.
Flowers above her ears, too, joined to a band of
pearls over her hair, holding a wonderful frothy veil
that framed the delicate beauty of her face.

Pearls on her earlobes, pearls around her throat,
and *his* pearl in pride of place on her left hand, hidden behind a bouquet of flowers, but Kit knew it
was there. He'd placed it there and she'd accepted
it and all it now meant.

His woman.

A woman to love for the rest of his days...and he
knew the child she was carrying would be just as
special because somehow she would make it so—
part of her, part of him, but a unique person to be
loved for what he or she was. That was Fleur's
gift—learning, knowing, accepting, helping, caring.

Next month she would have a scan and they'd
know—boy or girl—but the sex of their child didn't
matter to either of them. It was purely a life they'd
created, a life they would value, and making sure it

thrived was probably the best project they'd ever share together.

In fact, they should have more children. An only child could be lonely. With his family here, he remembered the fun they'd had together in their childhood. Kit made a mental note to discuss it with Fleur. After all, wasn't the adventure of life the biggest challenge of all?

She reached his side.

He took her hand, loving the feel of it in his—such a small hand but so strong in its commitment to making everything right for *their* life together. A magic touch, he thought, feeling totally spellbound as he looked into the eyes turned up to him—bright, shiny eyes, reflecting a heart full of love and happiness.

Could she see his?

Had he ever told her how much she meant to him?

The wedding ceremony began.

Kit concentrated on the words. It didn't matter that they were old words spoken regularly to whatever couples were getting married. Today they were for him and Fleur and the vows they made to each other were very personal.

Husband and wife…'til death do us part.

So it was declared.

So it would be.

Finally he lifted her bridal veil, drew her into his embrace, held her against him, loving the feel of her, loving everything about her, and because he needed to voice this before he kissed her, he said, 'I love you, Fleur. With every part of me.'

She knew it was true, knew it in every part of her.

'I love you too, Kit,' she whispered.

The congregation stood and clapped as they kissed.

Neither Kit nor Fleur heard them.

They were in a world that belonged only to them.

And it was perfect.

JACK'S BABY

BY
EMMA DARCY

CHAPTER ONE

BABIES, Jack Gulliver darkly reflected, undermined every normal, congenial intercourse between intelligent adults. They infiltrated people's lives even before they entered the world, then took over like tyrannical dictators. Nothing was safe from them.

Jack brooded over these truths as he drove through the tunnel under Sydney Harbour, taking the shortest route to Paddington and the Royal Hospital for Women. He wished Maurice had been satisfied with hearty congratulations on the birth of his son. It was totally unreasonable of him to insist Jack actually come and view the new pride and joy. Paternal enthusiasm run rampant. Jack wondered how long it would last.

One by one his friends had succumbed to the lure of fatherhood, only to find themselves knocked off their happy perches of being the main focus of attention in their households. They'd groaned out their misery and their complaints to him, envying his freedom from the chaos they had brought upon themselves.

'Good sex is impossible.'

'You're lucky if you get any sex.'

'Who wants sex? I'd like one—just one—full night's sleep.'

'Forget spontaneity. The baby comes first, first, first and first.'

'I haven't got a wife. She's turned into a slave to the baby.'

'There's no time for *us* any more.'

'It's like moving an army to go anywhere. I'd rather stay at home. Save the aggravation.'

There was no doubt in Jack's mind that babies were destructive little monsters. They probably should be born with a 007 warning engraved on their foreheads—licenced to kill. He knew of several couples who had broken up under the stress of parenthood, and the rest were struggling to adjust to changes they resented.

Jack now had a fair appreciation of why his own parents had limited their progeny to one only, why he had been brought up by nannies and shunted off to boarding school at age seven. Quite clearly he had interfered too much with their lives. From his current view as an adult, he understood they had taken practical steps to minimise the damage to their rights as individuals, but as a child, Jack hadn't liked being on the receiving end of their solutions.

The lonely, shut-out feeling of his youth was still an unhappy memory. No way would he inflict the same process on a child of his. On the other hand, he was quite sure he wouldn't like such a disruptive influence in his life, either. The solution, as he saw it, was simple. Don't have children.

Any curiosity he might have had about the experience of fatherhood had been more than fulfilled by what he'd observed with his friends. Apart from which, he felt no urge to perpetuate his bloodline. He enjoyed his life, loved his work, had the financial freedom to do what he liked when he liked. What more could he want?

Nina...

Jack grimaced as he tried to expunge that thought and the gut-wrenching sense of loss accompanying it. Nina had shut him out even more thoroughly than his parents had, not even giving him the chance to open the door again. All over a stupid argument about babies.

Or maybe there'd been other reasons. He shook his head, still frustrated by the way she'd cut him out of her life, leaving him wondering what he'd done wrong. He'd chosen that very night to ask Nina to move in with him, sure in his own mind he'd found a woman he'd enjoy living with, and just because he'd made a few entirely appropriate comments about the baby who'd wrecked the dinner party they'd attended, Nina had gone off her brain and dumped him, then and there. No comeback. Total wipe-out.

It made no sense to him. He was probably well rid of a woman who could act so irrationally. Yet there'd never been a glimmer of such behaviour in all the time they'd spent together—months of sheer joy. He could have sworn they were completely compatible, even to their pleasure in the creative work they did. She was the first and only person he'd ever felt really at home with.

There were times he missed her so badly it was a physical ache. He could still visualise her as clearly as if she were with him now, sitting beside him— dark velvet eyes with stars in them, a smile that made his heart dance, shiny black hair swinging around her shoulders, her soft, feminine curves a sensual promise he knew to be absolutely true. He could hear her infectious laughter and the sexy murmurs that excited him when they made love.

Futile memories. He wished he could forget Nina Brady and how he'd felt with her. There was no shortage of women wanting to interest him. Sooner or later he'd meet one who'd strike that special spark. It was only a matter of waiting. Eight months hardly rated as a long time. In a year or two, Nina's rejection wouldn't mean a thing.

The traffic lights favoured him right up to Taylor Square. As he turned into Oxford Street, he switched his mind to Maurice and tried to work himself into a lighter mood. Maurice Larosa was a good friend and a valuable business associate. He not only gave Jack all the French polishing work on the antiques he sold, but frequently sent clients who wanted to have pieces made to match furniture they'd bought. Favours like that deserved favours in return, and if it meant smiling benevolently at a baby, Jack was resolved on obliging. At least this once.

He spotted a car pulling out of a convenient space and shot into it, grateful not to waste time hunting for a parking slot. The hospital was only a short distance away. The dash clock showed seven-fifteen, plenty of time to get there, perform as expected and take his leave with the excuse of giving Maurice and his wife privacy to say their good nights.

He picked up the gift-boxed bottle of champagne from the passenger seat, smiling over this particular forethought as he alighted from the big Range Rover and locked it. Other visitors would undoubtedly shower presents on the baby. Some French bubbly might give the new and soon-to-be-frazzled parents a pleasant hour or two together. He knew from his other friends that babies killed any sense of romance stone dead.

Although it was April, there wasn't so much as a nip of autumn in the air. The lingering Indian summer made it a pleasant hour for walking. A waste of a nice evening, Jack thought, as he entered the hospital and headed for the inquiries desk. Having received directions, he caught the elevator to the correct floor, mentally bracing himself to endure baby talk with jovial indulgence for a minimum of twenty minutes.

The elevator doors opened. He stepped out. Something familiar about the woman waiting to step into the compartment caught his eye. He looked sharply at her and he had the weird sense of falling down an empty shaft instead of standing flat on a firm floor.

'Nina?'

Her name exploded from his throat.

Her hair was cropped short, but he couldn't mistake that face, those eyes as she stared straight at

him. Recognition, shock, disbelief, fear, anger…
each expression pulsed briefly at him from a stillness
that shrieked with tension. Then she whirled past
him, jabbed a finger at the control panel inside the
elevator and hugged herself against the back wall,
glaring a fierce rejection of him until the doors
closed.

The message burned into his brain. She didn't
want him. She didn't want anything to do with him.
He quelled the raging instinct to chase after her, find
her, make her listen to him. Useless. She'd made her
decision to shut him out. It hadn't changed. It wasn't
about to change. She'd just done it again.

He forced himself to walk away, to check the
room numbers he passed along the corridor. He'd
come here to oblige a friend. Never mind that he
had no heart for it. It gave him something purposeful
to do. He had to forget Nina.

But why had there been fear in her eyes? He'd
never given her any reason to be afraid of him.

Why anger? Surely she realised this meeting was
purely accidental.

Damn it all! What had he done wrong?

CHAPTER TWO

JACK...

His name kept pounding through Nina's mind, creating waves of pain that seemed to suck at her body, leaving her weak and trembling. When the elevator doors opened, she had to push herself away from the wall. Her legs were like jelly, her stomach a churning mess. Somehow she made it to the ladies' rest room on the ground floor, blundered into an empty cubicle, fastened the door, then gratefully sank onto the toilet seat, safely hidden until she could pull herself together.

Tears welled into her eyes. She hunched over, burying her face in her hands, rocking in anguish at the unkind stroke of fate that had brought her face to face with Jack at such a time and place. It wasn't fair. It was grossly unfair. She'd spent the past eight months trying to forget him, forcing herself to accept there could be no happy future with him. Seeing him again now opened up all the hurt she'd done her best to bury.

For one heart-stopping moment she'd thought he knew. But he couldn't. And, of course, he didn't. The surprise on his face told her he hadn't expected to run into her.

The husky urgency in his voice had rattled memories better suppressed. Jack wanting her, making love to her with such intense passion they seemed to flow together in a fusing heat that had made her feel it was impossible to tear them apart. They'd been a perfect match in so many ways...if there were only two of them. She hadn't known then, hadn't realised there was a fatal flaw in their relationship, silently waiting to explode in her face, just when she'd fooled herself everything would be all right.

The hollow sickness she had felt that night swamped her again. Jack was lost to her. Irrevocably. Their paths had diverged so deeply, no meeting place was left for them. An unpredictable and accidental crossing like tonight was a cruelty, a glimpse of what might have been if Jack's attitude about babies and having children had been different.

Nina remembered her own father's attitude too well to inflict the same crushing sense of being unwanted onto any child, much less her own. Every time her parents had argued, they had invariably flung out the bitter accusation of being trapped by an unplanned pregnancy. Nina was to blame for her father not being in the career he wanted, for her mother being tied to responsibility instead of enjoying many more carefree years. The list of resentments was endless.

It would have been the same with Jack—different reasons for resenting the situation but no difference in the feelings aroused. He had left her with no doubt about that. Nina shut her eyes tight, squeezing back the futile tears, wishing she could erase the image of him, stamped so freshly on her mind.

He was still magnetically handsome, emanating the same powerful virility that had drawn her to him at their very first meeting. In just those few strung-out moments before she'd escaped via the elevator, the old familiarities had leapt to vivid life again—the small mole near his jawline, a tantalising little disfigurement on his smoothly tanned skin. His streaky toffee hair, at its shaggy state, needing a trim. The startling directness of his green eyes tugging at her heart.

He shouldn't affect her like this. Not now, when it was so impossibly hopeless for them ever to get together. And this was the last place he should be. Why on earth would Jack be visiting a maternity hospital?

Someone must have pressed him to come, blindly intent on showing off a new son or daughter, not realising a baby had no appeal whatsoever to Jack Gulliver. Social politeness or professional sensibilities would have pushed him to oblige. It was the only answer Nina could come up with. She desperately hoped that seeing her wouldn't prompt a curiosity to know why she was here. If he found out…

She couldn't bear it. She just couldn't bear it. Arguments, recriminations, an insistence on shouldering some responsibility, financial if nothing else. Trapped by a child he didn't want but felt obliged to support. A tie between them going on and on…the bitterness of it. She'd hate it. She'd taken every step she could to avoid it—leaving her job, changing house, no telephone number in her name— all to make the break from Jack a completely clean one.

She wanted to howl out her fear and frustration, but if someone heard her it would draw unwelcome attention. A nurse might be fetched. Her chest hurt. Her throat ached. She grabbed some toilet tissue and mopped her eyes and cheeks, determined to rise above this dreadful stress.

Yet if the decisions she had put into action were sabotaged now, how would she cope? Her emotional state was shockingly fragile as it was, without Jack intruding on the life she had to establish and maintain. With Sally's help she could manage. She didn't need Jack's money, and her child certainly didn't need his attitude.

Maybe she was worrying for nothing. Jack's surprise didn't necessarily mean he was still interested in her. He could be attached to some other woman by now. There would have been plenty wanting to interest him in the past eight months. A good-looking man of substance didn't go begging for female company.

But what they had shared had been special. And Jack was choosy. He didn't give out to many people. The look in his eyes after the initial shock of recognition—eagerness, hope—would he shrug it off and let it go?

With any luck he might have assumed she was another visitor, passing through, leaving as he was arriving. Had he noticed she wasn't wearing proper clothes? She groaned as she realised it was more than clothes adding up the evidence against being a visitor. No make-up, hair in disarray, no handbag. She hoped she hadn't given him enough time to register those details.

Time… She glanced at her watch. Seven thirty-six. She couldn't risk running into Jack again. Best to stay hidden in this rest room until after the eight o'clock curfew for visitors. Sally would stay with the baby until she returned to the ward. There was no cause for panic. Sally expected her to spend twenty minutes or so browsing through the magazines available at the kiosk. Nina had left her happily chatting to the other two new mothers and their visitors—husbands, happy husbands and fathers.

The tears welled again. It was miserable being a single mother when she was faced with families celebrating their new offspring. Sally was a great friend and wonderful support, but it wasn't the same.

If only Jack…

Damn him! Why couldn't he have been different? Why were children so wrong for him?

CHAPTER THREE

SMILING benevolently did not come easily. Jack had to work hard at repressing the angry frustration that seeing Nina had stirred. He wanted to snap and snarl. He felt a deep empathy with his dog's behaviour when a great bone was moved out of his marked territory. He felt no empathy whatsoever with the drivel coming out of Maurice's mouth.

'He's got my ears, poor little blighter.'

Jack smiled. 'Well, one can always resort to plastic surgery.'

Maurice laughed indulgently. 'They're not that bad. He'll grow into them.'

'Bound to,' Jack agreed, his face aching with smiling.

Maurice looked besottedly at his wife. 'I'm glad he's got Ingrid's nose.'

Jack obediently performed the comparison, studying the straight, aristocratic nose of Maurice's buxom blonde wife and the longer, slightly bumpy one of his friend. He forced another smile. 'Yes. Much the better nose.'

Why was it obligatory to divide a baby's features between the parents? It was inevitably done, like a ritual, perhaps affirming true heritage, or an assurance that a little replica would fulfil its parents' expectations. Not only was it a deadly boring exercise to Jack, it almost drove him to snap, 'Let the kid be himself, for God's sake!'

But that wasn't the done thing.

He wondered whom Nina had been visiting on this floor. Not that it mattered. No point in trying to find some contact point with her. From the attitude she had flashed to him, it would probably constitute harassment. Besides, Jack had a built-in inhibitor against going where he wasn't wanted.

'Give me the baby, darling, while you open Jack's present,' Ingrid commanded, brandishing the new-born power of being a mother. This was definitely one time she could boss Maurice around. The proud and grateful Dad would undoubtedly lick her feet if she asked him to. Jack knew from observation that the flow of uncritical giving wouldn't last.

He watched Maurice lay the precious bundle in his wife's arms with tender care. It was really a pity such blissful harmony didn't last. They looked good—loving mother and father with child. Idyllic. The rot didn't set in until they went home from hospital.

Ingrid's long blonde hair gleamed like skeins of silk falling over her shoulders. Jack frowned at the reminder of Nina's hair, which some idiot had clearly butchered. What had possessed her to have her beautiful hair cut? She'd looked like a ragamuffin, wispy bits sticking out as though she'd run her fingers through the short crop instead of brushing it.

The style didn't suit her. It made her face look thinner.

Maybe her face *was* thinner.

Had Nina been ill?

It was a disturbing thought. Frustration boiled up again. He hated not knowing what had been happening to her. Her face had looked paler than he remembered, too, all healthy colour washed out of it. If she'd been ill, was ill…no, it still made no sense for Nina to look at him with fear and anger.

It was no reason to cut him out of her life, either. She could have stayed with him. He would have looked after her. Did she have anyone looking after her now?

'My favourite champagne, Veuve Cliquot!' Maurice beamed at him. 'Great gift, Jack.'

'I won't be able to drink it,' Ingrid wailed. 'It'll sour my milk.'

New regime rolling in, souring more than her milk, Jack silently predicted. He grimaced an apology. 'Sorry, Ingrid. I'm an ignorant male.'

'Never mind, love.' Maurice dropped a kiss on her puckered forehead. 'We'll keep it until the little guzzler here goes onto a bottle.'

'I don't know when that will be.' She pouted. 'Look how big my breasts are swelling up with milk. They're even beginning to leak.'

They were certainly stretching her nightgown to its limits of stretchability, Jack observed, and suddenly had a flash of Nina in the elevator, her arms hugging her rib cage, her breasts pushed up, surely far more voluptuous than they used to be.

She'd been wearing a loose, button-through dress, her shape disguised by it initially. Besides, his attention had been riveted on her face then, the expression in her eyes. But when she'd turned around in the elevator, pressing back against the wall, holding herself defensively, her breasts had definitely bulged.

His heart skittered. He gave himself a mental shake, pushing the idea away. To associate Nina's breasts with Ingrid's—swollen with milk—was a neurotic vision he could well do without. Nina couldn't have had a baby. It was only eight months since she'd left him.

After an argument about babies.

His mind whirled at sickening speed. Maternity hospital…not a dress, a free-flowing housecoat… tired, careless of her appearance…shock, disbelief, fear at seeing him here…anger…

He felt the blood draining from his face. He clenched his hands, gritted his teeth and willed his heart to pump his circulation back into top working order. He had to think clearly and rationally, not leap to wild conclusions. If Nina had been pregnant, surely to God she would have told him. Flung it in his face, most likely, in the middle of that argument. She couldn't have thought he'd turn his back on her.

Maybe she had thought it, deciding to take that initiative herself rather than confront what he might say or do, given his negative attitude to having children.

Nausea cramped his stomach and shot bile up his throat. If she'd gone it alone because she hadn't trusted him to respond supportively…

'Are you all right, Jack?'

Maurice's question broke through the glaze of horror in his mind. They were looking quizzically at him. Had he missed something? *Apart from a nine-month pregnancy?*

'Sorry.' He sucked in a deep breath and swallowed hard. 'I was just thinking how great the three of you look together.'

Ingrid laughed. 'Time you found yourself a wife and started a family, Jack.'

Join the club. They all said that. Once they were caught in the family trap, it was as though anyone who was free of it was an offensive reminder of what they'd given up. The hell of it was he might very well have a child somewhere on this ward, a child whose mother had decided was better off fatherless than having Jack in their lives.

'Aren't you thirty-something?' Ingrid persisted.

'Darling, I'm forty,' Maurice reminded her. 'Age has nothing to do with it. If I hadn't met you, I'd still be a freewheeling bachelor like Jack.'

Jack didn't want to be a freewheeling bachelor. He wanted Nina. He didn't care if she came with a child. He wanted Nina. The need and desire for her burgeoned out of the emptiness that had haunted the past eight months, growing with compelling force, overpowering all his objections to babies.

A little scrap of humanity like the one in Ingrid's arms couldn't beat him. He'd learn how to handle the child. He'd never had a problem handling anything once he set his mind to it. If Nina needed proof of that, he'd give it to her.

Babies were probably only destructive monsters because parents allowed them to take over. Jack was made of sterner stuff. Having seen the damage babies wrought on relationships, he could take protective steps and save Nina and himself a lot of unnecessary stress. It was all a matter of attitude and organisation.

What he needed was a plan.

He also needed definite facts instead of suppositions. A plan could very quickly come unstuck if he didn't have his facts right. Therefore, step one was to grab a nurse and make a few pertinent inquiries.

'You know, Jack—' Ingrid eyed him speculatively '—I have a few girlfriends you might enjoy meeting.'

The good old matchmaking trick.

Jack smiled. He didn't even have to force it. His heart had lifted with a swelling sense of purpose. 'Actually, Ingrid, I'm on my way to meet a lady I'm very interested in. If you and Maurice will excuse me… It's a delight to see you so happy, and I hope the new son and heir thrives as he should under your loving care. He's sure to be a great kid.'

Pleasure all around.

Having delivered his benevolent performance, Jack was well-wished on his way. In truth, he *was* feeling benevolent towards Maurice and Ingrid. Even their baby. They'd done him a great favour. If it wasn't for them he wouldn't have come here, wouldn't have seen Nina and put two and two together.

Only in this case, two and two were going to make three. Jack had no compunction about changing the mathematics of the situation. He was determined on being counted *in*, not *out*.

CHAPTER FOUR

VISITING hours had ended ten minutes ago. Nevertheless, Nina apprehensively checked the ward corridor, glancing swiftly to both right and left, confirming an all clear before scooting out of the elevator. It was only fifteen metres to her room. She covered the distance as fast as she could without actually running. Hearing Sally's cheerful voice still rattling away was an assurance that everything was normal.

No-one called out her name. Jack didn't suddenly emerge from one of the rooms in front of her. She reached her door, and with a thundering sense of being home free swung into the room and quickly closed the door behind her, safeguarding against a casual glance inside from any passer-by.

'There you are,' Sally said with satisfaction. 'I was about to send out a search party.'

'Sorry.' Nina turned to her friend, flashing an appeasing smile, and the world tilted as Jack filled her vision, Jack cradling her baby in the crook of his arm. She feebly fumbled for the door, instinctively seeking support, feeling herself sway alarmingly.

'Are you okay?' Anxious question from Sally.

'Here! Quick!' Jack, commanding.

Double vision. Two Jacks bundling babies into

two Sallys' arms, furniture wavering all over the
place. Nina closed her eyes. Too difficult to get
things straight. Hopelessly dizzy.

Strong arms hooking around her, scooping her off
her feet, carrying her, sitting her on the side of the
bed, holding her safe, thrusting her head down.
'Deep breaths, Nina. Sally, put the kid in its bassinette and pour Nina a glass of water.'

The kid.

A murderous haze billowed into Nina's fuzzy
mind. Her baby—the baby who'd grown inside her
for nine long, miserable, lonely months—dismissed
as a kid! If she had the strength, she'd put her hands
around Jack's neck and strangle him. How dared he
come in here, after all he'd said, and actually hold
the child he didn't want, pretending he didn't mind?

The kid. Not the baby. Not our daughter. The kid.
That said it all to Nina. He probably hadn't even
asked what sex the baby was. Didn't care. Her heart
pumped with furious vigour, clearing her head so
fast she didn't need the glass of water Sally pressed
into her hand.

She was tempted to hurl it in Jack's face. It might
sober him up. Whatever impulsive and stupid ardour
had driven him into this room needed dampening
down. He wasn't thinking straight, any more than
she'd been seeing straight. But she could see straight
through him! Having figured out what she was doing
in a maternity ward, he had a hot case of guilt.

'You need looking after, Nina,' he said gruffly.
'And I'm the man to do it. Drink up now.'

She sipped, just to moisten her throat. Then she glared her outrage at him. 'Don't you tell me what to do, Jack Gulliver. You have no right.'

He returned a determined look. 'I contributed to this situation and—'

'You did not.' She cut him off with more belligerent determination. 'You trusted me to get the contraception right, and I messed up. It's all my fault.'

'Accidents happen,' he said grimly.

'Well, you don't have to pay for this one. I take full responsibility.'

'Sure! And you're doing a fine job of it, letting yourself get so run down you almost faint at the sight of me.'

'Shock. You holding a baby was more than my mind could encompass.'

'Then you'd better get used to it, Nina, because that kid happens to be my kid, too.'

Her teeth clenched. Her eyes sizzled him to a crisp. 'She is not a kid.'

'You're right,' he snapped. 'More like a mind-bending drug than a natural member of the animal kingdom.'

'Huh! Now you're showing your true colours.'

'Just pointing out how distorted your judgment is.' His eyes flashed green fire. 'Denying me the right to know I've fathered a child. Denying me the right to make my own decisions. Denying me any chance to stand by you through what has obviously been a rough time. Even a murderer gets his day in court.'

The fierce flow of accusations stunned her for a moment. Justification sped off her tongue. 'You told me you don't want children, Jack Gulliver. So don't come the injured party to me. I left you free and clear.'

'I didn't say I wanted to be free and clear. I don't,' he retorted emphatically. 'I was just asking your friend, Sally, how quickly a wedding could be arranged.'

'A wedding!' Shock rolled through her mind again, sapping her energy. She took another sip of water, then handed the glass to Sally, who was still standing by, dumbstruck by the verbals zipping back and forth. Nina gave her a hard, warning look. 'What have you been telling him, Sally?'

'Me?' she squeaked. Her mobile face worked through alarm and wary consideration and settled on rueful resignation. 'Well, uh, he asked me who I was and I, um, gave him my business card.'

The card! Customised Weddings—We Deliver Your Dream. With her address and telephone number clearly printed on it!

Nina groaned, realizing the milk was spilled and couldn't be put back into the bottle. She sagged onto her pillow, swung her legs onto the bed and turned away from them, closing her eyes, unutterably depressed by an outcome she would have done anything to avoid.

'If I've done the wrong thing…' Sally's anxious voice floated over her.

'Don't blame Sally for letting the cat out of the

bag, Nina,' Jack quietly interposed. 'I would have found out anyway.'

That was probably true. Jack didn't let go of anything until he was satisfied. Like restoring a piece of antique furniture. He'd work at it and work at it until it was finished precisely as he wanted. Seeing her had done the damage, not Sally's blabbing.

Nina was suddenly aware of the silence in the room. The other visitors had gone. The babies were quiet. No-one had turned on a television set. Undoubtedly this little real-life drama was more interesting, the unmarried mother confronted by the father of her child. And Jack was so good-looking, so impressively steadfast in rebutting her charges. The two secure wives who shared this room would be looking with favour on him, not knowing what Nina knew.

It was sickening.

'A cup of tea,' Sally said as though plucking the idea out of a tank of possible solutions to the situation. 'I'll go and make one for her, Jack.'

'Good idea,' he approved warmly.

She heard Sally leave. The sound of a chair being shifted and the squeak of its upholstery told her Jack had sat down, settling in for a siege on her solitary position.

No point in hiding from him, Nina decided reluctantly. The music had to be faced, and it was better to get it over with here and now. She rolled onto her back, opened her eyes and steeled herself against the tug of attraction that hadn't diminished at all with either time or circumstances.

He met her gaze with direct intensity, his expression a moving mixture of compassion and resolution. Tears pricked her eyes. He cared about her. The baby was a complication he didn't want, but his feeling for her hadn't changed. It made the necessity of rejecting him again all the more difficult and painful.

It would be so easy to reach out and take the comfort and warmth and pleasure of being with him again. He'd wrap her in his arms and stroke her back and kiss her hair, and she'd feel his body stir with desire for her and… She'd missed him so much. But if she gave in to the need aching through her now, Jack would be encouraged to stick around, and the inevitable consequences would be worse than her current sense of deprivation.

Better to remain independent.

'I don't need your help, Jack,' she said flatly.

'That's not how it looks to me, Nina.' He reached out and took her left hand, fondling it warmly, persuasively pressing a link between them as he added, 'I think we should get married as soon as possible.'

'No!' She snatched her hand away, feeling as though he'd burned her. Her eyes blazed fierce conviction. 'I won't marry you, Jack.'

'Why not? It's the most sensible, practical thing to do.'

'I will not subject my baby to a father who doesn't want her.'

'If you're worried about the kid, let me assure you—'

'Her name,' Nina interrupted furiously, 'is Charlotte.'

'Charlotte?' He frowned. 'It doesn't go very well with Gulliver. Let's toss a few other names around.'

'Charlotte Brady sounds fine to me.'

Jack studied the stubborn set of her face and made a political retreat. 'Fine. If that's the name you like, I'm happy to go along with it.' He brightened. 'On second thoughts, Charlotte isn't too bad. We can call her Charlie. Charlie Gulliver has a nice ring to it.'

'Charlotte is a girl, Jack,' Nina pointed out with seething emphasis. 'She is *my* daughter and she will remain Charlotte Brady. I am not going to marry you.'

He sighed. Heavily. His eyes glittered with devious intent. 'Okay. We'll just live together then.'

'I have no intention of living with you, Jack. I have my own place. I have everything set up as I want it, and neither I nor my baby requires your support.'

'Brave words, Nina, but what if something goes wrong with your well-laid plans?'

'I'll cope.'

'You'll cope better with me at your side.'

'No, I won't.'

'We'll see about that,' he declared, letting her know he was not about to be put off, put down or put out.

Nina sighed. Heavily. Jack was going to make a

battle of it, no matter what she said. A wave of
weakness dragged through her. She wished Charlotte
would start bawling her head off. That would soon
shift Jack. If her cries set the other babies off, too,
he'd be out the door as fast as his feet could carry
him.

Sally returned, darting apprehensive looks at Jack
and Nina as she put the cup of tea on the mobile
tray. 'Better now?' she asked hopefully.

Sally Bloomfield was the most assertive person
Nina had ever met. She was a brilliant saleswoman,
able to talk anybody into anything and make him
feel delighted about it. Her appearance was always
polished and professional, from her chic auburn hair
to her beautifully shod feet. Her smile dazzled, and
her bright hazel eyes mesmerised. Sally sailed
through life with the blissful belief that no matter
what happened, it would turn out for the best. Her
optimism was good to be around, but right now Nina
needed her professional expertise.

'Tell Jack I'm perfectly capable of doing without
him, Sally,' she appealed.

'Right!' She sat herself at the end of the bed and
addressed Jack gravely. 'It's like this. Nina and I are
set up in business together.'

Jack looked surprised. 'Nina is organising weddings, too?'

'No, no, that's my specialty. I adore weddings.
Nina is a great seamstress. She fixes any bridal hire
gowns that need altering. Does extra beading and
tucks and stuff. Some of our clients have chosen

Nina's own designs, and she makes them so beautifully, it adds a lot to our reputation of delivering the dream.'

Jack frowned. 'She won't have much time for that with the baby. They're time-consuming little mo—' He caught his breath.

'Monsters,' Nina finished for him. 'Go on. Say it, Jack. That's how you think of them. Monsters!'

'I was going to say moppets,' he corrected her loftily.

'Huh!'

'Well, the thing is,' Sally said swiftly, 'Nina doesn't have to travel anywhere. Everything is very handy. The business is run from my home, and Nina has a completely self-contained granny flat at the back of the premises. She can bring the baby into the house with her when she has to do fittings. There's really no problem. She's got a solid income, good accommodation and nothing to worry about.'

'You see? I'm self-sufficient,' Nina declared triumphantly.

'Except for a man,' Sally muttered.

Nina glared at her.

Sally shrugged and flirted with her eyes at Jack. 'Well, you must admit, Nina, he is superb lover material. Why not have him? You can always get rid of a husband if it doesn't work out.'

'Excellent reasoning.' Jack leapt in eagerly. 'If she'd just give me a chance—'

'I am not going to marry him,' Nina interrupted.

'There's a lot of advantages to it, Nina,' Sally

argued. 'Where would I be without my husbands? I got a car out of the first, a house out of the second and the capital to set up the business from the third.'

Sally had it the wrong way round. Nina didn't want a sales pitch directed at her, but Sally had the bit between the teeth and was in full spate.

'Husbands can be very handy. You have a built-in escort, sex on demand, someone to look after you if you get sloshed at a party, financial backing, the muscle to stand over tradesmen and make sure they do the job right, and in your case, a no-cost baby minder when you want a break from mothering.'

'That's where it falls down,' Nina pounced. 'Jack hates babies.'

'It's different with my own kid,' he defended staunchly.

Nina swung on him. 'What's different about it? You think Charlotte won't cry? That she won't dirty her nappy and wake up in the middle of the night and take attention away from you?'

'I can adjust.'

'Ingrained attitudes do not disappear overnight, Jack Gulliver.'

A nurse came in and looked disapprovingly at the late visitors. 'I'm afraid I'll have to ask you people to leave. Hospital rules, you know.'

Sally hopped off the bed. 'Sleep on it, Nina,' she advised, her eyebrows waggling suggestively. 'It's very easy to get a divorce these days.'

Jack rose reluctantly from his chair. 'I'll be back

tomorrow, Nina,' he vowed, a challenge burning in his eyes. 'I'm not going to be shut out again.'

Then he turned to look down at the baby in the bassinette, giving her a salute as he moved past. 'Good night, kid. This is your dad talking, and don't let your mum tell you any different.'

'Her name is Charlotte!' Nina shouted after him.

CHAPTER FIVE

THE roses arrived just before the midmorning feeding time. One of the nurses carried in the huge arrangement, grinning from ear to ear. 'Three dozen!' she crowed, eyeing Nina with speculative interest. Being given so many was clearly a notable achievement.

'For me?' Nina asked doubtfully.

'It's your name on the envelope,' came the ready assurance.

They could only be from Jack. Which meant he really would be coming back today, bringing with him all the conflicts she had tried to keep out of the life she had planned for Charlotte and herself. With her heart aflutter with apprehension and her mind clogged with a host of desires she shied away from examining, Nina cleared the top of her bedside cabinet before she was aware of what she was doing.

The nurse set the vase down just as Nina realised she should refuse the extravagant gift. It was weak to give Jack any positive signals. But the deep red buds had a glorious scent, and they were so heart-liftingly beautiful, it seemed unnecessarily churlish to direct them elsewhere. It wouldn't make any difference in the long run, she argued to herself. The roses would die, just as Jack's interest in wooing her

232

would die when the crunch of actually having to deal with a baby came.

Having spent a restless night brooding over Jack's reappearance in her life, Nina remained unpersuaded there was any real hope of a happy future with him. All she could see ahead of them were endless disputes, damaging to everyone, especially Charlotte.

Recollections of her own childhood were still painfully vivid. Her parents had finally separated when she was ten, and she'd been shunted off to live with her grandmother, who was prepared to shoulder the burden. Despite being tolerated, rather than loved, by her grandmother, Nina had found it an enormous relief simply no longer being a bone of continual contention between her parents.

The nurse unpinned the envelope and gave it to her, still grinning. 'Red roses for love. Some guy wants to make an impression.'

'He already has,' Nina muttered darkly, and Jack had a lot of winning over to do before she'd change her mind about his fitness to be a father. 'Thanks for bringing them in.'

'My pleasure.'

Nina opened the envelope and withdrew the card. It read, 'For the woman who's given me more than anyone else in the world—Love, Jack.'

A lump filled her throat. She had to swallow hard to ease the constriction. The truth of it was Jack had given her more than any man she had ever met, but that did not make him right for Charlotte. Clinging to the conviction he could not be trusted to love their daughter as she should be loved, Nina opened the top drawer of her cabinet and dropped the card in, denying herself the indulgence of reading it over and over again, making more of it than it meant.

'Looks like your Jack is making up for lost time.'

The optimistic comment from Rhonda, one of her room-mates, struck a sensitive chord. Had she done wrong in denying Jack knowledge of her pregnancy? At the time she had imagined a horrified reaction from him. She had believed he would suggest an abortion and do his utmost to harass her into it. Maybe she had done him an injustice.

Nevertheless, the situation last night had been a very different one. A baby who was already born could not be as easily dismissed as an unseen fetus. It was a reality, a living, breathing human being, who was definitely a little person in her own right, one who couldn't be ignored or discarded as of no account.

Jack might want to diminish her importance, but no way was Nina going to let him relegate Charlotte to some distant place in their lives. Calling her the kid was so offensively impersonal. Nina still burned at the offhand attitude it typified. And corrupting their daughter's name to Charlie… No doubt if he had to have a child, he would have preferred a boy.

'Three dozen hothouse roses don't come cheaply,' came the knowing remark from Kim, her other room-mate.

'He can afford them. It's not money that worries him,' Nina said dryly, niggled by the unsubtle approbation both women had displayed towards Jack since his dramatic appearance on the scene last night. They couldn't seem to comprehend her reservations about accepting his volte-face on wanting a child in his life.

They were younger than Nina, and the course of their lives had run with conventional smoothness so far. They had every reason to cling to their romantic illusions, not having run into any serious snags themselves.

Kim, at twenty-three, was a rather plump but pretty blonde who'd married the guy she fell in love with at high school. The only career she wanted was being his wife and the mother of his children. Her husband had a permanent job on the railway, and she felt absolutely secure.

Rhonda, at twenty-five, was more sophisticated, a professional hairdresser who intended to keep working until she and her husband had their house paid off. He was a sales representative of a major food company, and their goals had been meticulously planned—their wedding, the baby, the house, their car traded in for a family station wagon.

Rhonda's catalogued milestones had driven Nina to reflect that none of her own goals had been achieved. She'd worked her way through design school, dreaming of making a name for herself in the fashion industry. Clinching an apprenticeship with a successful designer had seemed a helpful step, yet it had very quickly punched home to her that she'd never have the capital to launch her own brand name in such a highly competitive field. The closest she'd got to establishing her own business was this partnership with Sally.

As for her love-life, there had been no-one of any deep significance until Jack. She'd been twenty-eight at the time of meeting him, Jack thirty-two, and it truly seemed as though Mr. Right had finally come along. The shock had been totally shattering when he'd revealed how anti babies and children he was. Even if she hadn't been pregnant, it would have made her think twice about continuing their relationship.

Charlotte stirred, giving one of her little mewing cries. Nina swooped on the bassinette, eager to pick up her beautiful baby daughter and cradle her in her arms. She was so tiny and perfect, like a miracle, and Nina still marvelled at the way she latched instantly onto a nipple and sucked.

Having stacked the pillows on the bed for a comfortable position, Nina settled back against them, unbuttoned her nightie and smilingly watched her daughter home in on what she wanted. A rush of deep maternal love reassured Nina of the decisions she had made, despite the situation with Jack.

Although she had never felt a pressing need to have a baby, it had always seemed to her a natural thing to do somewhere along her lifeline. She would have wanted the choice to have a child and would have felt cheated as a woman to be denied it. Maybe it was some subconscious response to not having been wanted herself, but from the moment Nina had learnt she was pregnant, however unplanned it was, all her protective instincts had been aroused. This baby would be wanted and loved and cherished.

She might have been a failure as a daughter, a failure at making a name for herself with her own fashion label, a failure at picking the right man to love, but she was not going to be a failure as a mother. On that Nina was fiercely resolved.

'If your Jack doesn't worry about money he must have a great job,' Rhonda remarked, obviously interested in the financial angle. She had a budget worked out for everything.

'He runs his own business,' Nina explained.

'Doing what?' Kim pumped.

Nina sighed and gave in to their natural curiosity. 'Mostly French polishing. He restores antiques and makes cabinets and other bits and pieces. He's very good at it.'

A perfectionist, she thought. Like her with her sewing and dress designs. They both enjoyed making something beautiful. Their mutual understanding of the pleasure and satisfaction in creativity was one of the shared bonds that had made their relationship so good.

She wished she could believe in Jack's turnaround. Maybe she should risk the hurt of giving him a chance. If he persisted. The roses were a heady reminder of Jack's sensuality. A convulsive little shiver ran over her skin. She had missed the enthralling intimacy of his lovemaking. Sally had a point there. The nights were very lonely by herself.

'I wish my husband was a handy man,' Rhonda said ruefully. 'He can't even change a tap washer.'

'You can always get in a plumber. You can't hire a doting and devoted father,' Nina pointed out, reminding herself to be very, very wary of where she was heading with Jack, if indeed she was heading anywhere. There would inevitably be a lot of interrupted nights with Charlotte. Jack's groaning and grumbling wouldn't exactly be music to her ears.

'Give him time to feel like a father,' Kim advised. 'Does Charlotte favour him in looks?'

'Not particularly.'

She looked at their daughter. Her fair hair probably came from him. Not that Jack was fair now, but he must have been when he was a boy. Nina remembered her mother saying she was born with black hair, so Charlotte didn't take after her in that respect. In any event, Nina was certain Jack hadn't examined Charlotte for likenesses. She was just the kid to him.

'Well, whether she looks like him or not, babies have a way of winding themselves around fathers' hearts,' Rhonda declared, unable to imagine any other outcome. 'He wouldn't want to marry you if he didn't want her.'

The marriage offer had certainly come as a surprise. Probably a conditioned response to the situation, Nina had reasoned, guilt leading to a burst of doing the right thing by her. Given time, Jack would undoubtedly rue the impulsive idea.

'It won't last,' Nina said, casting a quelling look

at Jack's well-meaning supporters and determinedly dampening the little hope that kept squiggling through her.

Rhonda couldn't resist a last word. 'Look at it this way. If he's got plenty of money, you could always hire a nanny to take the hassle out of looking after the baby.'

A nanny for a kid. Rhonda had hit the nail on the head with that one, Nina thought. It probably would be Jack's solution to avoiding having anything to do with Charlotte. Well, he could think again if he was planning to separate her from her baby so he could have their twosome back without the hassle of being involved in parenting.

Charlotte hiccupped. Nina hoisted her up and gently rubbed her back to bring up wind. No nanny could feed her baby as she could. Jack had better appreciate her position on mothering—and fathering—if he really wanted to consider marriage. It was a family package deal or nothing, as far as Nina was concerned.

If Jack came today—she glanced at the roses. *When* he came today, she needed to get a few things straightened out. He'd better come today if he wanted to show good faith. Sally was taking her home tonight. Nina had no intention of waiting around with Charlotte, hanging onto a hope that might not materialise.

Charlotte burped, then started snuffling around Nina's shoulder for more milk. Nina lowered her onto her other breast and settled back contentedly to let her baby have her fill.

If Jack Gulliver thought he could walk into their lives and take over as he pleased, he was in for a big surprise.

Two hours later he breezed into the ward, radiating goodwill and bearing more gifts. Nina felt her pulse quicken. He had always excited her. She found herself cravenly wishing she'd put on make-up and a sexier nightie than the practical cotton one with the convenient buttons for breastfeeding. Which was absurd in the circumstances.

'I beat the lunch trolley,' he said, grinning triumphantly as he set his parcels down on her mobile tray and started removing their contents. 'I brought you a chocolate thick shake from McDonald's, that terrine you love—the one with bacon and chicken and pistachio nuts in it—from David Jones's food hall, your favourite Caesar salad, and fresh strawberries and cream to finish up. Enjoy,' he commanded, positioning the newly laden tray across the bed for easy accessibility.

She stared at him in amazement, not only that he'd remembered what she liked but had actually gone to the trouble of getting it for her. 'The hospital does feed me, you know,' she said, struggling against the seduction of being pampered.

'You need appetite tempters, not mass-produced stuff,' he argued earnestly. 'And none of this will upset the baby. I checked. So you can eat with a clear conscience.'

He looked so confident, brimming with bonhomie, his green eyes aglow with a gusto for life. It wasn't fair that he still had the power to dazzle her with his vitality, to ignite a flood of desire with his sizzling sex appeal. It was imperative she keep her head clear and her heart guarded. His words finally filtered through the attraction zone she had to disregard.

'You checked what would upset the baby?' she asked incredulously.

'No excuses for not eating, Nina. You look thin and run-down, and that's not a good state to be in. You need a full store of energy to cope with a new baby.'

He was sounding off like an authority, and being altogether too virtuous for someone who wanted nothing to do with babies. 'Since when did you become an expert on these matters?' she asked suspiciously.

'Made a few phone calls last night for some first-hand advice.' He grinned again. 'I've got plenty of friends ready, willing and able to hand it out.'

Determinedly cheerful in the face of disaster, Nina thought, though she had to concede he had made it through about sixteen hours without backing off and he was putting in considerable effort at this point. It won't last, she repeated to herself, but Sally's sales pitch swirled through her mind, whispering she might as well make the most of it while it did. The terrine was definitely a slice of gourmet heaven.

'Thank you, Jack,' she said sincerely. 'This is very kind and thoughtful of you.'

'You're welcome. Go ahead and eat,' he urged.

The hospital lunch trolley was wheeled in, and Jack waved it on to Kim and Rhonda. They were served with trays of what they had ordered, and Nina hoped they would be somewhat distracted from being interested spectators to the latest development between her and Jack.

She broke open the packet of crackers that accompanied the terrine and helped herself to a generous slice of the tasty delicacy, highly conscious of Jack watching her, exuding intense satisfaction. It was probably a big mistake accepting anything from him, encouraging him to stick around, Nina thought. It would end badly. But right at this moment, however wrong it was, it felt good having Jack here with her.

He stepped to the bassinette and looked at Charlotte, who was sleeping peacefully. This happy state did not test Jack's paternal staying power. It positively increased his cheerfulness.

'Hi, kid. This is your dad speaking,' he said, blithely confident of no reply. 'I'm looking after your mum now, so there's nothing for you to worry about. You can dream blissful dreams of plenty.'

The terrine was delicious. Nina had to acknowledge Jack had the capacity to be a good provider. And he couldn't blame Charlotte for messing up his chosen career, because that was solidly established. Apart from his earning power, he'd never been in financial difficulties, anyway. His parents had both been in the law profession, wealthy people who'd left a considerable estate to their only child when they died, both of them from heart attacks in their early sixties.

'Worked themselves to death,' Jack had remarked offhandedly, and Nina had received the strong impression there had been no great love lost between him and his parents.

Yet he must have been a wanted child. His mother had chosen to have him in her late thirties. Nina figured his parents had probably been disappointed and alienated from Jack when he'd chosen to do manual work rather than follow them into their high-brow profession.

In any event, Jack had no money problems.

He had an attitude problem.

And Nina didn't believe in overnight transformations, however much she might want to. She had seen Jack look benevolently upon babies before, even speak to them benevolently. She knew it to be an act, a social pretence. They were anathema to him.

'Good sleeper, isn't she?' Jack commented, warm approval in his voice.

'She'll probably turn into the baby from hell once I take her home,' Nina predicted.

'Well, we'll meet that problem when it comes,' he said, clinging to blind optimism.

'Why, Jack?' she demanded. 'Why are you even thinking of taking this on? I didn't imagine what you said to me about babies.'

His eyes were pained. 'Nina, if I could take that back…if I could take back these past eight months, I would. There's been one hell of a hole in my life since you took yourself out of it.'

Her heart flipped over. She tore her gaze from his and attacked the lettuce in the Caesar salad. However much he wanted it to be, this was no longer a one-on-one situation. She couldn't answer his needs. She concentrated fiercely on what she was eating. The dressing on the salad was superb. She loved the tangy taste of anchovies.

Jack pulled up the visitor's chair and sat down. 'I meant what I wrote on the card with the roses, Nina,' he said quietly.

'Sorry.' She choked the word out. 'I should have thanked you for the flowers. They're very nice.'

She kept shovelling the salad down her throat so it wouldn't tighten up. Her stomach wasn't receiving it so well, but she hoped it would soon settle down if she piled enough food into it. She was not—*not* going to let Jack Gulliver twist up her straight thinking or her carefully organised plans or her stomach.

'I've missed you. More than I can say,' he went on, undeterred by her lack of enthusiasm. 'You were the best thing that ever happened to me, Nina. I don't want to lose you again.'

He was remembering how it was. That was forever gone. No point in thinking it could be recaptured, not with Charlotte in the picture. Nina relentlessly crunched some croutons. They were more substantial than lettuce.

'You disappeared so quickly,' he complained. 'One week. Just one week, and you were gone. No forwarding address from where you'd been living. You didn't even work out your notice on the job you left. No one had a clue to your new where-abouts.'

Pure luck, she thought, seeing Sally's advertise-ment for a seamstress in the *Herald* the day after the critical argument with Jack. She wondered briefly if it had been good luck or bad luck.

'You made your stand, Jack,' she reminded him, her eyes sharply scanning his. 'You said last night I didn't give you a choice. I didn't think you gave me one. Can you honestly say, if I'd confronted you with my pregnancy one week after that argument, you would have reacted as you seem to be reacting now?'

He hesitated, searching his mind for an honest re-sponse. 'I love you, Nina. I would have done what-ever you wanted of me.'

A weight lifted off her heart. At least he wouldn't have suggested an abortion. The hope squiggled again. Love sounded good. Love sounded wonder-ful. On the other hand, his response was entirely concentrated on her, which left out the baby.

Nina shook her head sadly. 'It doesn't work like that, Jack. It's too one-sided. We had a lot of joy together....'

'Yes, we did,' he said eagerly, his eyes simmering with memories.

Sex, Nina thought. Wild, uninhibited, stupendous,

passionate sex. Total absortion in each other. That was what he was remembering and that was what he wanted back. She took a deep breath and deliberately dashed the highly distracting ardour emanating from him.

'I don't want to live with every bit of joy being whittled away by your resentment of the baby, Jack.'

He raised a hand in solemn fervour. 'Nina, I swear to you I can accommodate the kid.'

Nina gritted her teeth. *Accommodate the kid!* How dared he talk about Charlotte like that? It was hopeless. Absolutely hopeless. She picked up a strawberry and bit the fruit off its stalk, seething through its juice. Jack Gulliver might be the sexiest man alive, but he wasn't worth a father's bootlace. She shot him down with her eyes.

'If you're thinking of hiring a nanny—'

'A nanny! Who said anything about hiring a nanny?' He looked upset, frowning belligerently. 'No kid of mine is going to be brought up by nannies. If that's your plan, Nina, I've got to say right now I disapprove of it.'

Nina was so stunned, she popped another strawberry into her mouth, and the question, 'You do?' became something of a gobble.

'I most certainly do. My parents left me with nannies until I was seven years old and then they turfed me off to boarding school.'

'That's terrible!'

'We are not going to do that, Nina.'

'Oh, no!' She grabbed another strawberry, fascinated by these revelations about Jack's childhood.

He stood up and pointed at the bassinette. 'This kid is going to be brought up right.'

She nodded agreement, her mouth full of juicy fruit, her eyes feasting on a vision of Jack as a dedicated and devoted parent.

He leaned over and kissed her forehead. 'Must get to work now. I've got a shipment of stuff coming in. Keep eating, Nina. You need building up. Put some cream on the strawberries. It's good for the kid.'

She nodded again, totally dumbfounded by this turn of events.

He paused by the bassinette. 'See you tonight, Charlie girl. Be good for your mum. We've got to get her straightened out on a few things.'

He was almost out the door before Nina remembered. 'Sally is picking me up tonight,' she called after him. 'I'm going home, Jack.'

He halted, looking at her with determined authority. 'Correction. I'm picking you up. I've already fixed it with Sally. Very understanding woman, Sally. She let me into your granny flat so I could provision your fridge properly. No more skimping on meals, Nina.'

He left, having taken over as he pleased. Nina felt steamrollered. Maybe she did need straightening out. Hope jiggled in her heart and danced around her mind as she poured some cream onto the strawberries. She looked at Charlotte, who was still sleeping peacefully.

'Well, kid,' she said giddily. 'Maybe you've got a dad after all.' Then she sobered up and added, 'But I'll believe it when I see it.'

CHAPTER SIX

IT WAS strange, sitting beside Jack in his car, driving across the city. Nina felt she was in a time warp, as though the past eight months hadn't happened. Same big, four-wheel-drive Range Rover he had owned then, same sense of being king of the road with all the lower traffic around them, same man in control of where they went, drawing an intense physical awareness of him, same feeling of intimacy, enclosed in a world of their own.

To shake off the eerie feeling, Nina kept glancing around to check that Charlotte was, indeed, with them, securely tucked into her capsule and undisturbed by her new and strange surroundings. Life had moved on, and Charlotte added another dimension to it.

Jack had expertly anchored the capsule on the rear seat. He'd had his vehicle fitted for it today, learning where to put the bolt from the safety harness and get everything adjusted properly. Nina was amazed at his forethought. At least in this practical sense he had accepted Charlotte.

'Stop worrying, Nina. There's no problem.' He gave her a reassuring smile as he caught her glancing at the rear seat again. 'Babies always sleep in moving vehicles.'

'How do you know that?'

His smile turned lopsided. 'A guy I know drove around most of one night with his kid. His wife was desperate for sleep, and it was a surefire way to stop the baby from crying.'

'Maybe there was something wrong with the baby.'

'Just colic.'

He spoke so matter-of-factly, yet Nina was acutely conscious of the problems he listed and how they could affect their relationship. So far, Jack had only ever seen Charlotte asleep, like a serene little doll, demanding only a token acknowledgment. It was easy to think nothing much had changed. She was guilty of it herself, sitting beside him, remembering how it had been together...before Charlotte.

But they weren't going out on a date and they weren't going home to make love. Tension knotted her stomach as she wondered about Jack's expectations of tonight. Did he think they could pick up from where they had left off eight months ago?

He hadn't tried to kiss her, as yet. Not properly. Nor had he really touched her except in courteous and caring support. She stared at his hands, lightly guiding the steering wheel. Perhaps it was from his love of working with wood, bringing out the beauty of its grain. Jack had wonderfully sensitive hands. As much as Nina craved the physical reassurance of his love, it was too soon to let him resume their former intimacy.

Too soon in several senses. Her body needed recovery time from the ordeal of giving birth. Apart from which, Nina felt the need to test Jack's commitment to Charlotte before involving herself too closely with him. She couldn't risk accepting it on faith alone. The road to hell was paved with good intentions.

They were driving into the harbour tunnel now. Once they emerged on the north side, it wasn't far to Lane Cove, where Sally's house and business were handily situated to draw clients from both the northern and western suburbs of Sydney. Nina hoped Jack wasn't anticipating staying overnight in her granny flat. She hoped he wasn't assuming everything was settled between them. It wasn't. Maybe she should make that clear right now.

Something rolled against her feet as the Rover headed down the tunnel. She leaned over to pick it up. A can of dog meat. Nina stared at it, inwardly recoiling from what it meant. Jack still had the dog.

'Sorry about that,' he said, glancing over with a rueful grimace. 'Must have escaped from one of the shopping bags. Better put it in the glove box, out of the way.'

She did as he suggested, wishing Jack wasn't so attached to the mongrel dog he'd rescued from the RSPCA. It was big and fierce, and she was frightened of it. Jack had trained it to be a great watchdog, which was important, since the furniture he worked on was very valuable. Although he insisted Spike's bark was worse than his bite, Nina had never been able to bring herself to pat it and play with it as Jack did.

Maybe it was because she hadn't had any familiarity with dogs during her upbringing. Which reminded her... 'How come you never told me about your childhood, Jack?'

He shrugged. 'No joy in recalling misery, Nina.'

It was a fair answer. She hadn't detailed her childhood to him, either, only telling him her parents had divorced and she'd lived with her grandmother until she'd come to Sydney to go to design school. Since her family—if you could call it that—lived hundreds of kilometres away at Port Macquarie, the question of visiting them had been easily put aside.

Besides, with his own parents dead, Jack was not family minded. He'd never pressed her on the subject, accepting her independence as naturally as he took his own for granted. There had been no reason to tell him she had been an unwanted burden to everyone. It didn't do much for her self-esteem. Jack had accepted her as the person she was—no concern about her background—and that was how she liked it.

'Did you have a dog when you were a boy?' she asked, switching to her earlier thought.

'No. My parents wouldn't allow it. Too much trouble.' He flashed her a wry smile. '*I* was too much trouble, let alone a dog.'

So he'd been a burden, too, though not an unwanted one.

'Where I went to school, the caretaker had a dog.

He let me play with it,' Jack added in fond reminiscence. 'Honey. That was her name. A Labrador. One year she had nine pups. I would have given anything for one of those pups.'

Nina smothered a sigh. Jack was not about to be separated from Spike. Another problem. How could she let that ferocious dog anywhere near Charlotte? There were too many horror stories about dogs mauling children for Nina to even contemplate taking a chance with it.

They were out of the tunnel and heading up the Warringah Freeway. Jack would normally take the Willoughby Road turn-off to go to his home at Roseville Chase. He had a lovely place, Nina reflected, overlooking Echo Point and Middle Harbour. He'd turned the triple garage into his main work area, but he did the finishing in the rumpus room. It was an ideal set-up for Jack, but a child would certainly put a spoke in it.

They passed the turn-off and zoomed along to the Gore Hill Freeway. Nina steeled herself to spell out the situation as she saw it. Jack had to understand that giving an off-the-cuff commitment was not enough for her. She needed some very solid follow-up before she could even think of getting herself deeply entangled with him. She was about to open her mouth when he spoke first.

'Every kid should have a dog,' he declared, nodding over the idea. He looked to her for approval. 'Maybe a little one to begin with. I've heard that miniature fox terriers make great pets.'

Miniature sounded good. 'I think there's a few other things to settle first,' she warned, and they weren't in the miniature category, either. Jack was leaping ahead with apparently blind disregard of the adjustments he'd have to make to his lifestyle.

'Sure,' he agreed blithely. 'I won't rush you, Nina. Sally reckoned it would take at least six weeks to organise a dream wedding. I wouldn't do you out of a dream.'

Her mind freaked out. 'Jack!' She looked at him in horror. 'I don't believe in shotgun marriages.'

He frowned at her. 'No-one's pointing a gun at my head, Nina.'

'You wouldn't have thought of marriage except for the baby,' she said accusingly.

'That's not true. I was going to ask you to live with me the very night we had that damned argument. Same thing.'

'It's not the same thing at all!'

'It is for me.' His green eyes flashed intense conviction. 'You're the only woman I've ever wanted to live with, Nina.'

'You're forgetting something, aren't you?' she asked angrily. 'I come with a child.'

'It's because I'm taking our kid into consideration that I think marriage is a better idea,' he answered with controlled patience. 'Kids like to feel secure with their mum and dad.'

'That's all very well in theory,' Nina retorted fiercely. 'It doesn't work out so neatly in practice.

More than one in every three marriages ends in divorce. Where are the kids then?'

He sighed and slanted her a sympathetic look. 'I know you're speaking from your own personal experience, Nina. It must have hurt a lot when your parents divorced...'

No, it didn't. The hurt came long before the divorce.

'But that's no reason not to give us a chance,' he went on. 'We're different people.'

'I wouldn't be with you now if I wasn't prepared to give it a chance, Jack,' she said tightly. 'But will you please stop assuming I'm ready to commit myself and Charlotte to you? I'm not.'

Silence.

Nina could feel Jack brooding, searching for ways and means around her doubts and fears. It set her nerves on edge. She didn't want pressure. She couldn't cope with it right now. While life didn't hang out guarantees for anything, trust did require time to build.

It came as a shock when Jack pulled the Range Rover over to the kerb outside Sally's house and cut the engine. Nina had lost track of where they were. Home! Her heart fluttered in agitation. She hoped Jack wasn't going to be difficult, wanting more than she could give.

He released his seat belt and turned to her, reaching out to gently cup her cheek and capture her attention. 'Nina...' His eyes glowed with commanding intensity, and his voice was furred with deep emotion. 'I love you. I don't say that lightly. Let me show you....'

He leaned over. Before she could even think of stopping him, his mouth claimed hers with a seductive, tender yearning that melted any resistance she might have mustered if it had been a storming kiss. It was so gentle, so sweet, a sensitive tasting, begging a response, not trying to force one.

She ached for more, the emptiness of all the lonely months without him surging into a desperate need to be filled, to have doubts and fears obliterated by a flood of love so overwhelming it could carry everything in its stride. Her lips moved instinctively, encouraging, inviting, hungry for what he was offering, blindly seeking the reassurance of the passion she had known with him.

She lifted her hand to his chest, loving the warmth and strength she could feel through the light fabric of his shirt, the exciting thud of his heart, beating hard and fast with his need for her. It *was* the same as before.

Intoxicated by the wonderful familiarity of touching him again, Nina slid her hand over the smooth roundness of his shoulder, up the strong column of his neck and tunnelled her fingers through the thick springiness of his hair, exulting in the tactile reality of what had become only a haunting dream.

Jack...his mouth filling hers with enthralling sensation, feasting on her eager response, drawing on the desire that had always exploded between them. It flowed now, a torrent of wanting that craved fulfilment. Her body trembled with the force of it, weakness draining through her legs, ripples of arousal spreading to her stomach, her breasts straining to be caressed and held.

Slowly, reluctantly, Jack leashed the power of the passion they shared, leaving her still pulsing with sensation as he drew back, breathing roughly yet stroking her cheek and lips with feather-light fingertips. She dizzily opened her eyes, breathless, wavering between a protest at his parting from her and a plea for what had started to be finished.

He looked anguished. 'I could have been with you all this time....'

She didn't want to look back. She wanted...

'I would have been, Nina, if only you'd told me.'

Was that true? Had she robbed them of what should have been? This magic that was theirs?

His eyes swore it was so. 'I wouldn't have let anything get in the way of what we have together.'

Her desire-drenched mind thrilled to the constancy he avowed...until slowly, inexorably, it grasped the logic of what he was saying.

He wouldn't let Charlotte get in the way.

Which surely meant he would resent their child if she did. It was all too easy to forget her, not take her into account at all while she slept, a silent, non-interfering presence. But it wouldn't stay like that.

'Charlotte.' It was a husky croak, loaded with the guilt of her own forgetfulness.

'She's okay for a minute or two.'

'No.' Nina scrabbled for the release mechanism

on her seat belt, jerking her head away from Jack's tempting touch and dropping her gaze from the heart-searing heat of his. 'I don't want to talk about this now, Jack. I want to get unpacked and settled into my flat again.'

'I wasn't blaming you for the decision you made, Nina, just regretting the waste of time,' he said softly. 'It's made me very conscious of not wasting any more of it.'

'Fine! Let's get moving.'

The seat belt zipped away. She opened the passenger door and leapt out of the cabin before Jack could detain her further. Her legs almost crumpled under her. She had to hang onto the door to steady herself. The physical upheaval of giving birth to a baby was debilitating enough without adding sexual and emotional upheavals.

Nina instantly vowed to keep Jack at a firm distance until she could gauge his real reactions to having a baby in their lives. She didn't want to be torn in two by conflicting loves. If she gave in to what she felt for Jack now, it would only make everything ten times worse if she had to part from him for Charlotte's sake.

'Are you all right?' he asked in concern.

'Yes.' *Apart from being hopelessly vulnerable to you,* she added, silently railing at her weakness. She scooped her handbag from the floor in front of the passenger seat, shut the door and leaned against it, willing herself to be strong as Jack alighted from the driver's side.

He didn't press her. Much to Nina's relief, he set about the business of releasing Charlotte's capsule and collecting her suitcase from the back of the Rover. He carried both, leaving Nina to lead the way down the side path to her flat at the back of Sally's house. Her legs were still shaky, but she managed the walk with some dignity, grateful that Jack had assumed the role of porter.

All the lights were on, a welcoming gesture from Sally, no doubt. Nina unlocked the door and waved him inside, acutely conscious of the danger inherent in letting Jack invade her home, yet aware of how unfair and ungracious it would be to deny him entry. He would respect her wishes, she assured herself. All she had to do was take control of the situation and remain firm, no matter how persuasive Jack set out to be.

'Straight into the bedroom?' he asked quietly, nodding at Charlotte.

'Yes, please,' she whispered, flushing at the reminder of having shared a bedroom with him many times in the past.

Having been let in by Sally to provision the refrigerator earlier today, Jack was clearly familiar with the layout of the flat. Nina watched him manoeuvre the capsule and suitcase down the narrow hall, past the bathroom and laundry. The bedroom door was open. There was no need for Nina to accompany him or follow him. Better to keep her distance.

She stepped into the kitchenette, feeling more protected by the cupboards and countertops that hemmed the limited moving space. Having checked the electric kettle and found it full of water, she switched it on. After all the trouble Jack had gone to for her today, it was impossible to send him away without offering him at least a cup of tea.

As she waited for the water to boil, Nina took a deep breath in an attempt to calm her skittering nerves and flicked her gaze around the living area she had made her own, needing to regain the sense of independence it had given her. Jack probably thought it was small and cramped, but she had it arranged to suit her convenience.

The two-seater cane lounge and matching arm-chairs were grouped on the window side of the living room, a coffee table handily placed. On the other side was her sewing machine. Behind it on the wall was a huge corkboard, organised to hold all her reels of cotton, scissors, measuring sticks and other tools of her trade. At the end of the room was the television set and her sound system, so she could watch a program or listen to music as she worked or re-laxed.

The mottled beige tiles on the floor were easy to keep clean. She had made the cushion covers and curtains herself in a bright, fresh fabric patterned in lemon and white and lime green. A bowl of brilliant lemon chrysanthemums sat on the coffee table, a welcome home gift from Sally, Nina figured. She'd left Jack's roses at the hospital for Rhonda and Kim

to enjoy. An arrangement of three dozen was difficult to transport.

Jack had probably frowned over the wooden
planks under the legs of the dining table. They effectively raised it to a convenient height for measuring and cutting fabric. She didn't use the table for
meals, preferring to keep it for work. Normally she
perched on a stool at the kitchen counter to eat or
drink. But that didn't mean she wasn't looking after
herself properly.

She heard Jack coming from the bedroom and
hastily set out cups and saucers. By opening the refrigerator door, she effectively blocked the path into
the kitchenette. Nina only meant to get out milk and
direct Jack to the other side of the kitchen counter.
However, the stacked contents of the refrigerator
completely distracted her.

'All quiet on the Western Front,' Jack declared
cheerfully.

Nina barely heard him. Apart from an incredible
array of delicatessen goods loading up the shelves,
the meat tray contained great slabs of steak, at least
a dozen rashers of bacon, piles of chops and sau-
sages, and the vegetable containers were chock-a-
block with items from the greengrocers.

'I'll never eat all this,' she said dazedly.

'I'll help you,' came the confident reply.

Warning tingles ran down her spine. Nina forgot
about the milk. She shut the refrigerator door and
swung around to face a more pressing problem. Jack
shot his most dazzling smile at her across the counter

that separated them, and Nina felt her resolution fraying at the edges. He was making it so hard for her to hang onto common sense. Desperation drove a steely tone into her voice.

'Are you planning on having meals with me, Jack?'

His eyebrows lifted in appeal. 'I thought I'd come over after work and cook dinner for us. It'll give you a rest in between the two evening feeds for the kid.'

'That's very considerate of you.' He was taking over. Just walking in and taking over as he pleased. Intent on claiming whatever time she had free from the baby. Nina gritted her teeth in determined resistance to his infiltration tactics. 'Are you thinking of cooking breakfast for me, too?'

'Well, uh…' He hesitated, taking in the dangerous glitter in her eyes. 'It's not a good idea?' he asked cautiously.

'Not if you're assuming you can stay overnight with me any time you like,' she answered angrily.

'Not any time, Nina. Naturally I'll do whatever's best for you,' he hastily assured her, then changed his expression to anxious concern. 'But I am worried about tonight. Everyone says the first night home with a new baby is scary. No expert to call on…'

'And you consider yourself an expert?' Nina heard her voice rise to a shrill note.

'I meant it's lonely,' he swiftly amended. 'I don't like to think of you being by yourself, Nina. What if you have a bad night with the kid? No one to talk to…'

'No one to hold me and comfort me and kiss everything better. Is that the idea, Jack?' Wanting to satisfy his hunger for her, never mind what had to be done for the baby.

He frowned at her brittle manner. 'I just want to be here for you, Nina.'

He sounded so genuine. The look of caring in his eyes was almost her undoing. Her heart seemed to be pounding in her ears. She wanted his love, wanted to feel it surround her, seep into her, possess her to the point of losing herself entirely in him. But he only wanted to be here for her, and that wasn't enough. It simply wasn't enough.

If only he cared as much about Charlotte.

She closed her eyes, gathered the will to sort through her priorities again, knew she couldn't battle with her dilemma any more tonight and took the only escape route open to her.

'I want you to go now, Jack.'

'But, Nina…'

She opened her eyes, anguished by his persistence. 'Please.'

He looked hurt and bewildered. 'Why? What have I done wrong?'

'Don't argue with me,' she cried in desperation. Frantic to end the torment he stirred, she rushed to the door and opened it for him to leave. 'Please. It's been a long day for me. I need time and space for myself, Jack.'

He moved reluctantly, his eyes urgently scanning hers, wanting a reason for what he saw as incomprehensible behaviour. He lifted his hands, gesturing his willingness to appease whatever was troubling her. 'What if—?'

'No!' She shook her head vehemently. 'It's too much, too soon. Good night, Jack. Thank you for bringing us home, but I really do need you to go now.'

'All right,' he said gently, seeing she was too stressed to discuss the matter further. 'Good night, Nina. Say good night to the kid for me.'

The kid.

He left.

Nina closed the door after him and promptly burst into tears.

CHAPTER SEVEN

WHAT had he done wrong?

The question plagued Jack as he roamed disconsolately around the collection of antiques that had been delivered this afternoon. Normally he would be excited by the challenge of restoring the damaged pieces, keenly studying how it could best be done. He couldn't find any enthusiasm for it tonight. Nothing was working for him. Except for his dog, who was trailing him around, offering his loyal companionship.

'She shut me out again, Spike,' he said, heaving a woebegone sigh.

Man's best friend cocked his head, giving him a doleful look of sympathy, then sprang up to rest his front paws on Jack's chest, his tongue out, ready to lick everything better if Jack obliged by bending his head close enough. The weight of the huge, black and white shaggy beast would have knocked most people down, but Spike knew how to balance nicely when it was a matter of love and respect.

Jack looked fondly on him. 'You're a great dog, Spike, but I've got to tell you, your breath isn't as sweet as Nina's.'

A whistling whine, begging favour.

Jack gave him a rueful smile and ruffled the fur

behind his ears, earning a look of adoration that let Jack know Spike was absolutely steadfast in his love and devotion, no confusing or obscure responses and reactions coming from him. Jack was the central focus of his world, and there was no shifting him from that outlook. Spike knew what was good for him.

It was a pity people weren't more like dogs, Jack thought, brooding over all he'd done today to get things right between him and Nina. He was good for her. He knew he was. Why didn't she recognise it? Why wasn't she welcoming it? What more could he have done to show her he meant what he said?

'Maybe dogs are smarter than people,' he confided to Spike. 'People should think less and trust their instincts more.'

Spike panted agreement.

Jack reflected, with perfect justification, that there had been no confusion at all in Nina's response when he'd kissed her. He'd felt the electric current of desire charging through both of them, highly mutual, fantastically mutual. No possible mistake about it. Nina still wanted him. Whatever was muddling her mind was a frustrating mystery, but her body was definitely in harmony with his.

Jack felt himself stir just thinking about it. He'd been celibate for so long, all his hormones were zinging with excitement at the promise of knowing satisfaction again. Real satisfaction. Special satisfaction. It had always been special with Nina. She was his woman, pure and simple. Somehow he had to work out how to convince her he was her man. There was no point in even looking at any of this furniture until he'd figured out what to do about his problem with Nina.

With more than one appetite reawakened, Jack realised the empty feeling inside him could be attributed to a more pedantic hunger. 'Let's go and find something to eat, Spike.'

With a bright yelp of encouragement, the part kelpie, part collie, part Doberman, part several other breeds including, Jack suspected, great Dane, leapt down and bounded over to the door that led into the house. Why couldn't people be as simple and direct? Jack wondered with another niggle of frustration. He and Spike had no problem understanding each other.

They headed for the kitchen together. It was handily situated to what had once been the triple garage. Jack didn't mind his two apprentices ducking in to make coffee or get a snack. He'd always figured work flowed more easily if people felt at home. Sharing meals had seemed a good way of getting Nina to feel at home with him.

Too much, too soon, she had said, but he couldn't see why. The path to getting back together again was going to be very difficult if she kept shutting him out.

Jack opened the refrigerator and took out one of the meaty bones he'd got from the butcher that morning. 'Here you are, Spike. It's your favourite. Ham.'

Spike clutched it eagerly in his jaws, growling approval and appreciation, wagging his bushy tail in delight as he retired to his corner of the kitchen. He settled down, his position protected from attack from behind and on the flank by the two walls, his fiercely watchful eyes defying any approach from the front. Spike jealously guarded his bones, instinctively suspicious of any movement towards him. Protection was top priority. Even Jack was persona non grata if he moved too close.

Too close. The thought caught and held. Was that what Nina was guarding against, letting him get too close? Protecting herself and the baby in case he hadn't really changed his attitude about children? She kept harping back to that argument. Understandable enough, since she'd been feeding it through her brain for the past eight months.

Jack pondered this possibility as he collected some cheese and pickles, took some crackers from the pantry and settled down at the bar counter to chew over the situation. It could be the kid confusing Nina, distorting what was perfectly plain and straightforward to him.

Basically the kid was a side product of what they felt for each other. Naturally he accepted it, now that he knew about it. What kind of man would he be if he didn't? He would have accepted it eight months ago, too. Nina had got herself all cock-eyed about that.

Maybe she didn't want to share it with him. Like Spike with his bone. He reconsidered Nina's behaviour in the same light as his dog's current attitude— wary and watchful and ready to pounce on anything questionable and fight like the devil. Possessive and protective. It could explain a lot.

Though there was one difference. Jack knew he could still get to Nina on a one-to-one level. Maybe that was what she was afraid of, knowing he could slip past her defences despite being hell-bent on protecting the kid. Yet what was she expecting him to do? Take the kid away from her? Be jealous of her natural mother love? It was ridiculous.

'You can vouch for my character, can't you, Spike?'

The dog looked up, alert and attentive.

'Have I ever done you wrong?'

Spike growled at the idea.

'Of course not. You'd defend me to the death, wouldn't you?'

A bark of assent.

'We know I'm the salt of the earth. And Nina should know, too. But if she's gnawing at that old bone of contention all the time... It could be the answer, Spike.'

A darker growl.

'You're right. She should know better. Thanks for helping me out, Spike. You're a great source of inspiration.'

Understanding that the conversation was over and having given satisfaction, man's best friend returned to feeding his own satisfaction. He knew there was more in a bone than there was on the surface.

The idea of Nina shutting him out because she didn't trust him to behave as a father should did not sit well with Jack. It was extremely offensive to him. If that was Nina's belief, he had to set her straight. He could be as good a father as anyone else. Better. After all, he'd heard most of the complaints new parents made about each other, so he could work out how to circumvent them.

First thing tomorrow he'd call Maurice and arrange to have nappy-changing lessons from Ingrid. The criticism that fathers were inept or useless at such a task was not going to apply to him. As for Nina scoffing about him being an expert on babies, well, why couldn't he become one? There had to be plenty of books on baby problems.

He'd much prefer Nina to be leaning on him for advice and support than shutting him out. In fact, the more she leaned on him, the more likely she was to want what he wanted. Once they could make love again, Jack was sure everything would be fine between them. The fabulous fusion of their bodies into one, the glorious sense of ecstatic fulfilment, the deep intimacy of sharing the excitement and the aftermath…Jack wanted all that very badly.

This kid thing was not going to beat him.

Or break them up.

Feeling much more cheerful about the situation, Jack cut off a big chunk of cheese, spread it with pickles and bit into it with relish. Tomorrow was another day. Tomorrow he would knock Nina's worries about his fatherly fitness right on the head. She wouldn't shut him out again. No, sir.

'Here comes your dad, kid,' he said out loud, enjoying the ring of it. 'Here comes your dad.'

CHAPTER EIGHT

THE knock on the connecting door from the flat to the house had to be Sally's. Nina smiled as she called, 'Come in!' It was eight-thirty, the time Sally usually checked in with her each morning to discuss the business of the day. The return to routine gave Nina a comforting sense of normality and security. She needed it after the tumult of uncertainty Jack had stirred last night.

The door near the far corner of the living room opened, and Sally popped her head around, waggling her highly mobile eyebrows. 'I'm not disturbing anything?'

Nina shook her head. 'I'm all organised. Just washing up breakfast things. Have you got time for a cup of coffee?'

'If it's no trouble.' Having been welcomed, Sally sailed in, looking sunnily superb in a wheat-gold suit. She perched on the stool by the kitchen counter, her bright hazel eyes alight with curiosity and interest. 'How's the babe this morning?'

'No problems so far. She only woke to be fed once during the night. I couldn't ask for a more contented baby.'

'Let's hope it lasts.'

For more reasons than one, Nina thought as she

271

put the kettle on and spooned instant coffee into a mug for Sally. Jack might come to love a good baby, though babyhood was only the start of a long, trying journey with children. Would Jack last the distance?

She pushed the worry aside and gave Sally a warm smile. 'Thanks for organising the nappy service for me.'

'Piece of cake.'

Nina waved at the coffee table. 'And the lovely flowers. They're perfect.'

'Oh, Jack bought those. I only put them in the bowl.' She gave Nina an arch look. 'That guy is worth marrying, Nina. He cares a lot about you.'

'Mmm, we'll see,' Nina answered offhandedly. The kettle whistled. Glad of the distraction, Nina turned away to make the coffee to Sally's taste. 'Any bookings for me?' she asked, turning the conversation to business. She didn't want to discuss Jack. Her feelings about him swung from wild longing to helpless despair.

Sally was not slow on reading signals. She obligingly picked up the cue. 'I've tried to keep this week clear for you, but weddings always throw up last-minute little traumas. Juliette Hardwick has lost weight and wants her dress taken in. I've scheduled a fitting for seven o'clock tonight. Can do?'

'Of course.'

If Jack came for dinner, as he planned, he'd have to understand she wasn't always available when he wanted her to be. Most clients came after normal working hours. It was the only time they were free, and Nina had to accommodate them. Running one's own business was a lot different from working for someone else. Customers came first. The baby's needs came ahead of Jack's, too. Nina could see his patience running out very quickly.

'Tomorrow's free,' Sally continued, 'but Friday night Belinda Pinkerton and her mother and her three bridesmaids are coming for a consultation. Seven-thirty. They want your advice on what would best suit them.' Sally rolled her eyes expressively. 'Could be a big job in it for you, Nina.'

It was a thrilling thought. Nina grinned, her eyes dancing with excitement. 'I'll sharpen up my sales pitch.'

'Nothing like a complete showcase to advertise your talent,' Sally encouraged. 'Belinda likes dramatic. Think about it. And the Pinkertons have serious money to spend, so think big.'

'Great!'

Sally drank some of her coffee then casually remarked, 'I would have dropped in last night but I didn't want to intrude on anything private.'

Nina's burst of pleasure dimmed. She just didn't know where she was going with Jack.

Sally noted the change and grimaced. 'I hope I didn't do the wrong thing in letting Jack bring you home.'

'No.'

'He was very eager.'

'Yes.'

The monosyllabic replies drew a deep sigh from

Sally. 'I know it's none of my business, Nina, but the guy seemed very sincere. I had a long talk with him after we left the hospital the other night. He's dead-set on marrying you.'

'Maybe.'

Sally gave her a sharp, penetrating look. 'You don't want him?'

Nina winced. 'It's not that.'

'Well, if you're worried about the business, Jack assured me he'd respect and support any outlet you wanted for your creativity. He said he understood how you felt about it and knew how important it was for your own sense of achievement and fulfilment. The guy really impressed me, Nina. I don't think you'd have any trouble with him on that score.'

Sally was right. Jack wouldn't interfere with any opportunities that came her way. He valued his own work and would apply the same value to hers. It was only the time spent on the baby he'd resent.

'When he was here yesterday, he noted how you'd raised the table and said he'd make you one that fitted all your work requirements,' Sally went on. 'Save you from getting back problems.'

Nina couldn't help smiling. Jack would enjoy getting it right for her. He was quite obsessive about getting things right. Unfortunately, babies and children threw unpredictable spanners into perfect plans. Could Jack learn to live with that? Her smile drooped into a grimace. He'd been totally fed up

with the way his friends' baby had disrupted the in-
famous dinner party.

'I'd snaffle him if I were you,' Sally said confi-
dentially. 'The guy is pure gold. He's got money.
He's got brains. He's got great muscles. And he's
not going to mess with our partnership.'

Nina sighed and confessed the wretched truth. 'He
doesn't want children, Sally. That's why I broke up
with him in the first place.'

Sally's eyebrows disappeared into her flyaway
fringe. 'He turned his back on you when you got
pregnant?' she squawked in outrage.

'No. I didn't tell him I was pregnant. I knew he
didn't want children. He'd told me so in no uncertain
terms.'

Sally ruminated over these facts as she finished
her coffee. She set her mug down and gave Nina the
benefit of her wisdom. 'Well, he hasn't exactly been
put off by Charlotte, has he? Why didn't he run the
other way once he found out you'd had his baby?'

Nina shrugged helplessly. 'He still wants me. I
don't think Charlotte is real to him yet. He remem-
bers how it was between us and he wants that back.'

'Hmm.' Sally clacked her perfectly manicured fingernails on the counter. 'Is he coming to visit this
evening?'

'That was the plan. If he hasn't had second
thoughts.'

'Right!' Sally's authority finger shot out to em-
phasise points. 'Leave Charlotte with him while you
deal with Juliette Hardwick. If he wants to skip out

of minding the baby, he's history. If he takes it on, he'll start finding out Charlotte is real. Put him to the test, Nina.'

Having settled the matter to her satisfaction, Sally slid off the stool, supremely confident of pertinent results.

'But it mightn't prove anything,' Nina argued, not liking the idea of leaving Jack in charge of her baby. 'Charlotte sleeps most of the time.'

'It's a question of attitude,' Sally claimed, making a jaunty exit. She paused at the door for a curtain line. 'And don't forget to give him a reward if he does good. I'm a great believer in the reward system. It encourages performance.'

The door closed.

Right! Nina thought, mentally girding her loins. There was no good to be gained in mushing around with negative pessimism. If she wanted decisive answers, risks had to be taken. If Jack came tonight, she *would* leave Charlotte with him. After all, he was her father. His reaction to the idea of being left in sole charge of a baby should tell her something.

Attitude.

It should be a dead give-away.

CHAPTER NINE

A GLANCE at her watch warned Nina to stop dithering. It was almost five o'clock. Jack finished work at four. She wasn't quite sure what his plan was, but it didn't take long to get from Roseville Chase to Lane Cove. She wanted to be ready for him. For tonight's appointment with Juliette Hardwick, as well.

She always wore black for business. It was classy while also being unobtrusive. It was important for the women being dressed for a wedding to outshine everyone else. Since it was Nina's job to ensure they achieved that result, she didn't want her own appearance to be a distraction. Black was also the perfect foil to show up their dresses in the mirror as she moved around them, tucking and pinning.

With having to breastfeed Charlotte, it was far more practical for her to wear a button-through tunic, but vanity kept pulling her towards the silky two-piece, which featured a cowl neckline and a gold-link belt. It was definitely her sexiest outfit, soft and swishy, the fabric clinging to her curves, accentuating her femininity.

She had worn loose clothes through most of her pregnancy. Now that she had her figure back, more or less, the temptation to really feel like a woman

again argued against common sense. Besides, Jack
had seen her looking a frump in the hospital. It
wouldn't hurt to remind him of how she could
look—a sort of welcome, and a reward if he really
was as good as his word about being a dad for
Charlotte.

She wasn't sure how far a reward should go at
this stage. Sally did have a point. Some positive encouragement might help to establish a more positive
attitude. It was worth trying, anyway. If Jack saw
her making an effort for him, he might make more
of an effort with Charlotte.

Decision made, Nina whipped her favoured outfit
off its hanger and quickly pulled it on. Her waist
wasn't quite back to normal, but her breasts were
bigger, so her figure still balanced in a satisfactory
fashion. She slipped on a pair of soft gold slippers
and hunted through her earrings for the black and
gold dangly set that complemented her short hair-
style.

She'd washed and blow-dried her hair into perfect
shape earlier this afternoon. The longer sections on
either side of her face now curved smoothly along
her cheekline. It was a sophisticated style, cleverly
shaped to her head and cut higher at the back to
accentuate the curve of skull and neck. A gamine-
style fringe softened the overall sleek severity of the
cut and served to make more of a feature of her
large, dark eyes.

In keeping with Sally's policy of always looking
good, Nina had taken time with her make-up, using

both a light and dark grey shading to add emphasis to her eyes. Her thick black lashes looked even more lustrous with mascara. She'd balanced deep red lipstick with a subtle application of toning blusher, making her cheekbones slightly more dramatic. Sally insisted that hands were important, too, so a matching red varnish glossed her well-kept nails.

Now that her hair was short, Nina enjoyed wearing earrings. She had a long neck, and they really added style and made a statement with whatever she was wearing. Having found the pair she wanted and fastened them to her lobes, Nina felt a definite lift in spirits as she surveyed her reflection in the mirror. Not bad. Not bad at all. She grinned at herself. Jack would see a big difference between yesterday and today.

Not that she wanted to encourage him too much, more laying a promise on the line if he was prepared to toe it where Charlotte was concerned. No mother without daughter. A package deal. And Charlotte was not to be short-changed. Nina was determined on that.

She moved over to the double bed where the capsule occupied one side, propped around by pillows for extra safety. Leaning over the snugly sleeping baby, she inhaled the fresh, sweet scent of her. It had been a delight bathing Charlotte this afternoon, tiny arms splashing, legs kicking, her eyes wide open, staring up at Nina as though querying the experience while obviously enjoying it. The world was so new to her. Nina hoped nothing would spoil it for her daughter for a long, long time.

She moved quietly out of the bedroom and was passing the kitchenette when the knock on the door came, startling her into an abrupt halt. Her heartbeat accelerated with a hop, skip and jump. It had to be Jack. Fate had dictated that their paths cross again. She silently begged not to be disappointed as she composed herself as best she could and took the last few steps to admit the father of her child.

With a hopeful little smile appealing to all that was good in Jack, she opened the door. The same kind of smile was waiting for her, but she barely saw it. Her heart contracted at the sheer male vitality that hit her. Jack was dressed in jeans and a cream and navy body shirt, and his tall, muscular frame seemed to leap at her.

He'd had his hair trimmed, and his face looked so clean-cut and handsome, Nina couldn't help staring, drinking in all his attractive features, the high, wide forehead punctuated by strongly arched eyebrows, eyes of deep river green sweeping over her with drowning intensity, the striking sculpture of his nose and cheekbones and the teasing sensuality of his full-lipped mouth. She could smell the spicy after-shave lotion he had splashed on his shiny smooth jaw and had a mad urge to taste it, to run her tongue over the slight dimple just above the strong, straight line of his chin.

'Nina.' Intense relief and awed pleasure. His face broke into a dazzling grin. His hands came up, gesturing appreciation of the picture she made. 'You look fantastic.' He laughed. 'I feel like I've been run over by a truck, you're so stunningly beautiful.'

She laughed, too. He'd had the same impact on her.

'Even your hair…' He shook his head in wonderment.

'You preferred it long?'

'No…it's different, but it does suit you.' Emphatically positive.

'I know you liked it long, but it got in the way with bending down to get hems right on dresses.' She prattled, tingling with nervous excitement.

'Doesn't matter.' His eyes said he adored her any way at all.

Nina's stomach curled. 'You look great, too, Jack.'

He took a deep breath. 'May I come in, Nina?'

'Oh!' She expelled the breath she didn't know she'd been holding. She felt as skittish as a teenager on a first date, wanting everything to be perfect yet frightened of doing the wrong thing, going too far, not going far enough. It was silly. They'd had a baby, for heaven's sake, yet somehow the remembered intimacies made it worse. So much hung in the balance.

'I'm not going to jump you, Nina,' Jack said softly. 'I realise you need time.'

He understood. Relief and pleasure coursed through her, resulting in a brilliant smile. 'I'm glad you came, Jack.' The words bubbled from her as she stood back and waved him in. 'I'm sorry about last night, pushing you out so—so…'

'It's okay,' he assured her. 'It must have been a big strain, the baby, me, everything.'

'Yes, it was. I didn't know what to think,' she blurted.

'We'll work it out, Nina.' His eyes were serious, wanting her agreement.

Her heart swelled with hope, and the love they had once shared shimmered through it. She wanted to throw herself at him, hug, kiss, make love with wild abandonment, revel uninhibitedly in the joy of being together again, of touching, feeling, knowing he was her man and she was his woman. She shut the door and forced herself to be sensible.

'I'd like that, Jack,' she said with overwhelming sincerity.

The air between them was suddenly hyper-charged with hopes, dreams and desires. Jack seemed to teeter forward on his toes, then rocked firmly back on his heels. His hands lifted towards her. He clapped them and said heartily, 'Well, how's the kid been today?'

The kid.

It cleared Nina's mind of its heat haze, but she didn't take offence at the term this time. Jack meant well. He was trying. 'Fine!' She smiled. 'She loved her bath. You should have seen her, Jack. It was so…'

Her throat seized up as the realisation hit her she was blathering on like a besotted mother who had no conversation bar her baby's trivial activities. It was one of Jack's criticisms of the effect of having children.

'Go on,' he urged.

She swallowed. Her mind seized up. She couldn't think of anything bright to say. 'You'll think I'm a vegetable.' The words slipped out on a helpless sigh.

'Nina, I want to share everything with you. Don't shut me out.' The anguished plea in his voice, in his eyes, tore at her heart.

'But you said…'

'Forget it. It doesn't apply to us.'

She shook her head, unable to sweep the argument that had parted them under the carpet and pretend it never happened. 'I don't want to bore you, Jack.'

'You won't.' He stepped forward, his hands lifting instinctively to her upper arms to press persuasion. 'Seeing your face light up with joy, your eyes dance with delight—it could never bore me, Nina. I want to know what's behind the happy glow. I want it to spill over onto me. It's warm and wonderful and…' He expelled a long breath, and his thumbs fanned her flesh, wanting to draw her into him, enforced restraint allowing only a gentle caress. 'Please don't hold back from me.'

Her chest felt as tight as a drum, and her heart was playing percussion instruments on a wild scale. The desire in his eyes played havoc with any control she had, yet some thread of sanity wove through the swarm of feelings, reminding her what had triggered this passionate outpouring from Jack.

'You mean you want to hear about Charlotte's bath?'

'Yes. Anything. Everything,' he replied vehemently.

She gave a nervous little laugh, her lashes sweeping down as a wave of self-consciousness increased her inner turmoil. 'It's nothing, really,' she dismissed in an agony of doubt.

'Nina, don't throw it away.' A gentle finger tilted her chin, drawing her gaze to his. He smiled an appeal. 'You always made such fun out of telling me what you'd been doing. Let me enjoy listening to you again.'

She tried to relax, tried to respond, but it felt hopelessly flat now. It would sound forced and false. 'I'm sorry, Jack. I've gone cold on it.'

'Let me get you a drink.' He released her and strode into the kitchenette, talking brightly, trying to coax her into being her old, natural self with him. 'You used to keep sherry. Are you allowed a small tipple or do we stick to cups of tea? Tell me what you'd like.'

'A small sherry wouldn't do any harm,' she decided. 'There's a bottle in the cupboard next to the fridge. Just a splash over lots of ice.' She needed cooling down, too.

'Okay! Coming right up.'

She sank onto the stool on the other side of the kitchen counter, not offering to help, letting him find things himself, needing time to settle herself down and get a grip on what she should be doing. It was difficult not to simply feast her eyes on Jack, moving competently around, fixing them both drinks as though he was perfectly at home here. Except it might be different once she really introduced the baby into the equation, making it a test situation.

'How's that?' he asked, placing a glass full of crushed ice tinted with amber sherry in front of her.

'Great! Thank you.'

'My pleasure. Now tell me what you fancy for dinner. I'm cooking tonight.'

Nina took a sip of her drink as she tried to formulate the best way of telling him their time together was curtailed.

'You just sit there and relax and I'll prepare everything,' he went on, letting her know he was not going to crowd her.

'We're not going to have much time together, Jack. I have an appointment to fit a wedding dress in Sally's showroom at seven o'clock and I have to feed Charlotte before then. If you don't want to bother—'

'No, I'm not going to let you fall into bad eating habits.' He shook his head at her in frowning concern and checked his watch. 'Five forty-two. I can have a proper dinner cooked by six-thirty. What time do you usually feed the kid?'

'Six o'clock.'

'How long does it take?'

'About twenty minutes.'

'Then we should slot the meal in nicely before you have to go to work. I'll clean up afterwards.'

His face lit with inspiration. 'You can leave the kid with me. Save any distraction while you work.'

His off-the-cuff suggestion left Nina confounded. She had been winding herself up to test his attitude over minding the baby and he'd whipped the mat out from under her feet, so to speak. Her disbelief and confusion must have been written on her face. Assuming he was about to get a negative response, Jack instantly proceeded to argue his case.

'I am a responsible adult, Nina. You can safely leave the kid in my care. I promise if I'm worried about anything, I'll come to you. How does that sound?' he asked eagerly.

She was stunned. 'I...well, if you think—'

'Trust me,' he commanded, his green eyes boring directly into hers, unwavering in his sense of purpose, insistent that she accept his word.

Nina took a deep breath. Far be it from her to protest his offer or dampen his eagerness to please. The focus of his caring was still centred on her, but did that matter if it motivated him to spend time looking after Charlotte?

'All right,' she agreed. 'If you're sure you don't mind.'

He grinned as though he'd won a lottery. 'Glad to be of help.' Vitality bubbled from him as he danced to the refrigerator, swinging its door open wide to peruse the contents. 'How about a big, juicy steak?'

'A small one for me, please.' She wasn't sure she

could eat anything. Jack was not only taking over, he seemed to be turning everything around.

'Salad, jacket potatoes?'

'Yes,' she agreed dizzily.

It was a relief to hear Charlotte's first tentative cry—something normal, expected, and no problem knowing what to do about it. 'I'll have to leave you to it, Jack,' Nina said quickly, slipping off the stool.

A louder, 'Hey! Did you hear me?' cry told Jack where she was going. He swung around to catch her attention as she headed for the hall. 'Are you, um, self-conscious about breastfeeding, Nina?' he asked somewhat diffidently. 'I mean, would you mind bringing the kid out here so we can be together?'

Like a real family.

The thought zinged through Nina's mind, ballooning the hope, edging it with a silver lining. Her smile sparkled. 'I'll be back in a few minutes.'

His smile positively scintillated. 'Great!'

Nina didn't exactly dance down the hall, but her heart certainly jigged. Once in the bedroom she swooped on the capsule, picking Charlotte up in mid-wail and twirling around with her. 'Your daddy wants us with him,' she whispered gleefully.

Charlotte returned an arch look and spluttered.

Nina laughed and carried her over to the change table, performing a swift nappy change as she wondered what to do about her own clothes. Her top would have to come off. Then she remembered the lovely silk Christian Dior dressing gown Jack had given her for her birthday over a year ago. Its dramatic black and white print wouldn't clash with her make-up. Besides, Jack would recognise it and feel pleased she was wearing it.

Nina could hardly believe how well everything was going. The tension of testing Jack was completely wiped out. When she returned to the living room, he fussed around, making sure she and the baby were comfortable in one of the armchairs, offering to fetch anything they needed and emitting all the pleasure of a proud dad as he watched Charlotte in action.

'This kid sure knows what it wants,' he commented, a warm, appreciative gleam in his eyes.

Nina's stomach curled. Her breasts were highly sensitive at the moment. The tiny mouth sucking at her nipple sharply reminded her of many nights of love with Jack. Was he remembering, too?

The sense of intimacy being so strongly generated suddenly alerted Nina to the realisation it was still very early days in this new situation between them. 'Tell me what's been happening to you, Jack,' she invited quickly. 'Your work and everything.'

The conversation flowed smoothly enough, Jack very aware of keeping her at ease with him. The eight months of separation and the reason for it had to be laid to rest before they could really go forward. Nina couldn't be sure Jack's current attitude would last past the first flush of being together again. Charlotte would inevitably become more intrusive.

By the time Nina finished tending to Charlotte's needs and had changed back into her clothes, Jack had their meal ready. She carried the capsule out to the living room, setting it down near the cane lounge. Charlotte was still awake, happily crowing to herself, and Nina wanted to keep an eye on her, making sure it would be all right to leave her with Jack.

Surprisingly, Nina found she had a hearty appetite. She thoroughly enjoyed her dinner, relaxing in Jack's company while they ate. He even persuaded her into telling him about Charlotte's bath, chuckling at her description of the baby's initial stiffening at the touch of water and Nina's interpretations of the startled expressions on her face.

It was the kind of shared fun they used to have, and Nina was in buoyant spirits as she prepared to leave for her appointment. A last-minute check on Charlotte completely shattered her happy bubble of optimism. The tiny fists were clenched, and her face had the screwed-up air of concentration that Nina recognised only too well.

'Oh no! Not now,' she groaned.

'What's wrong?'

'Charlotte is working up to dirtying her nappy. What am I going to do?' she wailed, frantically checking the time. 'I can't be late. I'll have to come back and clean her up after I let Juliette in. If Charlotte starts crying—'

'Stop worrying.' Jack gripped her shoulders to calm her agitation, and his eyes beamed confident assurance at her. 'I'll take care of it. I trust I'll find everything I need in the bedroom? A clean nappy, baby oil, tissues, talcum powder?'

'Yes, but—'

'I can do it, Nina. Leave it to me. You go on and attend to business. Not a problem.'

'You've never done anything like this, Jack,' she cried, horrified at the idea of throwing him in at the deep end with a mess that would surely turn his stomach.

'Had a practice session this morning,' he asserted. 'I'm an expert.'

'What?' Incredulity blitzed the horror.

'Maurice Larosa has a new baby son. That's why I was visiting the hospital. I got his wife to give me nappy-changing lessons,' he said smugly. 'I bet I can do it as good as you.'

She shook her head dazedly. Jack taking nappy-changing lessons?

'Now, off you go.' He good-humouredly turned her towards the connecting door to Sally's house. 'I'll take charge here.'

She went.

She wondered if Maurice's son had dirtied his nappy or simply wet it. There was a huge difference. Huge! As a test for having the intestinal fortitude for hands-on fatherhood, Charlotte was certainly supplying a hardliner. Nina had to acknowledge there was a terrible fascination in finding out if Jack could really handle it and still come up smiling.

CHAPTER TEN

JACK was curious. And intrigued. How did Nina know the kid was doing heavy business? He couldn't see any telltale signs. The baby bomb was looking up at him as placid as you please, big eyes widely alert as though reviewing the conversation it had heard and checking Jack out before accepting him as substitute minder.

'I'm your dad, kid,' Jack advised. 'Better get used to me.'

The little face suddenly assumed a belligerent expression. The tiny arms stopped waving and straightened out, hands clenching.

'Want to fight, huh?'

No reply. A gathering of concentration on internal matters, eyes narrowing, face going red. Several seconds passed. It dawned on Jack that the kid was pushing. Then the job was done. Relief came. Relaxation. A look of blissful peace. Jack chuckled. It was so obvious.

'Good to get rid of that lot, eh?'

He recalled Nina's description of the range of expressions reflecting the kid's reaction to a bath and shook his head in amusement. Who would have thought personality was developed so young? He could see there might very well be a fascination in watching it grow. Maybe besotted parents weren't as foolish as he'd thought. On the other hand, it was patently ridiculous to let a pint-sized infant rule the roost.

He picked up the capsule and carried it into the bedroom. No point in lifting the kid out until he had to. Stuff might run down its legs. He put the capsule on the bed and examined what Nina had laid out on the change table. He figured a towel and a wet washer might be useful and fetched them from the bathroom. Nappy-changing carried unsuspected dangers. Maurice's kid had gone off like a fountain this morning, hitting him in the face before he could block the spray off with the absorbent pad.

Having assembled everything within easy reach, Jack felt supremely competent and confident as he gathered up the danger zone and moved it to the change table, holding the little body horizontally to prevent possible leakage. Mission successful. Jack grinned triumphantly as he unsnapped the fasteners on the terry-towelling body suit, freed the tiny feet from it, and pushed the garment up out of the operation area.

'Got to hand it to your old dad, kid. Think ahead. That's what you have to do in this life to avoid mishaps.'

The response from her pursed lips was a spit-and-splutter raspberry.

'No respect,' Jack chided. 'You'll have to watch that, kid. I'm supposed to be the authority in your life. You don't want to start off on the wrong foot.'

The odour started rising as Jack unfastened the plastic tabs on the nappy. It was incredibly foul. Worse than rotten egg gas. Jack's throat convulsed as he fought against gagging. Manfully he peeled down the front section of the nappy. The source of the smell revealed itself in all its slushy, yellow-green horror.

'Yuk! No wonder you wanted to get rid of that!'

A gurgle denoted agreement.

Jack hastily but carefully removed the liner that contained most of the mess, burying it in a heap of tissues. He set to work cleaning up the kid's bottom. The stuff had oozed everywhere. Tissues, he decided, were a great invention, but he was glad he'd had the foresight to have a washer and towel on hand to do a proper job of removing every putrid smear.

The assault on his olfactory nerves lessened as they got used to the stench. Or he got rid of it. One way or another, it wasn't too revolting after a while. Not the most pleasant of jobs, Jack reflected, but paint stripper wasn't pleasant, either, and it was an unavoidable adjunct to his work with furniture. Some things just had to be done.

He did, however, gain an insight into the fixation parents had about potty-training. There was definitely reason behind their madness. Cause and effect. He appreciated how important—indeed, obsessive— the issue could become when a person was faced with this every day. Jack resolved to be more sympathetic to potty-training discussions in future.

'That does it,' Jack informed the kid, having achieved absolute cleanliness.

He slid a fresh nappy under the pearly white bottom, positioning it with well-trained precision. A bit of baby oil, a shake of talcum powder, and all was sweetness and light. Gently moving the tiny legs apart in order to bring up the front piece of the pad, Jack was suddenly struck by the irrefutable fact he was looking straight at unfamiliar territory.

Maurice's kid had recognisable equipment. A boy was a boy. This was…a girl.

Jack blinked. Somehow she didn't look right. It took him a second or two to realise he'd never seen what a girl looked like before the age of puberty. No sisters. No girl cousins, either. Having been in a boys' boarding school from age seven, he simply hadn't been exposed to a young girl's anatomy.

Not that it changed, he reminded himself, but it obviously got more disguised. This was…so bare. It gave him a funny feeling—a strong rush of tenderness mixed with a fierce urge to protect.

A girl. A daughter…

Jack shook his head in bemusement. Was this what the father-daughter thing was about? A girl looked so vulnerable. She needed a dad to keep her safe from the bad guys. Mothers were fine. Mothers were irreplaceable, he amended, the memory of Nina breastfeeding still highly vivid and captivating. But fathers definitely had their role to play in looking after little kids.

'Don't you worry, Charlie girl,' he told his daughter as he covered her up and fitted the nappy firmly with the tabs. 'Any bad guy is going to have to get past me, and I'm no pushover.'

She made a popping sound with her mouth.

'Blowing me a kiss, huh?' He grinned as he put her feet in the body suit and did up the press studs. 'There you are. All snug. How about another kiss?' He gave her tummy a little tickle as he leaned over and made a popping sound with his lips.

She gazed at in him in wide-eyed fascination. Jack prompted her with a repeat demonstration. She caught on and gave it right back to him.

'That's Daddy's girl!'

He suddenly heard the drooling indulgence in his voice and jolted upright, appalled at how quickly, how insidiously he had been drawn into baby drivel. It was a highly sobering experience. Never in his worst nightmares had he imagined himself succumbing to such soppy nonsense.

He eyed the kid with glowering suspicion. There was a power here that had to be resisted. No kid was going to turn him into a blathering idiot. No, sir! He was master of his own behaviour.

'Back to your capsule, kid,' he commanded, picking up the thimble-sized piece of dynamite and transporting it to the restricted area where it belonged, doing no harm and coming to no harm.

'A place for everything and everything in its place,' Jack recited sternly, ignoring the wail of protest as he dealt with the mess on the change table.

The wailing continued. Jack set everything to

rights in the bedroom, then carried the capsule out to the living room. There was still the cleaning up to do in the kitchen. The kid was demanding more attention. Jack recognised the conflict of interests and decided it had to be nipped in the bud.

'Listen up, kid,' he addressed his demanding daughter in the voice of paternal authority. 'You and I need to come to an accommodation.'

It got through to her. She stopped wailing and gave him her attention.

'The human race rubs along best if people consider each other,' Jack explained. 'I'm not going to have your mother come back to dirty dishes in the sink. You've had your time quota from me. It's your mum's turn now. So quit being selfish.'

A spit-and-splutter raspberry.

Jack wagged his finger at her. 'No more lip from you, young lady. I'll put on some music. We can both listen to it while I do the work. That's it. Your dad has spoken.'

A satisfactory silence followed this little homily. Jack hummed happily to himself as he selected the Beatles anthology album from Nina's collection and slid it into her disk player. Proper instruction and education. That was the trick, he decided. He turned the volume down low on the sound system, considering delicate eardrums, and started off Charlie girl's musical education with a gentle blast from the past.

'How's that, kid?' he asked on his way to the kitchenette.

No reply. Totally enthralled with the new experience.

Jack congratulated himself. He was wise to the baby game. Kids could dominate a relationship in no time flat. They looked helpless and cute, but they were really dyed-in-the-wool tyrants, given free rein. Things had to be kept in proportion. There had to be respect, discipline, an understanding of limits.

It was really quite simple to handle, once one appreciated the power game being played. As the old saying went, it was the hand that rocked the cradle that ruled the world. Anyone who let the kid in the cradle do the ruling was asking for trouble.

CHAPTER ELEVEN

'It will be done first thing in the morning,' Nina assured Juliette Hardwick for the umpteenth time, barely restraining herself from pushing the bride-to-be out the door.

'Don't worry, Juliette,' Sally chimed in, having joined them to do her public relations priming of the client. Sally never missed a trick in delivering the dream. 'I'll bring you the dress myself tomorrow evening. You'll look absolutely perfect on your wedding day.'

'You don't think I've got too thin, do you?' came the anxious question.

More lingering, Nina thought in exasperation, desperately eager to get back to Jack and Charlotte. Jack must have coped somehow, since he hadn't come looking for assistance, but it could be pride holding him back. Nina was full of trepidation at what she would find when she returned to her flat.

Sally soothed and flattered, and finally Juliette bid them good night and left. The door had barely closed behind her when Sally grabbed Nina's arm, detaining her from dashing away on the instant. Her bright hazel eyes gleamed with the need to know.

'Obliging attitude?' she queried, her eyebrows waggling madly in the direction of the granny flat.

'He offered to mind Charlotte. I didn't have to ask.' Nina rushed the words out.

'*Great* attitude!'

'He said he'd had nappy-changing practice.' Incredulity was still bombarding her mind.

'*Fantastic* attitude!'

'And Charlotte was working up to dirtying her nappy when I left.'

Sally laughed in delight. 'That'll test him.'

Nina was too concerned about the outcome to laugh. She pulled out of Sally's hold. 'I've got to go. I'll collect the wedding dress in the morning.'

'Don't forget the reward,' Sally called after her and merrily started trilling her favourite song, Mendelssohn's 'Wedding March'.

Which was certainly jumping the gun, in Nina's opinion. Even if Jack had managed to get through tonight's testing ground without major damage to the attitude he'd adopted, it was only a start in the right direction. Nina couldn't blind herself to the consequences of making a wrong decision with him, no matter how much she wanted everything to turn out well.

Hope and desire were traps. When Jack was with her, Nina found it impossible not to respond to him. He tapped so many feelings in her it was all too easy to fall into those traps. If she wasn't careful, she'd find herself making excuses and compromises instead of facing up to realities.

A panicky tension gripped her as she reached the door to the flat. With her fingers grasping the handle, she paused and forced herself to take a long, deep breath. To appear in an emotional flap would give the wrong signals. Jack had asked her to trust him. She had to assume everything was fine.

She also had to watch out for signals herself, bring an objective view to the scene. Jack might try covering up his real thoughts and feelings about the baby for her sake, but they would come out in the end. No one could hide the truth forever, and once resentments could no longer be contained, they had the potential to explode with devastating effect.

Having cautioned and calmed herself as best she could, Nina turned the handle and started to open the door, keenly listening for the sound of trouble— a cry from Charlotte, a curse from Jack, a muttered imprecation against children in general and the twist of fate that had bedevilled his life plan.

Music. Nothing but music playing at a reasonable volume. Nina recognised one of the Beatles' songs. Not exactly a lullaby. Ringo's drumbeat was not in the somnolent category, more in the foot-tapping, hand-clapping class. Jack was very fond of the Beatles' music, but what of Charlotte?

Nina peered around the door, seeking some hint of what she was about to confront. Jack was sprawled in the cane armchair closest to the kitchenette and facing in her direction. He was half-hidden by the *Herald*, its large pages propped on his thighs and held up in front of him so Nina could only see his hair above them. Apparently he was engrossed in reading an article and hadn't heard the door open.

Charlotte's capsule lay on the floor between Jack's armchair and the lounge. Nina couldn't see over the raised end of it to check the baby, but concluded she must be asleep. There was not a peep out of her. A glance at the kitchen counter assured Nina Jack had cleaned up after their meal, as promised.

Relief washed through her. His relaxed air, Charlotte's silence, work all done, no evidence of any trauma—nothing for Nina to worry over. Relief was swiftly followed by pleasurable amazement. Jack's confidence in his competence was not misplaced. This was a better start than Nina could ever have credited, given the unpropitious circumstances.

Curious to see how well he had managed the nappy-change and reclothing Charlotte, Nina very quietly closed the door behind her and tiptoed forward. Her heart missed a beat when she saw that the capsule was empty.

'What have you done with Charlotte?' The question flew off her tongue, alarm rising rapidly and giving her voice a sharp edge.

The newspaper was instantly twitched down, Jack's face appearing above it, beaming surprised delight. 'You're finished already. Everything go well?'

'Jack, where is Charlotte?' She gritted the words out, holding herself back from flying at him tooth and claw.

'Right here,' he answered blithely, lowering the

newspaper to his knees so she could see. 'Just like a puppy,' he said, smiling at the baby clinging like a limpet to his chest. Without any support whatsoever!

'A puppy?' Nina repeated, dazed, alarm subsiding into shock.

'You know how puppies snuggle up to their mother, hanging all over her. Or if she's left them alone, they go into a huddle, clutching onto each other,' Jack expounded happily. 'Must be the warmth or the comfort of another heartbeat.'

'Right!' Nina agreed limply.

It was a strain, holding herself back from rushing forward and snatching Charlotte off his chest. She told herself Jack's arms were in a good position to halt Charlotte from rolling off him, and he was leaning back in the chair, so it wasn't likely she would flop backwards. Apart from which, Jack liked dogs. It was okay for him to compare Charlotte to a puppy. It was a good sign he was viewing her favourably. Fondly.

'Must be instinctive,' he concluded.

It could be called bonding, Nina thought, trying to look on the bright side as she cast an eagle eye over her baby. Charlotte wasn't moving. The nappy bulge looked right. The press studs on the body suit were all matched up, fastened properly. Nothing was askew.

'How come you picked her up?' Nina asked, curious to know more of how Jack thought about their child. She hadn't expected him to bother with her beyond the necessary.

He gave a funny grimace. 'She took a dislike to one of the songs and started yelling her disapproval. I tried telling her why she should appreciate it but she wouldn't listen until I got her up close to me.'

'And then she fell asleep on you?'

Jack heaved a rueful sigh. 'I think I must have bored her with musical technicalities. Or it was too much for her to take in. She *is* only little.'

Nina giggled. She couldn't help it. Jack didn't have a clue how to handle Charlotte. First he had referred to her as *the kid*, trying for an impersonal distance. Then he reasoned she was like a puppy, to account for her need to be comforted when she cried. Talking to her as though she were a fellow adult did, however, take the cake. No way was a week-old baby going to understand a word of what he said.

Jack looked at her quizzically. 'What's so funny?'

Nina quickly shook her head as she swallowed her laughter. 'Hysterical relief,' she explained, not wanting to put him off any effort to come to terms with the problem of having a child he didn't want. 'I was a bit wound up, having left you with one of the worst aspects of taking care of a baby.'

He shrugged. 'No worse than stripping paint.'

As he folded the newspaper to lay it aside, Nina bit her lips to stop the giggles erupting again. Jack's logic was certainly novel, but if it worked for him, she was not about to criticise or make fun of it. Any practical parallel he could find to keep his toleration level up was fine by her.

Having got rid of the newspaper, he placed a supporting hand around Charlotte's shoulders and head, his other hand cupping her bottom, and he leaned forward, plucking her from his chest. 'Down you go, Charlie girl,' he crooned, swooping her smoothly into the capsule. 'Mummy's turn now,' he added as he tucked the bunny rug around her.

'Turn?' Nina queried, bemused by Jack's indulgent manner with their daughter. He was even calling her by name now. At least, his version of her name.

He stood, grinning, a wicked gleam in his green eyes. 'For a cuddle,' he enlightened her, stepping forward purposefully.

Was he expecting, demanding a reward? Had he calculated what he had to do in order to get what he wanted? Turn and turnabout?

Tension zipped along Nina's nerves. *Control*, her mind screamed. She whipped up a hand to stop him. 'I'm not a baby, Jack. I'm a woman.'

'I know,' he said warmly, taking her hand and putting it on his shoulder as he slid an arm around her waist. 'I've got the music on. Let's dance.'

Her body hit his and didn't want to leave it. Besides, dancing was relatively harmless, she argued, nothing more than a social convention, done in public all the time. Except she knew perfectly well Jack was a great dancer, a sexy dancer, and she was playing with fire. Heat was racing through her veins even before he gathered her closer.

'I need to hold you,' he murmured, his mouth hovering near her ear, his breath tingling over her skin. The ache of yearning in his voice sent an echo reverberating through her body, stirring the need to be held, to feel his weight, his strength, his warmth, his sheer animal maleness.

'It's been so long,' he groaned, his hands sliding over her back, relearning its curve, revelling in the sensual rub of silk on flesh, his and hers.

Yes, so long. The words moaned through her mind, wanting freedom of expression. It would be treacherously easy to close her eyes to the future and seize the moment, taking what she could while she could. Would that be so wrong when it felt this right to be held by Jack? But if it was so right, it would still be right tomorrow, she cautioned herself. And all the tomorrows that made up the future.

They swayed to the music. Tempted beyond caution, Nina slid both arms around Jack's neck, pressing her breasts against the satisfying solidity of his chest, loving the firm delineation of his muscles as he sucked in a quick breath, then slowly released it.

It was dangerously wanton of her. She knew it but didn't care. She had been too long apart from him, too long feeling only half alive. Her body was singing at every brush with his, exulting in the moving pressure of his thighs, arching sensuously to the moulding of his hands. She felt the growing hardness of his arousal, and excitement speared through her, leaving a shivery weakness that forcefully reminded her she wasn't ready for this.

A paralysing thought crashed into her mind and stopped her feet dead. 'Jack...'

'Natural response,' he soothed.

'Jack, have you been with other women?'

He met her gaze with sizzling sincerity. 'Not since you, Nina. I don't want any other woman.'

'Oh!' She flushed at his directness, at the desire blazing from him, searing her conscience with doubts about her decision to go her own way and leave him to his.

'You're the only woman I've ever loved. The only person I've ever loved, Nina,' he said huskily.

Her heart turned over. Jack was like her, alone in the world, no family to speak of, and though friends were good, it wasn't the same as loving and knowing yourself loved. Without thought, without reason, Nina's whole being surged to meet him as he bent his head to kiss her.

Their mouths melded, emotional intensity swiftly moving to a passionate expression of their craving to be one again. It was only when Jack scooped her into a more intimate fit with his erection, wildly accelerating the need to merge together, that Nina's swimming senses whirled back to some common sense.

'Jack!' she gasped, tearing her mouth from his, her hands scrabbling to hold his head back. She choked out the words in incoherent little bursts. 'I can't. The birth. I'm sorry. I'm not—I didn't mean…'

'Not fit yet,' Jack interpreted, sighing raggedly as he eased away and met her frantic eyes with rueful understanding. He stroked her cheek, transmitting tender caring as he smiled, warm pleasure welling over desire. 'It's enough to know you feel the same, Nina.'

'I have an appointment for a medical check-up next week,' she babbled, not realising she was implying a promise, rushing to excuse the frustration of not following through on the promise she had recklessly implied in flying with her instincts here and now.

'It doesn't matter. I don't care how long we have to wait. What's another week or a month?' His smile spread into a happy grin. 'I'm already on top of the world knowing you want me as much as I want you.'

Her heart stopped its mad beating, hanging suspended for a mind-blowing second. She'd done it! Committed herself without thinking! Only to making love with him, she feverishly excused. Her pulse picked up again, drumming through her temples, definitely a rush of blood to the head. And other parts of her anatomy.

Jack planted a gentle kiss on her forehead. 'I promise I'll keep it cool until the doctor says it's okay. I wouldn't hurt you for anything, Nina.'

Cool, yes. Better to stay cool for as long as she could. Though it would be wrong to lead Jack on

and not deliver. If she just took one step at a time…
The big risk was in taking too much for granted.

Jack tilted her face up to his, his eyes probing hers
with compassionate concern. 'Was the birth very
rough on you, Nina?' he asked softly.

She grimaced. 'There was a clock on the wall. I
kept telling myself if I survived one more minute I
might make it through actually having the baby.'

'That bad,' he muttered, distressed by the description. 'I wish I'd been with you.'

'It's behind me, Jack. I've got Charlotte now, and
she's worth far more than one day's pain to me.'
Needing him to realise and appreciate the importance she placed on their daughter, she added, 'She
was going to be my world. She'll always be an essential part of it. If you hurt her, you hurt me.'

He looked taken aback. 'I'd never hurt a kid,
Nina. What on earth gave you that idea? I know I
said kids were…' He hesitated over what words to
choose.

'An abomination,' she finished dryly.

'Well, they can be,' Jack quickly qualified, 'but
the way I see it, that's more often the fault of the
parents. Kids need a bit of firm direction now and
then or they just run wild. Which isn't good for anybody.'

Nina couldn't argue with that reasoning. She
agreed with it. Though the word *firm* needed discussion.

'Anyway,' Jack went on, 'Charlie girl and I are

getting along fine. Don't be worrying about things I said, Nina. I'll be a better dad than most.'

He spoke so earnestly, Nina let the subject slide. Picking at old wounds didn't do any good. Besides, he'd certainly displayed a promising attitude. She smiled. 'Thank you for looking after her so well tonight, Jack.'

He grinned, relieved that she had accepted his efforts to deliver peace of mind on favourable paternal attributes. 'I've been more than rewarded,' he said magnanimously.

The idea of reward again. It struck a false note with Nina. She didn't like it. Not one bit. Sally might advocate a system of rewards as eminently workable, but Nina didn't want her relationship with Jack to work that way. She wanted him to care for Charlotte because she was a much-loved daughter, not because he might be rewarded with a session of lovemaking with the woman who happened to be Charlotte's mother.

It preyed on Nina's mind long after Jack left that night. Love wasn't based on manipulation. Love, to her mind, was a natural reaching out to each other, an open and honest expression of genuine feeling. To reduce it to a bargaining counter or a stick-and-carrot manoeuvre was anathema to her.

She did not doubt Jack loved her. Everything he did and said reflected it. But if he couldn't come to love Charlotte... A deep sadness dragged at her heart. Their baby, their child.

She had to tell him, lay it on the line what it meant

to her and why. If he understood where she was coming from, would it help? Would it make the difference?

A sense of futility washed through her. Impossible to force what wasn't felt. Not all the words in the world could achieve that. The only realistic course was to wait and see.

CHAPTER TWELVE

'TONIGHT is the night, Spike,' Jack informed his dog, who stood in the bathroom doorway, watching him shave.

Spike settled down on his haunches, rested his big shaggy head on his front paws and closed his eyes. He'd heard the same words all day. Clearly they excited his master, but since nothing new had happened, there seemed no point in responding until a change did occur. This shaving business every afternoon was no longer new.

'Sleep if you like, but I won't be sleeping. No, sir. Not if the doctor gives the okay. Good thing it's Friday. Maybe Nina will let me stay over the weekend.'

Spike opened an eye. The tone of voice was different.

'Don't worry. I'll come back and feed you. Bring Nina and the kid with me. She's not a bad little kid, Spike. Good as gold. You'll like her.'

A querying whine seemed appropriate.

Jack grinned at him. 'You can learn to play dad, too. Look after her as you would a puppy. Keep her in check, give her a lick, warn off the bad guys.'

The last words were growled, so Spike growled in agreement.

Jack laughed, unable to contain his high spirits. Cautioning himself with the possibility that Nina might need more recovery time made no difference to the tingle of anticipation. If that were the case, well, he'd take it on the chin and rise to the occasion. Or not rise, he corrected himself, instructing his anatomy to behave in an appropriate manner. Love came first, desire second.

But he sure hoped everything was fine. Celibacy did not suit him. His sex drive had been in overdrive ever since he had sighted Nina again. Being with her so much over the past couple of weeks had exercised his powers of restraint to the limit. Nevertheless, he'd hold off like a gentleman as long as he had to. Nina needed cossetting. She'd been through a bad time.

Jack put down the razor, splashed water over his face, towelled off, then closely examined the result of his shave in the bathroom mirror, running his hand over the shiny, smooth skin. Not a trace of stubble anywhere. Satisfied, he opened the new bottle of aftershave lotion and dabbed it on. Obsession by Calvin Klein. Cost him over seventy dollars.

Spike stirred, leaped to his feet. He sniffed the air and barked.

Jack grinned at him. 'You like it, Spike?'

A yelp of agreement.

'Appealing. That's what the salesgirl said. I wonder if appealing means sexy? What do you think, Spike? Does this smell sexy?'

Spike's howl sounded like a mating call.

It put Jack in a great mood for getting dressed and on his way. New clothes, too. Casual smart. The open-necked olive green shirt had a nice feel to it, soft and silky. The snugly fitting fawn trousers didn't need a belt. The less obstacles to undressing, the better, Jack figured. Fumbling did not feature in his plans for tonight.

It would also be good if Charlie girl cooperated by sleeping through as many hours as she could. Give Nina a real break so she could relax and not worry about interruptions and hurrying things. All going well on the medical side, he'd have to speak to Charlie girl about considering her mother's needs. Her father's needs, as well. He rehearsed a few lines as he slid on a pair of leather moccasins that didn't require socks.

'Listen up, kid. You and I need to come to an accommodation. Give your mum a good rest tonight, and tomorrow I'll introduce you to my dog. How's that, Spike?'

A bark of approval.

'We'll be having a few changes around here soon, Spike. I've got myself a family. Well, almost. Nina's holding out on marrying me, but I'm sticking in there, and sooner or later she'll say yes.'

He bent to give his faithful companion a good ruffle behind the ears. 'Happy days are coming, Spike. We might even get a little dog for you to boss around and lick into shape for Charlie girl. You are a bit big for her.'

The growl could have been pleasure from the

scratching, but Jack saw a doubtful gleam in the beady brown eyes.

'You're right. I'm big, too. The trick is to be gentle with her. No rough stuff. Okay?'

Spike nodded.

'Good dog. Come on. It's early dinner again for you, but I got a great bone from the butcher to make up for it. Lots of meat left on it.'

Bone was the magical word. Spike perked up and pranced towards the staircase, his great bushy tail swishing with eagerness. Jack was just as eager as his dog. They raced down the stairs together, barking and laughing.

Once in the kitchen, Jack wasted no time in handing over the special treat. Spike growled his delight and approval and retreated to his corner to gloat over it. Hours of gourmet pleasure in this bone. He watched his water dish being filled and was content. This man was definitely the best of all possible friends. He even smelled good.

'Well, Spike,' he said, 'I'm off now. Wish me luck.'

Having been given his heart's delight, Spike howled encouragement.

'Right on, Spike. Tonight could be the night.'

CHAPTER THIRTEEN

NINA settled Charlotte for the night, fussing with the bunny rug, delaying the moment when she'd have to face Jack alone with no more responsibilities to claim her attention. At least, not for hours. It was only ten-thirty. Sometimes Charlotte slept through until almost three o'clock.

It wasn't as though she didn't want to make love with him, and the doctor had assured her there was no reason to hold back, yet a host of inhibitions were crowding her mind and playing havoc with her nerves, making her tense and apprehensive. She simply couldn't put aside the fact that it wasn't the same as it had been before she fell pregnant with Charlotte.

She wasn't carefree. She didn't have only herself to consider. Most of all, she was afraid that having sex wouldn't feel as satisfying as it should, either to her or to Jack. Giving birth to a baby had to have caused some physical difference, and if making love was a disaster, it would be awful.

As she straightened up from Charlotte's capsule she flashed a smile at Jack, who had accompanied her into the bedroom, ostensibly to say good night to his daughter. 'I have to go to the bathroom. Won't be long.'

She fled before he could say anything, shutting herself in the bathroom like a panic-stricken virgin. It was ridiculous. Jack had been so patient, understanding, kind and thoughtful. She loved him. And tonight he was so excitingly attractive she'd barely been able to eat any dinner. Her stomach kept curling. Even the smell of his aftershave lotion had a tantalising appeal.

Aware that she was slightly sticky from breast-feeding, Nina whipped off her dressing gown and panties and stepped under the shower. Perhaps a warm spray all over would help her relax. Feeling freshly clean was an appealing idea, too, although she had showered before Jack's arrival this evening.

Her breasts weren't so tight since Charlotte had taken her fill. They weren't a worry. Fortunately, her skin was not disfigured by stretch marks, although she hadn't regained good muscle tone yet. The flesh on her abdomen felt slightly loose to her. Would Jack notice? It shouldn't matter, she sternly told herself. All in all, she was in good shape.

Except for the stretching inside. There was surely some. Her internal muscles had to be fairly elastic to have coped with a baby's passage, but Nina doubted they were as good as new again. What if she was, well, spongy? She wished Sally had had children. She could have asked her about it. Her doctor had said there was nothing to worry about, but he was a man. It was times like these when a woman needed a mother who cared enough to have an intimate discussion with her daughter.

Nina sighed and turned off the taps. She vowed to be on hand when Charlotte grew up and had a baby. Her daughter was not going to lack a sympathetic female ear, nor the loving reassurance a mother could give. There were many problems in being a woman. Many pleasures, too.

As she towelled herself dry, Nina concentrated on the pleasures. She didn't want to spend the rest of her life in a sexual vacuum. Jack was a great lover. Impossible to imagine anyone better. He really cared about making her feel good, and he knew how to do it.

Whether he turned into a loving father to Charlotte or not, Nina reasoned she owed it to herself to extend the loving experience with Jack, as long as he wasn't stirring up tensions and problems with their child. Tonight was the night. If she didn't jump this self-conscious barrier about her body, it was only going to get bigger and bigger in her mind. Maybe she should suggest dancing. Jack had a very seductive way of making her forget things when he danced with her.

Nina slid on the Christian Dior dressing gown again. She looked at her panties and decided no. She was going to do it. Make love with Jack, no matter what. Barriers were out. She moved over to the vanity bench and slid open the mirror cabinet above it. She took out the tiny bottle of perfume Sally had given her the morning after Charlotte was born, saying it was to remind her she was still a woman, as well as a mother.

Spellbound, by Estee Lauder. She dabbed some on her pulse points. It had a sexy scent. Definitely sexy. Jack would certainly get the message. No backing off tonight.

Nina returned the bottle to the shelf, slid the mirror door shut, took a deep breath and left the bathroom on a wave of unshakable determination and a waft of telling perfume. She heard Jack's voice in the bedroom. Without hesitation she went to join him.

'That's it, Charlie girl,' he was saying as she walked in, his voice low and intense.

'What's it?' Nina asked curiously. Jack had a weird way of talking to Charlotte, as though she understood everything he said. Nina sometimes wondered if it was a subconscious defence against his dislike of babies. If he spoke to Charlotte as though she were an adult, she wasn't *one of them.*

He straightened up and swung to face her, a satisfied little smile hovering on his lips. 'Oh, I was just telling her about my dog.'

A light switched on in Nina's mind. Jack spoke to his dog as though it understood everything, too. She'd found it rather endearing, although it only minimally reduced her unease with the huge, intimidating animal. Jack had said Charlotte was like a puppy. Since he loved his dog, maybe it was best he kept likening Charlotte to a puppy.

'That's nice,' she said. Or was she going stark, raving mad in her need to have everything turn out right?

'She's going to sleep now,' Jack assured her as he left Charlotte's side. 'Are you okay?' His eyes raked hers, checking for any sign of reluctance, assuring himself there was no last-minute change in the current of aroused sexuality that had been flowing so strongly between them all evening.

'Yes.' Unmitigated consent, throbbing through her, reaching out to him, pulling him to her in wanton dismissal of the cares that had trip-wired the churning desire to know and feel every dimension of intimacy with this man.

The cautious query in his eyes winked out. A few strides and she was in his arms, no hesitation, an urgent claiming that couldn't wait any longer to savour the freedom to sate their senses in each other. For several seconds he simply held her crushed to him, as though soaking in the imprint of her body.

'You feel so good.' His cheek rubbed over her hair as he swayed, rocking with an exultation of spirit that swirled through her, setting her heart pounding with anticipation. He inhaled deeply, the air suddenly sweeter to him than ever before. 'Smell so good,' he added with a raw sigh.

'You, too,' she whispered.

'I'm dying to taste all of you, Nina.'

'Yes.' A hiss of elation, wild recklessness seizing her.

Her arms locked around his neck, and she arched against him, revelling in the tension of his hard, hot muscles as she tilted her head back, her eyes a dark, sultry invitation, her lips already parted for him. She needed to be swept into a fast and furious maelstrom of passion, needed to have sensation bombarding her mind, needed to feel, not think, and for the feeling to be so intense, so pervasive, so exciting, there wasn't room for anything else, only Jack and her, man and woman, fusing in a feast of feeling.

She met his mouth eagerly in a kiss of urgent hunger, their tongues dancing with wildly erotic intent, dipping deeply, sweeping, darting, thrusting, coiling around each other in a tantalising tango, driving towards the ultimate coupling, a feverish fore-runner fuelling their desire for fulfilment. She moved her hips provocatively against his, and his hands swept down to her buttocks to incite a more raunchy rolling contact, aggressive and fiercely possessive.

It was intensely exciting.

Jack tore his mouth from hers, groaning with pre-climax tension. 'This is too fast.'

'Not for me,' Nina said, wanting to lose herself in the throes of passion.

He swung her over to the bed and wrenched her gown open. In hot haste he swept the silk from her arms, his hands quickly scooping up to cup her breasts tenderly, weighing them as though they were newly precious to him.

'The magic of a woman,' he said huskily, and bent to curl his tongue around her distended aureoles, sending piercing shafts of pleasure through Nina, totally immobilising her for several enthralling moments before the need to touch him snapped her into movement.

She dragged his shirt out of his trousers. It was all the prompt he needed to break off his absorption in her to discard his clothes. Their eyes shone with rapturous delight in each other, and their hands revelled in the blissful sensuality of skin against skin, fingers grazing, luxuriating in touch, warm flesh seething with sensation.

'I never stopped remembering you,' Nina whispered, 'but feeling makes it real.'

'Let me make it lastingly real, Nina.'

He clamped her naked body to his as he carried her with him onto the bed, then beguiled her with a shower of kisses that sucked and caressed, teased and ravished. She writhed voluptuously under the smouldering heat of his lips and tongue, uninhibitedly offering him the freedom to do all he wanted. Her breasts tingled. Her stomach rippled with spasms of excitement. Her thighs quivered. Then the sweet ecstasy of the most intimate of all kisses drove her mindless with need for the exquisite feeling of him filling her.

She raked his shoulders in frantic urging. 'Come into me now, Jack. Now,' she cried.

He surged over her, into her, and she wound her legs around him, lifting herself to the fast, beautiful, slide of his flesh, the glorious strength and power of it pulsing forward, crowding the waiting emptiness, taking it by storm, injecting an explosion of sensation that held her on a pinnacle of pure bliss.

'Again,' she begged.

The sheer poignant splendour of it held her impaled as the thrust was repeated and repeated in the vibrant rhythm of intense possession, transporting them both into the inner world of oneness, where neither had any existence without the other and desire was answered and satisfied in the wild, orgasmic heat of giving and taking.

Wave after wave of exquisite delight convulsed Nina's body, overriding the memories, turning dreams into the vibrant substance of a reality that was beyond imagination. Love had so many forms, but this was the heart and soul and body of it, this union that communed with instinct, rejoicing in its sublime rightness. On one final crest of ecstasy she felt the added spill of Jack's climax, like hot foam rushing to mingle with the swirl of her sweet release, and her arms curled around him, bringing him down to her to kiss once more in a seal of completion.

Her man, the only one who had ever made her feel this incredible sense of fragility and strength, both vulnerable and invincible, stirring her trust in him to let herself go and exult in a togetherness that went beyond anything earthly. There was awe and wonder in their kiss, a celebration of love fulfilled, their lips tingling deliciously as they drew apart.

'Jack…' She breathed his name with a sigh of blissful happiness, hugging him tightly to her.

'You and me, Nina,' he murmured, wrapping her in his arms and carrying her with him as he eased his weight off her and rolled onto his back. 'Nothing could ever be as great as this,' he concluded, his contentment settling around her like a warm cloak of lovely security.

'It was all right for you, then?' she asked, not really needing the assurance but wanting to hear it.

He laughed, a deep rumble of pleasure. 'Nothing in the world could be more right, my love.'

She smiled. 'It was great for me, too.'

For a while they simply luxuriated in lying together. Nina loved rubbing her legs against Jack's powerfully muscled thighs and calves. He had such a magnificent physique. His broad chest rose and fell under her cheek in a quiet hum of happiness. She played her finger pads teasingly over the erotic places she knew, just under his hipbone, down the side of his rib cage, near his groin, enjoying the spasmic shiver of pleasure she aroused.

Jack ran his fingernails over her back, lightly raking her skin. It made her feel like purring. She adored it. He could do it for hours, and she'd love every minute of it. Being naked with Jack was a hedonistic delight, packed with a multitude of sensory pleasures.

'I like your aftershave lotion,' she said.

'It's called Obsession.' She heard his grin. 'I very much want you obsessed with me.'

She laughed. 'I am. My perfume is called Spellbound.'

'Ah! You have me entranced.'

'Mmm…' She snuggled languorously, indulging herself in stretching and curling over him, so delectably different to being coldly alone. 'I could stay like this forever,' she murmured.

'Well, it would be a step in the right direction if you married me.' Jack rolled the words out confidently.

She wanted to. But… 'It's not that easy, Jack,' she said regretfully.

'We can make it easy, Nina. We just get Sally to arrange everything. I'll happily pay her fee, so it's no trouble to you.'

'I didn't mean the business of making arrangements.'

'What then?' He turned her onto her back and heaved himself onto his side so he could look into her eyes and watch the play of expression on her face. 'Tell me the problem, Nina,' he gently insisted.

There was no avoiding the truth, and she didn't want to. Honesty was the only way to go in this open intimacy between them. She had to hope Jack would understand, and she trusted he would appreciate where she was coming from.

'It goes back a long way, Jack,' she said ruefully.

'I'm listening.'

She held nothing back, telling him about her childhood, her parents' constant bickering, their resentments at being trapped by the responsibility of looking after the child neither of them had wanted, her hatred of asking them for anything, the misery of slinking away from arguments, making herself as unobtrusive as possible, the lonely sense of not really belonging anywhere, her grandmother's attitude of paying for her keep when she went to live with her after the divorce.

The memory of her mother's and grandmother's attitudes did not concern Nina so much. She knew she would do her utmost never to load her daughter with negative feelings. It was the memory of all the hurtful rejections from her father that weighed on her heart.

'My dad always found me a nuisance, Jack. Everything he ever did for me was a chore. He looked at me as though I were a constant irritation. It made me shrink inside.'

'Did he hit you, Nina?' Jack asked softly.

'No more than the occasional smack. It wasn't physical abuse, Jack. It was his attitude towards me that hurt. He simply didn't want me in his life.'

'He shouldn't have married your mother. Bad decision. You would have been better off adopted by a couple who wanted a baby, Nina.'

She took a deep breath. He wasn't applying what she was saying to himself. She had to bring it home to him. 'Jack, you didn't want a baby, either.'

He frowned, not liking the parallel she was drawing. 'You think I'd act like that with our daughter?'

'I don't want Charlotte to ever feel what I felt, Jack,' she said earnestly. 'I know you mean well, and you've been very good with her, but I'm afraid you won't be able to keep it up.'

He pondered that for a while, his eyes sad and sympathetic as they scanned hers, taking in the doubts they harboured. 'I really dug my grave with my mouth, didn't I?' he remarked wryly.

Nina was relieved to see he wasn't offended. She reached up and stroked his cheek. 'I love you, Jack. You're a wonderful person. I don't want to drag you into parenthood if it doesn't suit you. It would end up hurting all of us.'

He nodded. 'I see what you mean, but I honestly don't think you have a lot to be afraid of with me, Nina. I can't promise you I won't make mistakes. This is new territory for me.'

'For both of us,' she acknowledged fairly.

He placed a gentle finger on her lips. His eyes pleaded for her belief. 'I can promise you I'll never knowingly make our kid feel she isn't wanted or doesn't belong. I've been through that myself. I sure as hell wouldn't do it to my own kid.'

His sincerity was beyond doubt. Nina recollected what he'd said about nannies and the alienation from home life by being sent to boarding school at a young age.

'Don't you worry,' he went on strongly. 'Charlie girl is going to have a very special place in our lives. She'll know it, too. Look at Spike.'

This last comment threw Nina. 'What has our daughter got to do with your dog?'

'When I took him home from the animal shelter he was a cowed and beaten dog. Whoever his previous owner was had woefully mistreated him. Broken his spirit. I gave Spike confidence in himself.

Now he thinks he owns the place,' Jack declared, proving his capability of restoring faith in a dog.

Nina couldn't help smiling. 'Charlotte isn't a puppy, Jack. Human beings are a bit more complex.'

He gave her a wise look. 'Maybe human beings make things complex when they should be kept simple.'

'Maybe. In any event, let's give it some time. There's no need for us to rush into marriage.'

His sigh carried reluctant resignation. 'Living apart doesn't give me the best chance to prove I can be a good dad, Nina,' he pointed out.

That was true, yet she couldn't bring herself to make a commitment she wasn't absolutely sure of. 'Be patient with me, Jack,' she pleaded. 'I've seen my parents go through the marry in haste, repent at leisure experience. I don't want to be rushed.'

'Fair enough,' he agreed, kissing her lightly to show there were no hard feelings. He followed it up with a dazzling smile. 'How about you and our daughter spending the weekend at my place? It lets me be a full-time dad for two days so you can judge how I'm doing,' he added persuasively.

Jack's emphasis on the words *our daughter* was not lost on Nina. It would be an even better sign if he called her Charlotte, but Nina was content with one step forward at a time.

'Fair enough,' she agreed happily, reaching to pull his head to hers again and turning to feel the warm, wonderful length of his body against hers.

Jack needed no further invitation to resume lovemaking, and Nina revelled in every exquisite nuance of their intimacy.

One barrier gone, she thought exultantly.

She fiercely hoped Jack could remove the other.

CHAPTER FOURTEEN

JACK learnt a highly sobering lesson the next morning. When it came to babies, triumph could be turned into disaster in no time flat.

There he was, thinking he'd achieved a great step forward. Charlie girl had slept right through the night, as her dad had tactfully suggested, giving her mum a good rest, not to mention the freedom to reacquaint herself with the highly pleasurable satisfaction of lovemaking between a man and a woman. A splendid kid, Jack had thought, one who knew the meaning of artful cooperation and followed it to the letter.

Then what happened? Because Charlie girl hadn't woken for her regular feed in the wee hours of the morning, when she had called for it at the respectable time of sunrise, Nina's breasts were so tight with milk, at the first bit of sucking it ran down the kid's throat like the gush of a tap having been turned on full blast. Too much to cope with. She'd choked and spewed everywhere, distressing Nina and not feeling too good herself.

Jack could not have imagined such a little kid being a projectile vomiter. He took over the cleaning-up detail, relieving Nina of that mess. And he certainly had to admire Nina's fast thinking. She figured out if she lay on her back and the kid had to suck up from her breasts, the flow wouldn't be such dynamite.

It solved the feeding problem. Unfortunately, a baby's stomach was only so big. It couldn't take the double helping of milk Nina's inbuilt maternal machinery had manufactured and stockpiled. Her breasts were still uncomfortably tight after the kid had filled up.

'I'll have to use a breast pump, Jack,' she said worriedly. 'Will you find a chemist shop and buy one for me, please?'

'A breast pump,' he repeated, incredulously thinking of the sucking contraptions stuck onto cows' teats for milking. When he was in primary school he'd gone to a dairy farm on an education excursion and seen them in operation. Nina had to use something like that? The idea horrified him.

'Yes. I guess I should have had one on hand, but I didn't expect Charlotte to start sleeping through the night this soon.'

Guilt writhed through Jack.

'I think there's a twenty-four-hour chemist shop at Epping if you wouldn't mind going for me,' Nina urged.

'Of course, I'll go.' He checked his watch. It was almost seven o'clock, too early for normal business hours. They were only a couple of streets away from Epping Road. 'Should be back in about twenty minutes or so. Will you be all right, Nina?' he asked anxiously.

'Yes. I'll get you some money.'

'No. I'll pay.' Apart from his desire to look after

her, this dreadful outcome was his fault. 'Take care now. I'll be as fast as I can.'

'Thanks for helping, Jack.'

'Only too glad to.'

It was the truth. He'd bungled badly. Nina was right. Human beings were more complex than he'd thought. As he raced out to the Range Rover and hit the road, he castigated himself for not even realising the dire consequences ensuing from his initiative with Charlie girl. And the poor little kid—she couldn't have realised, either. She'd trusted her dad and almost ended up drowning in her mother's milk.

It was like the environment, Jack thought. If one little part of the pattern was changed, it set up a chain reaction that messed up everything. Big mistake! It was just as well Nina didn't know about his father-to-daughter chat. He'd have a black mark against him.

She'd probably see it as selfish, cutting down on the kid's needs to have more time with her. Which was true, in a way. But he hadn't meant any harm. It was a salutory lesson. He'd be a lot wiser in the future about how he arranged things.

Luckily it was Saturday morning, and the traffic was light on Epping Road at this early hour. He made good time to the shopping centre. He found the all-night chemist and rang the bell for attention. A guy came to let him in, and Jack spelled out the problem. He was mightily relieved when the breast pump turned out to be relatively small with an easy-to-use hand pump attached to a suction cup and a little bottle.

'I'd recommend you buy a jar of wool fat, too,' the pharamacist advised.

Jack's mind leapt from cows to sheep. 'What for?' he asked warily.

'Your wife could get sore nipples from the breast pump. They're probably sensitive anyway. If they crack it'll be very painful for her. Wool fat's the best to use on them.'

Cracked nipples! Things were going from bad to worse. Huge mistake!

'Right! I'll take a jar,' Jack said quickly. 'Anything else we might need?'

'No. She should be right if she takes care. If not, see a doctor.'

'I'll see she takes every care,' Jack vowed, hating the idea that any action of his would result in Nina having to see a doctor.

Nothing was simple, he decided, paying over the money and collecting the goods. Babies could really complicate the normal run of life. He'd observed this with his friends without fully appreciating how complicated it could become. He'd always thought control was the key to keeping the little monst—uh, moppets in their place, but it was now clear that control was a very tricky business. He'd have to give it more thought, more care.

Having climbed into the Range Rover, he set off for Lane Cove, determined to get on top of the baby game. No more finagling without knowledge of possible repercussions. He couldn't afford to let Nina catch him out on too many mistakes. After last night, he was certain the door was well and truly open for him. He wasn't about to shut it in his own face.

At least he had the whole weekend to make up for this mishap. If he ever met those parents of hers, he'd have a few things to say to them. Fancy not wanting Nina, giving her a hard time. He was lucky his own parents had only ignored him for the most part. Nina had had it much rougher than he had. No wonder she needed a lot of reassurance.

As for Charlie girl, Jack figured he had no problem there. She was a good kid. Listened to her dad like a little trooper. He'd have to find some private time to have a quick word with her today, tell her there was a new plan and she'd better get back to her normal schedule. They'd upset the applecart.

Tonight…well, maybe he'd just cuddle Nina.

Unless she wanted more than that.

In which case, he'd oblige.

He might very well take obliging to a new art form. The pharmacist had assumed Nina was his wife. Jack was going to turn that into a reality as soon as he could. It surely wouldn't take long for Nina to see he wasn't like her father. He wasn't like his father, either.

All it would take was some mutual understanding with Charlie girl. *She* recognised a good deal when she was handed one. Kids knew instinctively which side their bread was buttered on. It was simple mathematics. A girl needed a dad, and he was obviously the right one to have.

Jack fiercely hoped it *was* simple.

CHAPTER FIFTEEN

SOMETHING was badly wrong, and Nina couldn't ignore it any longer. It was getting worse, not better. Much worse. Ever since the first night Charlotte had slept through, her breasts hadn't felt right. This morning, both feeding times had been pure agony.

Over the past week she'd used the pump to drain off the excess milk. It hurt, but she'd persisted with it until yesterday. Maybe her inexperience was at fault there. Whatever the reason, her breasts now had a hard, hot, red lump towards her armpits and were extremely painful. She was definitely running a temperature. On top of which, Charlotte was fretful, as though she wasn't getting enough.

It hurt to lift the capsule. Nina realised she wouldn't be able to manage getting to her doctor on her own. Her head was in a swoon from the fever. It could be dangerous if she fainted. She took the most sensible course and rang Sally, who was close at hand and wouldn't mind doing her a favour.

'It's Nina,' she announced quickly, cutting through Sally's customary greeting spiel. 'I'm not well. I need your help.'

'Be right there.'

Nina put the receiver down with a grateful sigh. Sally never blathered on when action was required.

She had a mind like a razor blade underneath her glittering sales persona. Within seconds she was at the connecting door, and she burst into the flat in a blaze of efficient purpose.

Nina turned groggily from the kitchen counter on which she had leaned to use the telephone. Sally took one look at her, grabbed hold and supported her over to the closest armchair. She clamped a hand on Nina's forehead and started questioning.

'Flu? Gastric? What?'

Nina haltingly explained what was wrong.

'Mastitis,' Sally diagnosed. 'Infection in your breasts. Might even be abscesses. My sister had the same problem. It can happen when you're weaning a baby.'

'But I'm not weaning Charlotte,' Nina wailed.

'She's sleeping through. Same thing. You'll need antibiotics to knock out the infection. Maybe pills to stop producing any more milk. Best to get you to your doctor right now.'

Tears welled into Nina's eyes. 'You mean I won't be able to feed Charlotte any more?'

'Depends on how bad the infection is. Babies do survive on bottles, Nina. This is no time to quibble about what's best for them. We've got to do what's best for you.'

Nina felt too weak and upset to resist as Sally moved into top organisation mode, calling her secretary, who arrived pronto with Sally's handbag and car keys. Instructions were given to take business calls on the mobile telephone. The secretary was to stay in Nina's flat and look after the baby. If any problem arose, Sally could be reached on her car phone or at the doctor's surgery. Within minutes they were on their way.

'Does Jack know about this?' Sally asked.

'No.'

'You didn't tell him you were having problems?'

'I didn't want to worry him.'

The tears gathered again and started trickling down her cheeks. Jack had been wonderful last weekend, though he hadn't liked her having to use the breast pump. She had seen the recoil in his eyes, the frown, the silent wish it wasn't happening. She had given the excuse of a heavy workload to put him off coming to her flat the past two nights, not wanting him to see her discomfort.

He would undoubtedly blame Charlotte, and everything would start going wrong. Maybe it was cowardice on her part, avoiding problems that might put him off the fatherhood scene. Testing his resolve didn't seem like a good idea any more. Making love had probably been a big mistake. She wanted him too much.

'Give me Jack's number,' Sally commanded.

'What for?'

'You can't manage this alone, Nina.'

'Other single mothers must,' she argued.

'What's the point in hiding it? Jack's either there for you or he isn't. Better find that out now, Nina.'

Relentless logic.

The fear of losing him persisted. 'It's only about

eleven o'clock. He'll be busy at work, and it mightn't turn out to be as bad as you think, Sally.'

Her desperate optimism earned a derisive snort. 'Your temperature's sky-high. If Jack won't take over with Charlotte when you're sick, he's not worth having,' Sally declared, her vision unclouded by emotional bias. 'She may have to be bottle-fed. And that means shopping for all the necessary stuff. Now is the time for all good men to come to the aid of the party. Give me his number.'

Nina's head whirled. Too much to do, and she was too weak and woozy to do it. Besides, Sally was only speaking the inescapable truth. If Jack couldn't handle this, it boded ill for a future together. She gave his number, and Sally simultaneously pressed it into the car phone.

'Jack. It's Sally. Don't talk. Listen. We haven't got time for unnecessary chat. I'm almost at the doctor's surgery with Nina, and she's in trouble. Running a fever and pain in her breasts. She might have to go into hospital.'

'Hospital!' Nina groaned, the future getting blacker by the minute.

Sally ignored her. 'Are you okay to help with the baby?'

'Tell me what to do and I'll do it,' came the quick, decisive reply.

'Go to a chemist shop and buy up whatever you'll need to feed a newborn baby. Tins of formula, bottles, teats, sterilising solution. Ask the pharamacist. He should know everything. It might not be necessary, but it's better to be prepared. You can always exchange these items for other stuff. Next feed is two o'clock, but Charlotte might want it before then.'

'I'll go right now.'

'Hold it! If Nina has to go to hospital, can you step in and take over with Charlotte?'

'No problem. I'll take her home with me. Nina, too, if the doctor only gives her medication. I'll look after both of them.'

'Sure you can handle it?'

'They're my family. Thanks for letting me know, Sally.'

'I left my secretary with the baby at the flat. I'll report to her when I know more.'

'I'll go to the flat as soon as I have the stuff for Charlotte.'

'Right. Bye for now.'

Charlotte. He'd called her Charlotte. Surely that had to be a good sign, Nina told herself. And the possessive way he'd said *my family*... Jack had the best of intentions. She didn't know why she was crying. The tears rolled from a seemingly unstoppable well.

'That guy is coming through really well, Nina,' Sally asserted as she drove her BMW into the parking lot behind the medical centre. 'His heart is in the right place. Having met countless bridegrooms in my time as a wedding director, let me tell you Jack scores a high distinction in many areas.'

'Thanks, Sally.' Nina managed to choke the words

out. She wished she'd consulted Sally before she'd reached this awful state.

'Now let's get you inside to the doctor.'

It was out of her hands now, Nina thought. Fate had done it to her again, throwing her a curve she could never have anticipated. She couldn't exercise any control over where it would end. It was all up to Jack to make it come out right.

If he had the heart for it.

CHAPTER SIXTEEN

CHARLIE girl was yelling her lungs out and wouldn't listen to a word Jack said. He walked her up and down Nina's living room, rubbing and patting her back with no better result. The kid was beyond reason and comfort. Jack was desperate for news of Nina and more instructions when the telephone rang.

'I'll answer that,' he shouted at Sally's secretary, and quickly thrust the baby into her arms. 'Take her into the bedroom and shut the door. I don't want Nina hearing her over the phone and getting upset. Hurry!'

He grabbed the receiver the moment the door shut. 'It's Jack. How's Nina?' he demanded anxiously.

'Worst-case scenario. Abscesses. The doctor's given her intravenous antibiotics and booked her in at Royal North Shore Hospital. I'm taking her there now. A surgeon will see her this afternoon.'

'A surgeon?' Alarm shot through him.

'No big deal. It's called incision and drainage. Nina will have a general anaesthetic.'

'That could make her pretty damned sick,' he said worriedly, his gut twisting at what she had to go through.

'She is pretty damned sick. They'll probably hold

her in hospital for a couple of days. Have you got everything for Charlotte?'

It hit him with nerve-shattering force that he was on his own with the kid. Not for an hour or two. For a couple of days! And nights! No fall-back situation with Nina on hand. The responsibility was all his. He fought down an incipient sense of panic. Hadn't he said all along that a little kid couldn't beat him?

'All equipped and ready to go,' he said, firmly projecting confidence. 'Tell Nina not to worry. Tell her Charlotte couldn't have a more competent dad. I'll handle everything at this end.'

Charlotte… That's what Nina called her. Since he had to be both Mum and Dad to the kid, he'd better use that name, too. Give himself double-barrelled power.

'Good,' Sally said approvingly, as though she'd heard his thought. 'I'll come over to your place this evening and mind Charlotte while you visit Nina and reassure her. Okay?'

Relief flooded through him. He wasn't really on his own. Sally would help if needed. And there were Maurice and Ingrid and any number of friends he could call on. The panic receded somewhat.

'That would be great, Sally. Give Nina my love. And thanks again,' he said with sincere gratitude for her forethought and friendship.

Jack put the receiver down and took several deep breaths to unwind the knots in his stomach and get some oxygen into his brain. He was going to need a clear head and a cast-iron constitution. The kid's life and well-being were in his hands.

It suddenly struck him that depending on friends to deal with this baby emergency could be viewed by Nina as a cop-out. In actual fact it was a cop-out.

Charlotte was his kid. He'd told Nina no nannies. He was not going to shunt his kid off onto anyone else. This was the big one. The proving ground. He had to make a success of it, or Nina would wipe him off and shut him out forever. Rightly so. If he couldn't be a responsible father in a crisis, he didn't deserve any further consideration.

With steely resolution he marched down the hall and into the bedroom. Charlotte was still bawling. He took her from Sally's secretary and perched her against his shoulder so her ear was fairly close to his mouth. He pitched his voice low and intense and projected urgent command.

'Listen up, kid.'

The bawling hiccupped to a halt. Jack patted her back in warm approval as he spelled out the problem.

'You and I need to come to an accommodation. Just remember, we're in this together. You and me, kid. We did the damage, and now your mum's out of action. What's more, we've got to come through this with top marks.'

A loud burp exploded near his neck.

'That's good,' Jack encouraged. 'Don't start crying again. It'll only give you more wind. Going

onto a bottle after being on your mum's breast may
not be—'

A full-blooded scream told Jack in no uncertain
terms this communication was not welcome. It
raised the hair on the back of his neck. Sheer terror
was electrifying. He did his best to rectify his mistake and failed miserably.

Patting didn't soothe Charlotte. Rocking didn't
help. She paid absolutely no attention to his claim
that everything would be all right if she just trusted
him. The little legs kicked, tiny fists were clenched
and waving aggressively, face screwed up in constant yelling mode, body contorting against every
attempt to comfort. Jack had joked with his friends
about babies from hell. His heart quailed.

With another burst of determination, he forced his
mind clear of the paralysing noise. There was only
one answer to this. His friends had informed him
that car motion acted like a sleeping pill for babies.
He had to load Charlotte into the Rover and hit the
road. If she didn't calm down, he had no hope of
feeding her from a bottle.

Getting the formula right for her loomed ahead of
him. He couldn't expect to strike it lucky the first
time around. The pharmacist had suggested he take
three different tins of it, in case one or the other
didn't suit her taste. He had to try out different teats,
as well. Bottle-feeding was a complicated business.
He needed Charlotte's full cooperation if they were
to find an agreeable solution.

He lowered the wildly fractious kid into the capsule and used the bunny rug like a straitjacket to hold her tucked in. Charlotte did her fighting best to wreck his arrangement. Fortunately, he had everything ready to go. Sally's secretary had been most helpful, packing for Nina while he had loaded all the baby stuff into the Rover.

With Nina ill, he wanted the quickest and smoothest transfer to his home. It gave him a sick, hollow feeling to think of her going to hospital instead of coming home with him. Making it worse was the frantic fear of failing the fatherhood test.

He passed on Sally's report to her secretary as she accompanied him out to the street and watched him anchor the capsule to the back seat.

'Good luck!' she said with feeling.

He waved a salute and climbed into the driver's seat, thinking he needed all the luck he could get in these circumstances but admitting such a need sounded weak. This was a time for unshakable strength. He had to show Nina he was a rock she could always lean on. Charlotte, too.

He did his best to ignore the wailing from the back seat as he started the engine and headed for home. It took Charlotte the length of Mowbray Road to the Pacific Highway to quiet down. Jack blessed the friends who'd told him about the car-motion trick.

With peace momentarily reigning, Jack moved his brain into high gear and activated the car phone to set the next critical step in motion. He'd told his two apprentices he'd be bringing his family home and they were to be on standby to help.

Gary, his older apprentice, answered the call. 'I'll be at Boundary Street in a few minutes,' Jack informed him briskly. 'Nina's gone to hospital so I'm on my own with the kid. I need all the baby stuff out of the Rover and inside as fast as possible, so come running when I pull up.'

'We'll be ready for you, Jack. Anything else?'

Jack thought swiftly. 'Yes. Find the biggest pots in the kitchen, fill them with hot water and put them on the stove to boil. Quickest way to sterilise bottles and teats.'

'Right.'

'That's it for now.'

It wasn't a cop-out to use his apprentices, Jack reasoned. He was still the one in charge, and there was no telling how quickly Charlotte would wake up and demand to be fed. It was best to be ready to give satisfaction. If he could. Pleased with his forethought, Jack concentrated on picking the fastest lane through the traffic.

Gary and Ben were only in their late teens, but he'd found them completely reliable, and meticulous in following his instructions. They had the same innate drive to get things right as he had, an important character trait for French polishing. Anyone who worked with him had to take pride in doing and finishing a job properly, down to the finest detail.

Jack reflected it was lucky all his pots were stainless steel. No possible mistake with them. The pharmacist had warned him against aluminium pots for use in sterilising. Of course, once he was over the hump of the first couple of feeds, he'd use the sterilising solution and equipment he'd bought, but that took six hours. Deal with the emergency first, Jack reasoned, then establish a routine. He had to keep thinking positively.

Operation Arrival went as efficiently as Jack could hope for. 'We'll set up in the breakfast room,' he instructed, and the boys were right on his heels with the first load of baby necessities—the bath, the change table, the nursery bucket, the shopping. Spike fell into step on the other side of the capsule, keeping an eye on the new pup as Jack carried it inside.

The breakfast room was open to the kitchen. The boys usually ate their lunch there. It had a good solid oak table with half a dozen sturdy chairs around it. A TV set and one comfortable recliner chair for Jack's convenience comprised the rest of the furniture. There was plenty of space to set up the change table and all the paraphernalia that went with it. A bathroom was just off the kitchen, so the major work areas for a baby crisis were handy.

Jack put the capsule down near the TV set, out of the way of the action. 'Watch her, Spike. Anything wrong, let me know.'

The dog squatted, sticking his head over the side of the capsule for a closer look. It was a pity the pup was all covered up. It smelled as though it needed a good lick.

Jack unpacked the shopping, loading it along the kitchen counter for easy access. The boys brought in the bags of nappies, Nina's suitcase and the load of clothes and other stuff he'd packed for Charlotte.

'That's everything, Jack,' Ben assured him. He was seventeen, a cheery-faced, red-haired kid who was always eager to please.

'Great. You guys start sterilising the bottles and teats while I get the change table ready for action.'

'Why are we boiling up nine bottles?' Gary asked. He was a thin, wiry, intense nineteen-year-old who had a passion for knowing the whys and wherefores. As a statement of rebellion against standard conformity he tied his long brown hair in a ponytail and wore one earring. 'I didn't think a baby could drink that much,' he added with a frown.

'Mathematics, Gary. We've got three different formulas to try and three different teats, a fast flow, medium flow and slow flow. I want every combination ready, three bottles of each formula with each size teat on them. That way we can find out what suits the kid best without too much delay in between trial and error.'

'If we boil the teats in three different pots we won't get the sizes mixed up,' Ben suggested.

'Good idea,' Jack said, warmly approving. Nothing like effective and efficient initiatives to get a project off the ground. 'You're in charge of that, Ben. Only five minutes for the teats. Ten minutes for the bottles. I'd better get some towels out of the linen cupboard. This kid can be a champion spewer if we get it wrong for her.'

Jack privately congratulated himself on sounding calm and practical and in control. He collected a box of tissues and some face washers, as well. Being prepared for the worst would stop any panic setting in. He had to keep hoping the worst wasn't beyond his capabilities. He double-checked that he had every possible need assembled on the change table, then joined the boys in the kitchen.

Charlotte—bless her little heart—slept on as Jack and his two helpers started mixing the formulas. The assembly line of bottles was quickly achieved. Each set of three was placed in a pot of lukewarm water so the formula would come out at the right temperature.

Jack congratulated his boys on having done a great job. The initial pressure was off, and they were all feeling pleased with themselves when a mewling cry signalled time up. Spike leapt up and barked a warning. Action stations again.

Jack quelled a twinge of fear that all the preparation in the world might be of no avail if Charlotte felt they'd lost the plot her life had followed since she was born. Dogs sensed fear. For all he knew, babies did, too. *I'm a rock*, he sternly told himself, and rapped out an order to demonstrate his unshakability.

'Test the temperature of the formula while I change her nappy.'

'How do we do that?' Gary asked.

'Sprinkle some on your wrist. Shouldn't be any hotter or colder than your skin.'

He scooped Charlotte out of the capsule just as she was screwing up her face for a full-blooded yell. The shock of being lifted opened her eyes and turned the yell into a splutter.

'It's okay. Your dad's going to take care of business,' he assured her as he carried her to the change table.

She kept her eyes on him as he disposed of her wet nappy. Spike almost upset everything, standing on his hind legs and resting his forepaws on the table so he could get a proper view of proceedings. His weight pushed the lightweight table, rocking it for a moment, but he quickly adjusted his balance.

'Gently does it, Spike,' Jack admonished him, desperately controlling a wild flutter of apprehension. He didn't want Charlotte's confidence in him undermined before he'd even started to offer her a bottle.

Luckily Spike provided distraction, Charlotte transferring her wide-eyed and wary gaze to the dog. Spike sniffed the baby oil. He sniffed the talcum powder. He sniffed the fresh nappy Jack fastened around the pup. It was all very curious.

'There you go,' Jack said triumphantly, putting her legs into the body suit. 'Your mum couldn't do it any better.'

Big round eyes looked up at him. Jack sensed a belligerent challenge, possibly even a clash of wills in the offing. All was not right in her world. She knew it, and she was not about to be fooled.

'This next bit is going to be strange to you, Charlotte,' he warned respectfully as he did up the press studs. 'Nothing can really take the place of your mum, but there are some things you've got to accept in life, like it or not. It's up to you to make your choice of the options I've lined up. And Charlotte—' his voice gathered in eloquent appeal '—please try to understand this is all there is for you.'

The grave look she returned was full of suspicion. Jack was full of trepidation. But he'd told her the truth, and what more could he do? Life did bowl a curve sometimes. One had to adjust and move on. He hadn't planned on being a father, and here he was, taking on the role of both parents.

'Going to do a good job of it, too,' he muttered as he carried Charlotte over to the breakfast table and sat down, cradling her in the crook of his arm. He tucked a hand towel under her chin to catch spillage and spread a bath towel over his knees for bigger accidents.

'Temperature's fine, Jack,' Gary declared.

'Formula one, slow-flow teat,' Jack instructed.

Ben handed him the bottle. The boys stood by to watch the baby's response. Having sniffed the nappy that had been dropped into the nursery bucket, Spike lined up with them. All eyes were on the teat going into Charlotte's mouth.

'She's sucking,' Ben said excitedly.

'Yeah, but is she getting any?' Gary questioned.

The little jaws worked away for a minute or so and gave up. She spat the teat, screwed up her face and bawled her frustration.

Jack's stomach started tying itself in knots again. He checked the level of formula in the bottle. Hardly any gone. 'Medium flow,' he commanded, willing himself to stay on top of the crisis despite his misgivings about Charlotte's willingness to adapt to adverse circumstances.

Ben took the discard bottle. Gary handed him the next tryout. Spike whined at the strange pup. She stopped her weird barking and looked at him. Jack shoved the new teat into her mouth, and Charlotte latched onto it. She sucked. Not for long. Her mouth turned down, and the formula dribbled out the corners of it. 'Yuk!' was written all over her face.

'I can tell you, kid,' Jack said sharply. 'None of it's going to taste exactly like mother's milk.' He heard himself cracking and appreciated, for the first time, how a baby could reduce even the most reasonable adult to a quivering wreck. He pulled himself back from the brink and got on with the job, handing the bad-taste bottle to Gary. 'Formula one's a reject. Let's try formula two, medium flow.'

Jack wiped away all trace of the yukky dribble before offering the next bottle. He didn't want Charlotte to get confused, thinking it was the same taste. She needed food. One way or another, he had to get it right for her.

She attacked the new teat like a threshing machine. For the next five minutes it looked as though formula two was a winner. Then her stomach staged a revolt. The formula came back out like a gusher. The towels took a beating. Gary removed them to the laundry. Ben brought some more. Jack did his best to soothe Charlotte, holding her up to his shoulder and patting comfort. She vomited down his back.

Nightmare alley, Jack thought, struggling to keep his anxiety under control. Spike examined the mess and decided not to lick it up. Gary manfully took on the cleaning duty. Jack juggled Charlotte as Ben helped him strip off his soiled shirt.

Having emptied her stomach, Charlotte yelled for more food. 'Formula three, medium flow,' Jack called, an edge of desperation creeping into his voice. He settled her on his arm again and addressed her on the seriousness of the situation. 'This is the last stop, Charlotte. You've run out of choices. Think about it.'

'Maybe we should try slow flow again, Jack,' Ben suggested anxiously. 'Let her get used to the taste before it hits her tummy.'

Jack nodded, his mind almost numb with the possibility of all-out disaster. 'Good thinking. Go slow might do the trick.'

Ben quickly swapped the bottles, and they all held their breaths as Charlotte started working the teat, more cautiously this time. She had a brooding look on her face. Her eyes clung to Jack's. 'This is the good stuff,' he crooned. At this point, propaganda was his last resort.

Her face slowly cleared of the suspicion they were

poisoning her. Her sucking settled into a steady rhythm, and the content in the bottle gradually lowered.

'We've got it,' Ben crowed.

'That's the one, all right,' Gary happily agreed.

Jack's nerves sang a song of relief. To keep the sense of a positive roll moving forward, he directed the logical conclusion to this critical exercise.

'Okay, guys. We throw out the first two formulas and put the slow teats on the other two bottles of this lot. Store them in the fridge for later.'

He hoped Charlotte was storing this formula in her memory cells and would recognise it as the good stuff at future feeds. Scientific process was fine in theory, but human beings were both contrary and unpredictable. Jack had been shaken into an acute realisation that he was holding a miniature human being with a mind and stomach of its own, who was totally dependent on his meeting its needs. It was a highly sobering and humbling experience.

'Do we use the sterilising solution for the spare bottles now, Jack?' Gary checked.

'Yes. Wash them up and dob them in.'

High on success, the boys went back to kitchen duty. Spike remained on watch, his canine mind intent on collecting a bank of information on this new species of pup. Jack gradually relaxed, happy that Charlotte had apparently accepted the inevitable, at least for the time being. Maybe the surrender was due to exhaustion or hopeless resignation, but Jack preferred to look on the brighter side. His kid was not about to die of thirst or starvation. Thus far she was safe with him. As he'd promised her she would be.

'Your mum would be proud of you, Charlotte,' he told her. 'This is a big step to take for a little kid, and you're doing great.'

The teat dropped out as she hiccupped.

Was this another protest on the way? 'Got some wind?' Jack asked hopefully.

He put the bottle on the table so he could give her back a gentle rub. Two big burps. No sicking up. He grinned at the boys, who had stopped work to watch the outcome. 'No worries,' he assured them, almost dizzy with relief as he settled Charlotte onto his other arm.

'See? Your dad can change sides just like your mum. Here comes the good stuff.' He didn't care if he looked or sounded fatuous. He zoomed the bottle down to her mouth, and she latched on again. He felt a rush of paternal pride. 'You're a champion kid, Charlotte. A real fast learner.'

Spike barked agreement and trotted around the chair to take up watch on the other side. The hump of the current crisis was definitely over.

'Thanks for the teamwork, guys,' Jack said warmly. 'It could have been rough without your first-rate assistance.'

Gary grinned. 'New experience to chalk up.'

'Yeah,' Ben agreed, matching his workmate's grin. 'Operation Bottle-feed. That's a good one, isn't it, Gary?'

They laughed, happy to have been of help.

Jack smiled at Charlotte. They had all learned something today. It brought a new sense of closeness, a bonding that was different from anything Jack had felt before. This little-bitty human being was precious to him. He wanted her to be happy. With him. With the world. With everything. Whatever it took, he'd manage it somehow.

Spike shuffled forward and laid his head on Jack's lap, claiming his place in the family, too. Jack ruffled the long, shaggy hair. If only Nina were here with them. A wave of misery flattened any sense of euphoria at having come through the crucible of full, hands-on fatherhood.

Nina must be going through hell. He hoped the medical staff at the hospital were giving her adequate pain-killers as well as antibiotics. He'd raise a ruckus tonight if they weren't.

He hadn't seen her for almost three days. Her choice, not his. The suspicion rose that she hadn't felt well and had hidden it from him, though why she would keep it to herself was beyond his comprehension. Didn't she realise he would do anything for her?

Something was wrong with Nina's thinking. She had called for Sally's help, not his. Tonight he would have to find out why she hadn't turned to him. She should have done, instinctively, automatically. Did she still not trust him to do right by Charlotte?

Jack shook his head in bewilderment. His gaze fell on the baby. She'd stopped sucking. Her mouth was slack, her eyes closed, and her sweet little face glowed with replete contentment. It gave his heart a real boost, filling it with so many good feelings his underlying anxieties were momentarily forgotten. *My kid*, he thought. *Mine and Nina's.*

At least he could lift one worry off Nina's mind. Operation Bottle-feed successful.

CHAPTER SEVENTEEN

'NINA?'

Jack's voice, soft and strained with concern. Sluggishly she opened her eyes. The curtain was drawn around her bed. She'd been sleeping since the surgeon's visit. He'd examined her and explained what he was going to do in the morning. The pain tablets were good. If she kept still, the discomfort could be held at a distance. But she needed to see Jack, talk to him. She slowly turned her head.

'Don't move if it hurts,' he said anxiously, springing up from the chair to lean over her.

'Charlotte?' It came out like a croak. Her throat was dry.

'She's fine. Sally's with her while I'm here. She's taken to the bottle okay, Nina. I've fed her two lots of formula. She's not fretting or playing up. Everything's going well. When I left she was fast asleep. No problem.'

Nina knew she should feel relieved, pleased that Jack was coping with their baby. It was ridiculous to feel so bereft and useless. Tears welled into her eyes, great globs of self-pity. It wasn't fair this had happened to her. All the hard months of her pregnancy, fiercely resolving to be everything to her child, and she couldn't even feed her baby. She shut her eyes to stop the tears from overflowing, but they squeezed through her lashes.

Jack's hand gently brushed her hair from her forehead. 'Is it terribly painful, Nina? Do you want me to fetch a nurse?'

'No.'

'Then what's wrong, love?'

The deep caring in his voice twisted her heart. 'I'm a failure,' she blurted out.

'No, you're not,' he strongly asserted. 'Sally told me your designs for Belinda Pinkerton's wedding are brilliant. You've got great talent, Nina, and once people start seeing it…'

She moved her head fretfully. 'I'm a failure as a mother. I let you get in the way, Jack.'

His hand stilled, then withdrew. She heard the chair being drawn closer, the squeak of its cushion as he sat down. The sense of apartness made her feel worse, as though she was losing everything.

'How, Nina?' he asked quietly.

She had to swallow hard to get rid of the lump in her throat. She opened her eyes and looked at him with aching regret. 'I didn't want you to know I had a problem. I hoped it would get better. I wanted it to go away. If it wasn't for you and my delaying getting help…' Tears swam again. 'I'd still be feeding Charlotte.'

'Why didn't you want me to know?' He shook his head in hurt confusion. 'Love is about sharing. Both the good and the bad.'

'I didn't want the bad to rebound on Charlotte. You blaming her and resenting her.'

'I don't!' he cried, standing in agitation, his hands slicing the air in frustration as he pulled himself back from pressing his case with more physical persuasion. 'I wouldn't, Nina!' he pleaded. 'She's not to blame for anything. She's just an innocent little kid, for God's sake!'

His vehemence made her head pound. Her mind clutched wearily at the truth he spoke and limply let it go. Reason and logic could be argued until the end of time. It made no difference to the realities seeded by emotions.

'You hated seeing me use the breast pump,' she said flatly.

It silenced him, cut the feet out from under his principled posture. Principles were fine things. The problem was in living up to them. He sank back onto the chair. He expelled a long breath as though trying to lower a dangerous high of pent-up feelings. His face was grim, jawline tight, eyes shuttered as he leaned forward, resting his elbows on his knees.

'That's true. I did,' he admitted, as though tearing the words from his conscience. 'Though not for the reasons you attribute to me, Nina. It was because *I* felt guilty.'

She frowned, not understanding.

With an anguished look at her, he reached out and stroked his fingers gently over the hand lying close to him. 'Please listen to me, Nina. I'm sorry you read different things into my feelings. The last thing I wanted was to give you pain.'

Her fingers lifted instinctively to tangle with his, to link, wanting his warmth, wanting so much more from him. Her eyes clung to his in hope, aching for him to allay the apartness she felt.

'The first night we made love, I had a talk to Charlotte beforehand, telling her it would be good if she slept through,' he confessed. 'She did. With the result that you had to use a breast pump, which you obviously found unpleasant. I then told Charlotte she'd better wake up as usual, but she'd got the hang of sleeping through and there was nothing I could do about it. You shouldn't give a little kid confused messages, on again, off again. It wasn't her fault.'

Nina stared incredulously at him. He really thought Charlotte took in what he said to her?

'None of this is her fault.' His eyes begged her forgiveness. 'It was me. It was me!' His face twisted with guilt. 'I was being selfish, wanting us to have the night together like we used to. I'm dreadfully sorry, Nina. I just didn't realise how it would affect you.'

Nina's stomach clenched. She had misunderstood, misjudged. It was crazy for Jack to have felt guilty, but she could see that he did, given his propensity for fantasy communication with his dog and Charlotte.

'If you'd shared your worries with me, I could have helped,' he went on regretfully. 'Told you about cabbage leaves. It might have saved you all this pain.'

'Cabbage leaves?' she repeated dazedly.

'One of my friends told me about them. His wife got sore breasts from feeding their baby, and she used a cabbage leaf compress in her bra to get them better. It worked, too.'

'Why? How?' Nina couldn't believe it.

Jack shrugged. 'There's no known scientific reason for it, but it does work. You keep the cabbage in the refrigerator so the leaves form a cold compress. When they warm up in the bra you replace them with cold ones again. My friend was joking about how many cabbages he had in his fridge, but he wasn't joking about it fixing up the problem. We could have tried it, Nina.'

We… It was she who had set them apart, not Jack. She should have given him the benefit of the doubt and put fear aside.

'I know lots of things about problems with babies,' he added anxiously. 'My friends have poured them out to me. I guess that's why I thought they were little monsters. Nobody bothered telling me the best things. Like the funny expressions Charlotte gets on her face and how good it feels when she's happy.'

Her heart swelled with so many mixed emotions Nina couldn't find words for them. The realisation thumped into her mind that it was her fault it had come to this, her fault for not opening up to Jack, not trusting him, her fault she could no longer feed her baby. It would have been all right if only she had spoken, shared, as Jack said they should, the bad, as well as the good. How had she got so twisted up?

Her eyes filled with more tears.

'Don't cry, love,' Jack begged. 'Tell me what I can do.' He grabbed some tissues and gently dabbed the wet streams trickling down her cheeks. 'If there's something you want…'

'I'm sorry,' she choked out. He wasn't to blame at all. She was.

'It's okay. If it helps to cry, you cry. But don't think you're a failure as a mother, Nina,' he said earnestly. 'You're a wonderful mother. The best. Any kid would be lucky to have you as their mum. The breastfeeding bit doesn't matter. It's the love that counts, and Charlotte knows she's loved.'

The warmth in his voice washed over her, soothing the painful torments in her mind. He dabbed her cheeks again as she struggled for control of her tear ducts. Her head ached, her body ached and her heart ached. She was a mess. Nevertheless, she pushed herself to make the effort to speak.

'Thanks for coming to the rescue, Jack. With Charlotte, I mean.'

'I'm her dad,' he said gruffly. 'I wish you'd take that on board, Nina. You're not alone. Unless you really prefer it that way.'

His pained expression needed answering. 'I don't,' she said simply.

His eyes scanned hers, searing them with his

doubts as to her underlying wishes and feelings. 'It doesn't add up, Nina,' he said softly. 'You say you love me. You say you're giving me a chance. Yet you turned to Sally, not to me. It was Sally who called me to the rescue. You shut me out. Again.'

It was not a bitter accusation, more a restrained statement of fact, all the more powerful in tearing at the reservations she had held about him.

He took a deep breath, and there was a flicker of compassion in his eyes as he went on. 'I appreciate where you're coming from, Nina, but I have scars, too. We all carry baggage of one description or another. In many ways my parents shut me out of their lives. I wasn't abused. I was simply and effectively sidelined. Ignored for the most part.'

His tone was matter-of-fact, not begging pity or even sympathy, but the loneliness of a long-distance runner was behind the words.

'I understand why you shut me out of your pregnancy, though your decision took no account of my love for you,' he went on. 'It painted me as not worth consideration. Like today. How do you think it makes me feel, Nina, to know you chose not to call on me? To keep it all to yourself?'

She hadn't seen it that way. She hadn't wanted to bother him…a different form of consideration. 'You were very much on my mind, Jack,' she pleaded.

He shook his head. 'Negatively, not positively. I want to be involved, not set aside. And for you to risk this kind of suffering rather than open your door to me, it makes me wonder if I'm doing wrong in thrusting myself into your life again.'

'No. I do want you, Jack,' she cried. 'I want you so much, I'm frightened of anything that might drive you away.'

'Only you can drive me away.' His voice throbbed with raw intensity. 'I keep knocking on your door. You open it. You shut it. Putting me outside doesn't make me feel wanted, Nina. I don't even do that to my dog.'

She cringed at the blunt indictment of the way she had treated him. She had no excuse. She had seen everything from her own prejudicial point of view. Tunnel vision. With growing horror she realised she had done to Jack what her parents had done to her—rejected him, lowered his sense of self-worth, focused on her own feelings without considering the effect on him. Just because he was a man didn't mean he was immune to the same hurts she had known.

He grimaced. 'I probably shouldn't have brought this up when you're so ill. Not the time nor the place.'

'Yes, it is, Jack,' she whispered, squeezing his hand. 'You needed to say it, and I needed to hear it.'

He gave her a crooked half-smile. 'As long as you're reassured that Charlotte is safe with me.'

'I am. Thank you. For many things.'

It wasn't enough, not the touch or the words. She sensed his inner tension, the restraint he was constructing, sealing off the wounds of mistrust and moving silently but resolutely to that place of self-sufficiency he had learned to exist in long before they had ever met. No doubt he had returned there during the estranged months of her pregnancy. It was Jack's survival ground, come what may.

'I brought in your toiletries and a set of fresh clothes for when you leave,' he said flatly.

Easier to deal with the superficial mechanics of life than the hidden areas, Nina thought. Jack withdrew his hand and bent to unpack an overnight bag. The physical separation made her even more tensely aware of the effect her reluctance to involve him was having, the loss of true intimacy, the protective shield she had raised, driving Jack to start raising his own.

Having stowed her belongings in the drawers of the bedside cabinet, he resumed his seat, facing her with a bleak and determined expression. It alarmed Nina. He had come here caring about her, and she had blamed him for her own failure. The cost of that mistake was building up.

'Sally told me you'll be raw and sore for a week or so. I've planned for both you and Charlotte to stay with me. If it's not what you want, Nina... If you'd rather return to your flat and arrange other help—'

'No.' She had to stop his retreat from her. 'If it's not too much trouble for you...' That sounded weak and uncertain. 'I mean—'

'Don't feel obliged to come to me just because I

took responsibility for Charlotte while you're in here,' he added before she could find a more positive reply. 'If I've assumed too much, bulldozing you into a situation that's distressing you, it's better we settle it now. It was never my intention to hurt you. Say the word and I'll take everything back to your flat.'

'No. I want to come to you,' she said with as much strength as she could muster.

His direct gaze left no room for prevarication. 'As a halfway house or a serious commitment, Nina? Please be honest with me.'

Her heart started galloping. How could she promise the level of absolute trust he wanted when she couldn't trust herself to deliver on it? If it were possible to throw a switch that would alter or adjust all the negative circuits in her brain, she would. It wasn't her intention to hurt, either.

'Will you give me another chance, Jack?' she pleaded. 'I'll do my best to sort myself out.'

'It doesn't have to be done by yourself, Nina. My door is open to you, and I'm always ready to listen.' Frustration threaded his voice. 'If you'll only be honest with me.'

'Yes. I realise that now,' she said earnestly.

His face slowly relaxed into a half-smile of wry appeal. 'Charlotte is not just yours, Nina. She's part of both of us. It's not two against one. It's the three of us.'

'Yes,' she agreed, seizing the concept with desperate energy. 'Do you love her, Jack?'

He looked blank, as though he'd lost connection with her train of thought.

'Charlotte, our baby. Do you love her?' she repeated anxiously, needing to hear him say it.

The light switched on behind his eyes again. He reached out and took her hand, pressing it with convincing fervour as he answered, 'Yes. Yes, I do.' He sounded almost surprised at his own words.

Was it true?

'We're a family,' he added insistently.

Nina clutched at that concept, too, eager to push aside the single-parent status she had carried for so long. She didn't have to be a single parent. She didn't want to be. Jack was giving her a chance to have it all…the three of them.

'A family,' she repeated, fiercely resolving to embrace the idea in every way. No shut doors. The sense of togetherness had to be held and nurtured. Belonging to each other—that was what family should mean. Belonging so deeply that love and trust and support could be taken for granted.

Her inner turmoil eased. It slid into her mind that Jack was right in saying human beings made life more complex than it had to be. Of course, he must love Charlotte. He wouldn't be asking for honesty if he wasn't prepared to give it himself. She laced her fingers through his and closed her eyes, concentrating on the warmth and strength of his touch.

Together…

A family.

CHAPTER EIGHTEEN

FEELING raw and sore for a week was no exaggeration, Nina discovered. She could not have coped alone, even if she had wanted to. Going home with Jack proved to be the best solution to everything. It was a revelation in so many reassuring ways. Nina was constantly being shamed for having harboured any doubts and fears about a future with him.

He was kindness itself in looking after her and seeing to her needs. The community nurse visited every day to supervise her medication and recovery. Jack fed her, washed her, helped her do whatever she wanted and gave her loving company.

If she was awake he shared Charlotte's feeding times with her. It was too painful for her to hold the baby, but she was happy to watch Jack handling their child, talking away as though Charlotte understood him perfectly and always including Nina in the conversation, welding them into a family unit. He'd put a rocking chair in the bedroom, and he'd sit for hours sometimes, beaming with love and pleasure in both of them.

When she had first seen Charlotte taking eagerly to the bottle, Nina had felt a deeply distressing confusion. Had she only imagined the special bonding between mother and child arising from the physical connection of breastfeeding? It hurt to feel she wasn't necessary at all. Not even missed. Left fragile in every sense by the operation, she had been unable to block a rush of tears.

'It's no different to her,' she blurted out in answer to Jack's concern. 'The bottle is just as good.'

'It might be now she's got used to it, Nina, but let me tell you she gave us the rounds of the kitchen the first time up,' Jack said with an expressive roll of his eyes. 'All of us were on tenterhooks, trying to please her with a substitute, and she knew jolly well she wasn't getting mother's milk.'

It distracted Nina from her sense of loss. 'All of you? Who do you mean?'

'Gary and Ben and Spike. I talked Charlotte through it while they gave me backup support.'

Nina listened in amazement as he described his scientific method of trial and error, the assistance given by his apprentices, Charlotte's reactions, the advice he had given her and the final acceptance of the third formula. She wished it had all been taped on video film, the three men handing bottles around, the dog getting in on the act, the baby the focus of all attention and efforts to please, missing her mother in no uncertain terms.

'You did wonderfully well, Jack,' Nina said in sincere admiration, immeasurably cheered by this story.

His smile gave her heart another lift. Everyone wanted approval, she thought. And praise. Recognition of what was given. Love and appreciation went hand in hand.

'Try not to be upset about the bottle-feeding, Nina,' he urged, his green eyes soft with warm sympathy. 'I know it's a disappointment to you, but next time we'll know better. You'll be able to breastfeed as long as you want to.'

'Next time?' she echoed uncertainly.

'Uh…' He looked discomfited and tried to dismiss it. 'Just an idea I had. Bit premature. Forget it. The important thing is Charlotte's okay. Nothing for you to worry about.'

'You're not being honest with me, Jack,' she chided. 'Why not play the idea past me?'

He shrugged and grimaced appealingly. 'It sounds like I'm assuming too much. You said not to rush you. Let it go for now, Nina.'

'I've adopted an open-door policy. I'm listening, Jack,' she said persuasively, wanting to know his innermost thoughts and dreams.

He gave her the direct look that zinged straight into her heart. He hesitated for a few moments, needing to reassure himself he wasn't about to make a mistake. She returned his gaze steadily, projecting her desire to share in every sense.

'I didn't like being an only kid, Nina,' he said tentatively. 'Since we've got Charlotte…I thought, maybe in a year or two…if you felt up to it…'

'We add to the family?'

'What do you think?' he asked warily. 'If you'd prefer to leave it at one… It was just an idea. It's been growing on me this past week. I mean, I can't imagine life without Charlotte now. I really love this kid. If we had more, there'd be plenty of love around for everyone, wouldn't there?'

Nina had a mad desire to laugh. She had been so hopelessly and wildly wrong about Jack, it was almost funny. But it wasn't, really. It had very nearly been tragic. Again tears threatened. She struggled for control, then smiled to set him at ease.

'I was an only child, too. I know what you mean, Jack. It would be good for Charlotte to have a brother or sister.'

His face broke into a pleased grin. 'Hear that, kid?' he asked Charlotte, who promptly stopped guzzling to give him her full attention. 'You might rule the roost, but you're going to have company.'

She blew him a raspberry.

'There you go, getting impertinent again. I'll tell Spike on you if you don't show proper respect.'

The dog, who had squatted beside the rocking chair, leapt up to check what was going on. He looked at Charlotte. Charlotte looked him straight in the eye, as though imparting the message that he needn't think he could be interfering between her and her father, then lifted her gaze to Jack and opened her mouth for the teat again.

It was enough to make Nina start wondering if there was more to instinctive communication than she had credited.

Over the next few days, it became very evident that Jack had an innate talent for family. He called his apprentices 'his boys', giving them a strong sense of being on the team, and they looked up to him as though he was a second father to them. Spike dogged his footsteps everywhere and was naturally included in practically every activity. Charlotte, 'the kid' or, Nina suspected, 'the pup' in Spike's mind— was adopted by all of them.

Eventually the community nurse declared Nina healed. Having accompanied her to the front door, thanking her for the help and advice given, Nina went in search of Jack and Charlotte to give them the good news. She heard voices coming from the rumpus room, where Jack did his final polish on whatever he was working on. As she approached she remembered he had an appointment with Maurice Larosa, the antique dealer. She paused, loath to interrupt a business talk.

Their conversation drifted through the open door, holding her riveted.

'She's a champion kid, Maurice,' Jack declared with pride. 'Sleeps through the night. No worries at all. You'd better have a daughter next time.'

'I guess boys are noisier,' came the rueful reply. 'She's got your chin, Jack.'

'Chip off the old block. Though her eyes are just like Nina's.'

'The fair hair must come from you.'

'I guess so. She's going to be a stunner, Maurice. Blonde hair and big brown eyes.'

'Sounds like she's got you wrapped around

her little finger already,' Maurice remarked in amusement.

Jack laughed. 'That's my daughter. You'd better warn your son not to mess with her. I'm riding shot-gun on this kid.'

Nina couldn't help smiling. If there had still been any question about Jack's attitude towards Charlotte, it was more than answered by the doting expressions she was hearing.

'Well, I must be going,' Maurice said, dragging his mind back to business. 'Great job on the desk, Jack. My client will be delighted with it.'

'I'll get Gary to deliver it this afternoon. I'll show you out through the workshop, Maurice. Something else I want you to see.'

Self-conscious about eavesdropping, Nina moved beyond their sight as the two men started out of the room. 'Mind Charlotte, Spike,' Jack called over his shoulder. 'Won't be long.'

This cavalier instruction to his dog piqued Nina's curiosity. As soon as the coast was clear she returned to the doorway into the rumpus room. Spike was sitting on his haunches beside the capsule, cocking his head attentively as Charlotte waved her fists and burbled. An inquiring whine came from his throat. Charlotte raised her voice in a peremptory manner. Spike squatted down, dropping his head over the side of the capsule. Charlotte crooned at him.

Nina had the weird feeling Charlotte had this huge, intimidating animal wrapped around her little finger, too. Certainly she wasn't the least bit frightened of the dog. She grabbed a fistful of shaggy hair. Spike's huge lolloping tongue came out and gently swatted her chin. Charlotte crowed in delight. Having sensed Nina's presence, Spike turned his head and gave her a look as if to say, 'Well, she asked for it.'

'That's fine, as long as you don't eat her,' Nina heard herself say indulgently, and wondered if she had taken leave of all common sense. But the dog settled down contentedly and let Charlotte play with his hair, not so much as twitching an ear as the baby cooed her pleasure, obviously thinking it a great game.

'Don't worry. Spike thinks he's her stand-in mum.'

She half-jumped as Jack's arms slid around her waist then relaxed as he gently pulled her against him.

'He's such a big dog.' She sighed.

'All the better to keep her safe. Spike would lay his life on the line for her, Nina. But if you want a smaller dog for her...'

'No.' It was obvious that dog and baby had bonded in some perfectly natural way that both were comfortable with. Jack undoubtedly had something to do with it, and she trusted his judgment. 'I suspect you're losing your dog to Charlotte,' she warned good-humouredly.

'Mmm.' He nibbled her ear. 'There's something very seductive about little beings, babies and pups and kittens and chicks. I think this might be the first time Spike's been in at the beginning, and he's not going to miss out on knowing how things develop.'

She knew intuitively Jack was really speaking for himself. He didn't want to miss out on anything, either. Next time he would be with her throughout her pregnancy. There would be nothing lonely about it. Nothing lonely at all.

'The nurse said I've healed very well,' she informed him. 'And quickly, thanks to you taking every possible strain off me. I can get back to work now.'

His head lifted. She felt his chest expand, and a long breath wavered through her hair. 'Nina, the boys have been making you the perfect table to suit your working needs. We could turn the sunroom into a professional sewing room for you. It's only a fifteen-minute drive to Sally's for appointments.'

'I must call Sally,' she said, smiling over his plan. 'I'm sure she wouldn't mind.'

Nina turned in his embrace to let him see the happiness and certainty glowing in her eyes. 'I want to call her about a date for our wedding. If you still want to marry me.'

'Want to…' He laughed, unable to contain his joy. 'We're going to have all the frills Sally can think of.'

'Her charges are high, Jack,' she warned, laughing with him.

'Who cares? It'll be the best day of our lives. Charlotte can be a flower baby.'

She arched an eyebrow. 'Maybe we should have a flower dog, as well.'

He shook his head, his eyes adoring her. 'I love you, Nina Brady.'

She looked at him with all the brimming emotion in her heart, this incredibly caring man, her lover, her partner in life, the father of her future family. 'I love you, Jack Gulliver,' she answered with vibrant passion, and went up on tiptoe to kiss him.

It was a kiss of promise, of absolute commitment, but most of all, of love and trust and deep pleasure in their togetherness. It was the beginning of the song of belonging.

CHAPTER NINETEEN

JACK slowly surfaced from deep sleep, feeling decidedly groggy. He recollected it had been a big night, a superb dinner and lots of champagne, he and Nina celebrating with Sally, riding a high from the great spread Nina had been given in a bride magazine, beautiful photographs of her best designs. Then he realised what had woken him. The kid was yelling.

He struggled out of bed, trying not to disturb Nina, who hadn't budged. Big night. A well-deserved big night. He didn't want the kid waking her up and spoiling sweet dreams of success and recognition of her talent. She'd worked hard for it. A special night for her.

Everything had been peaceful when they'd arrived home. Ben, who'd volunteered to baby-sit, had assured them there'd been no problems. The kid was six months old now. Shouldn't be yelling at this hour. Jack frowned at the numbers illuminated on the bedside clock radio. Four-seventeen.

The night-light in the hall gave a dim glow, guiding him out of the bedroom. He frowned as he saw a brighter light coming from the kid's bedroom. Someone must have left the touch-lamp on. The yelling stopped, but Jack kept going, deciding he might as well see if something was wrong. Switch the lamp off, as well.

He reached the doorway and halted in his tracks. His three-year-old daughter, along with her ever-faithful friend and companion, Spike, were lined up beside the cot, eyeballing the baby. Charlotte planted her hands on her hips and held forth to her little brother.

'Listen up, kid! You and I need to come to a 'commodation. I don't like being woke when it's still dark. Spike doesn't, neither.'

Spike dutifully whined his displeasure.

'Now I'm going to teach you what's what.' She stepped over to the lamp and tapped it until it went off. 'This is dark. Have you got that, kid? Dark,' she repeated for good measure. 'You keep quiet when it's dark.'

A raspberry from the cot.

The lamp came on again. 'This is light. You can start yelling when it's light—' she wagged an authoritative finger at the baby '—but not before. And don't blow raspberries at me. Show some respeck. This is your big sister talking.'

A becoming silence from the cot.

'That's better,' Charlotte declared with satisfaction. 'You've got to be a fast learner in this family, kid. Give him a lick for being a good boy, Spike.'

Spike's tongue reached through the slats of the cot and swatted Patrick's hand.

'Right! Now I'm going to give you dark, and Spike and I are going back to bed. You might as well go to sleep again. You can wake up when it's light.'

The lamp went off. Jack scooted to his bedroom before the education brigade marched into the hall and to their bedroom. He listened for a while to make sure everything was all right. Silence reigned. He slid into bed and lay there with a huge grin on his face. Charlotte was definitely a champion kid.

Nina rolled against him and snuggled, sleepily mumbling, 'Love you.'

'Love you, too,' he murmured, kissing her forehead.

He had a great wife, a smart daughter, a fast-learning son, an obliging dog.

What more could a man want?

Maybe another kid. When and if Nina felt up to it. After all, Patrick needed a younger brother or sister to pass the family lore onto. Fatherhood, Jack decided, was addictive. Especially with a family like his. On that contented thought, he closed his eyes and went back to sleep, serene in the knowledge all was well with his world.

* * *

*If you have enjoyed these novels by Emma Darcy,
don't forget* The Italian's Stolen Bride *and*
The Ramirez Bride *are new modern Romances
on the shelves in May and September 2005.*

0305/01a

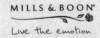

MILLS & BOON®

Live the emotion

Modern
romance™

POSSESSED BY THE SHEIKH by *Penny Jordan*

After being stranded in the desert, Katrina was rescued by
a Sheikh and taken back to his luxury camp. He decided to
marry her, though he thought her a whore. Then he
discovered – first hand – that she was a virgin…

THE DISOBEDIENT BRIDE by *Helen Bianchin*

Their marriage was perfect – and then billionaire Tyler
Benedict's wife left! Now he wants her back. Beautiful
Lianne Marshall can't refuse his deal – but this time she
won't play fair. However, Tyler is after more than a
business arrangement!

HIS PREGNANT MISTRESS by *Carol Marinelli*

Australian billionaire Ethan Carvelle left Mia Stewart years
ago. Now Mia's pregnant – claiming Ethan's late brother is
the father! Torn between duty and desire, he decides to
make her his mistress. But he knows nothing of the secret
Mia is hiding…

THE FUTURE KING'S BRIDE by *Sharon Kendrick*

Prince Gianferro Cacciatore is heir to the throne of
Mardivino and his father, the King, is dying. The pressure
is on Gianferro to find a wife and his heart is set on
English aristocrat Millie de Vere. But Millie hardly knows
the prince…

Don't miss out…

On sale 1st April 2005

*Available at most branches of WHSmith, Tesco, ASDA, Martins,
Borders, Eason, Sainsbury's and all good paperback bookshops.*

Visit www.millsandboon.co.uk

MILLS & BOON®

Live the emotion

Modern
romance™

IN THE BANKER'S BED by Cathy Williams

When Melissa Lee works for Elliot Jay, she expects their
relationship to be strictly business. He is seriously sexy,
but he keeps his emotions in the deep freeze! Melissa is
soon getting Elliot hot under the collar, and now he has a
new agenda: getting her into his bed!

THE GREEK'S CONVENIENT WIFE by Melanie Milburne

When her brother's exploits leave Maddison Jones at the
mercy of billionaire Demetrius Papasakis, the last thing she
expects is a proposal. But Demetrius knows she has to
agree to a marriage of convenience – and Maddison finds
herself unable to resist!

THE RUTHLESS MARRIAGE BID by Elizabeth Power

Taylor's time as Jared Steele's wife was short, but not
sweet. Within weeks she discovered that he had a
mistress and that she was pregnant. She lost the baby *and*
her marriage. Now she is stunned by Jared's return – and
his claim that he wants her back!

THE ITALIAN'S SEDUCTION by Karen van der Zee

It sounded like heaven: an apartment in a small Italian
town. But after a series of mishaps Charli Olson finds
herself stranded – until gorgeous Massimo Castellini offers
her a room in his luxurious villa. Though he's vowed
never to love again, Massimo finds Charli irresistible.

Don't miss out...

On sale 1st April 2005

Available at most branches of WHSmith, Tesco, ASDA, Martins,
Borders, Eason, Sainsbury's and all good paperback bookshops.

Visit www.millsandboon.co.uk

0305/01b

EXtra

Favourite, award-winning or bestselling authors. Bigger reads, bonus short stories, new books or much-loved classics. *Always* fabulous reading!

Don't miss:

EXTRA passion for your money! (March 2005)
Emma Darcy – Mills & Boon Modern Romance
NEW *Mistress to a Tycoon* and **CLASSIC** *Jack's Baby*

EXTRA special for your money! (April 2005)
Sherryl Woods – Silhouette Special Edition –
Destiny Unleashed. This **BIG** book is about a woman
who is finally free to choose her own path…love,
business or a little sweet revenge?

EXTRA tender for your money! (April 2005)
Betty Neels & Liz Fielding – Mills & Boon
Tender Romance – **CLASSIC** *The Doubtful Marriage*
and **BONUS,** *Secret Wedding*
Two very popular writers write two very different,
emotional stories on the always-bestselling wedding theme.

Available at most branches of WHSmith, Tesco, ASDA, Martins, Borders, Eason, Sainsbury's and all good paperback bookshops.

www.silhouette.co.uk

0305/154

On sale 18th February 2005

Available at most branches of WHSmith, Tesco, ASDA, Martins, Borders, Eason, Sainsbury's and all good paperback bookshops.

0205/024/MB124

MILLS & BOON

All in a Day

What a difference a day makes…

CAROLE MORTIMER

REBECCA WINTERS

JESSICA HART

On sale 4th February 2005

*Available at most branches of WHSmith, Tesco, ASDA, Martins,
Borders, Eason, Sainsbury's and all good paperback bookshops.*